THE
WEDDING
BEES

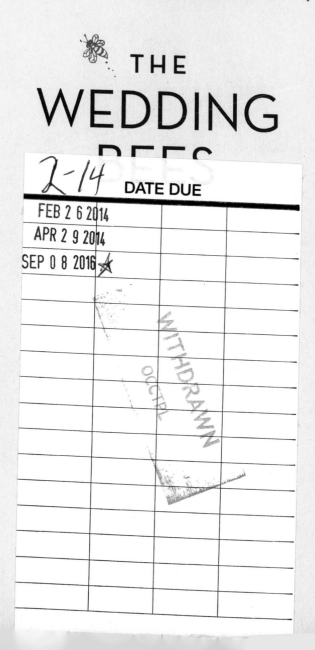

Also by Sarah-Kate Lynch

Finding Tom Connor
Blessed Are the Cheesemakers
By Bread Alone
Eating with the Angels
The House of Daughters
On Top of Everything
Dolci di Love

THE
WEDDING
BEES

A Novel of Honey, Love, and Manners

SARAH-KATE LYNCH

𝒲𝓂

WILLIAM MORROW

An Imprint of HarperCollins*Publishers*

This book was originally published in Australia in 2013 by HarperCollinsPublishers Australia Pty Limited.

P.S.™ is a trademark of HarperCollins Publishers.

HarperCollins books may be purchased for educational, business, or sales promotional use. For information please e-mail the Special Markets Department at SPsales@ harpercollins.com.

FIRST WILLIAM MORROW PAPERBACK EDITION PUBLISHED 2014.

Library of Congress Cataloging-in-Publication Data has been applied for.

ISBN 978-0-06-225260-9

14 15 16 17 18 ov/rrd 10 9 8 7 6 5 4 3 2 1

In praise of
random acts of kindness
good manners
and
guardian angels

THE
WEDDING
BEES

Sugar Wallace did not believe in love at first sight, but her bees did, and her bees could not even tell red from green.

They could, however, see forty different shades of purple.

In other words: those bees might not know everything, but in some respects they knew more than Sugar Wallace.

1ST

Sugar's bees hummed steadily in her lap as she wound down the window and strained to look up at the Flores Street apartment building. It was five stories tall, its perky orange brickwork hiding beneath a robust layer of dust. A fire escape zigzagged down the middle like an exotic scar, and a pink stoop below the red front door gave the impression the building was poking its tongue out, perhaps at the faded bunch of motley balloons tied to the basement's ivy-covered railing.

"Why, it has such character," Sugar told her friend Jay, who was drumming his fingers impatiently on the steering wheel. "And I've never lived around the corner from a knishery before. Plus if I get an accordion and it breaks, I know just where to get it fixed."

Sugar patted the Styrofoam square that sat on her knee and housed her precious queen and a sleepy fledgling kingdom of worker bees. Despite being little more than a stone's throw away from Manhattan's famous overpopulated canyons, Flores Street was surprisingly charming: a leafy cobbled dead-end lane nestled in Alphabet City just south of Tompkins Square Park. Once she had them settled, the bees would love it down here. Far enough away from the chaos of those uptown skyscrapers, they would have a smorgasbord of gardens, parks, street trees and window boxes upon which to feast. There was space, there was sunshine; it was splashing around them now, dancing right down at street level through the new growth on the linden trees.

She breathed in the city air as Jay spotted a parking space ahead: it was a perfect spring day, the sky a radiant blue, the temperature cool but with a change-of-season edge to it that hinted at better things to come. She was hardly the first person to arrive in this part of the city buzzing with excitement for what the future held. A hundred years before, the cobbles would have been all but invisible through the swarming throng of playing children and bustling adults, all new to America from across the oceans and going about the frantic business of carving out a life in their newly chosen city.

"Can't you just see it filled with little ragamuffin kids and loaded pushcarts?" she asked Jay.

"Yes, I can," he answered. "And I can smell it too, what with there being no bathrooms in those days and all."

Sugar allowed him his crankiness. He was still recovering from having the fruit juice scared out of him by the heaving traffic on Franklin Roosevelt Drive and now was having trouble fitting his van into the parking space. The sweat patches under his arms were spreading and Jay was not a sweat-patches-under-his-arms sort of guy.

"I think bathrooms are pretty much a routine fixture nowadays," she said. "Hey, do you think the accordion is difficult to play? As you may recall, I'm not real musical."

"The entire eastern seaboard can recall how musical you are not. Really, Sugar, I don't know what you're thinking."

"I'm thinking you're not going to fit in here."

"I'm not trying to," Jay said. "I found where I belong years ago and I just wish you would do the same instead of flitting about, leaving behind a trail of worried nutcases wondering how they'll ever survive once you're gone. I see it every year when I move you and it worries me half to death."

"Hold your horses, Jay. They're not nutcases. They're my friends. And I was talking about the parking space. You're not going to fit into the parking space. Let's give up on this one and drive around the block."

She wanted to get another look at the Indian spice bazaar and the pickle shop anyway. "A whole shop just for pickles? You don't find that in every neighborhood."

"And you also don't find murderers and rapists and pickpockets and homeless people," said Jay, driving somewhat unevenly along Flores Street and turning carefully into Avenue B where, as if to prove his point, a homeless man lurched out from the sidewalk, careening right in front of them.

Jay slammed on the brakes and managed to avoid him, but the homeless man continued to stagger across the road, narrowly missing a moving cab, before tripping on the curb and knocking over a tall man in a Hawaiian shirt, who just happened to be standing there talking on his phone.

"Oh, my goodness," Sugar cried, thrusting her box of bees at Jay, leaping out of the van before he could stop her and crossing the road in front of a honking utility truck.

The man in the Hawaiian shirt, mildly winded, scrabbled on the sidewalk for his cell phone and kept talking into it.

"Are you all right?" Sugar asked him, but he just pointed at the homeless man who was still lying in a crumpled heap and needed more immediate help.

"Can you hear me, sir?" Sugar asked as she pulled a McDonald's burger wrapper from the arm of the man's heavy coat. "Are you OK? Are you hurting anywhere? Goodness gracious, that was quite some tumble."

The homeless man turned awkwardly and looked up at her with dark, clear eyes, focusing on her as if she was exactly who he expected to see.

"No, ma'am, I am not hurting," he said, in a far from feeble voice. "At least not in the way I imagine you mean it."

"Well, that's a relief," Sugar said.

The man in the Hawaiian shirt snapped his phone closed and got to his feet.

"Sorry about that," he said, in a singsong accent that sounded to Sugar a little like creek water roiling over hot pebbles on a sunny day.

A shiver ran up her spine.

He had floppy brown hair and a nice nose in a handsome face, although thanks to the extreme loudness of his Hawaiian shirt he clashed horribly with the Mexican mural behind him. His eyes, on the other hand, were an intense shade of blue that exactly matched the street painting's vivid background. "Can I give you a hand?" he asked.

She couldn't quite place his accent. Couldn't quite operate her tongue.

"Perhaps to get this gentleman back on his feet," he suggested.

Irish, she thought, perhaps, although why she was thinking about his origins at all escaped her.

"Yes," she said, retrieving her wits. "To his feet. Right away. Good plan. We can't have him sitting there in the gutter another moment. It's just not a dignified place to rest."

"I couldn't agree with you more," said the old man. "And I like dignified."

Sugar and the man in the Hawaiian shirt stepped forward and pulled him up.

But as they stepped away again, the backs of their hands brushed—it was just the lightest touch, for the briefest of moments, almost nothing more than hair upon hair, yet Sugar felt it like a blowtorch on crème brûlée.

She sprang away and they looked at each other for a split second, then his phone started to ring again and she turned quickly to the old man, who had stopped teetering and come to a solid standstill.

"I can't thank you enough for your help," he said. "Lord knows I don't like heights but some places are just too close to the ground and the sidewalk is one of them. George Wainwright. A pleasure to make your acquaintance."

"Sugar Wallace," Sugar said, shaking his hand, noticing his clean, clipped fingernails. "And it's a pleasure to make yours too. But are you sure you're feeling all right?"

"I'm good, Miss Sugar, just sorry to make such a spectacle of myself, and embarrassed on account of knocking over this unsuspecting young man in such a fashion."

"He seems OK," Sugar said. "Leastways it has not interrupted his ability to be glued to his cell phone."

"Cell phones! I don't know what it is about the world at the moment," George said, shaking his head, "but I just can't seem to get a fix on it."

"You're not alone there; it's a slippery place," Sugar assured him, flapping a little at his coat, which she could see was not as tattered as she had first thought. It had epaulettes on the shoulders and buttons that looked as though they had been recently shined. "I mean, I'm still trying to get a handle on the microwave oven."

George looked at her with those clear dark eyes. "I hope you don't mind me saying so," he said. "But I don't get to meet many people like you these days. You new in town?"

"Just blew in this minute."

"What in the hell, Sugar?" Jay interrupted, appearing at her elbow, his armpit circles now halfway down to his waist. "I had to drive right around the Square and park half a mile away. I stood in dog poop, goddamnit!"

"You mind your language, young man," George said. "Miss Sugar here was only showing a little old-fashioned concern for a fellow human."

"You see, Jay," said Sugar. "I am not the only person in the world who doesn't appreciate cursing."

"You can keep your eyes off the cooler," Jay snapped at George, regardless, shifting the box of bees from under one arm to the other. "You'll get a buzz from what's in here but I assure you it won't be the one you're looking for."

"Jay, it's OK," Sugar said. "You've got it all wrong. This here is George, and he's not interested in the cooler, no matter what's in it. Anyway, you can let me take those now."

She reached for the box of bees just as the Hawaiian-shirt wearer snapped his cell phone closed again.

"And who might you be?" Jay asked.

"I'm just the guy who was standing here making sure this gentleman had a nice soft landing when he fell," he answered with a smile that revealed a single dimple in his left cheek and one front tooth that crossed slightly over the other one.

The smile was directed at Sugar. "I'm Theo Fitzgerald," he said.

For a moment she thought she felt her bees vibrate in a different rhythm against her chest, their tiny wings beating at twice the normal speed, agitating the air in the cooler at a crazy manic pace, but almost by the time she had noticed it they were back to their regular pattern again.

"I'm Sugar Wallace and this is my friend Jay," she said. "And he might not seem like it but he is one of the world's kindest individuals. He came up from Virginia to Rhode Island just to drive me to my new apartment right around—"

"Don't go telling everyone where you live," Jay interjected. "Sugar, you are not going to last ten minutes in this town."

"You're right, he does not seem like it," said George.

"I'm not Amish, Jay," Sugar said. "I've watched *Sex and the City* almost as much as you have. You can quit fussing any time you like."

"It's funny you should say that about not being Amish, because neither am I," said Theo. "Amish, that is. I'm Scottish, which is completely different. No relation whatsoever."

This time Sugar was sure she felt the bees change their vibration, for just a moment, to match her quickened heartbeat. It was those Mexican-mural-blue eyes of his: they seemed to look right into her, as though he could tell what she was thinking, even though she didn't quite know herself.

"Come on," Jay said, reaching for Sugar's arm. "We have things to do. Can't stand out here all day chitchatting."

Sugar felt a slow blush crawl up her neck and blossom in her cheeks as Theo's eyes stayed fixed on her. "If you're sure you're steady on your feet," she said to George, "Jay's right, we truly best be going."

"I'm steady," said George. "Steady as I've been in a long while. Best get going myself. But sure is nice to have you in the neighborhood, Sugar. I'll be looking out for you, just see if I don't."

He turned around and shuffled off, favoring his right leg, although moving swiftly enough all the same.

"Hardly here a minute and already the pond scum is muscling in," Jay grumbled.

"Actually, I'm not pond scum either," Theo said. "You know, as well as not being Amish."

"Yes, thank you, have a nice day," Jay said, pulling Sugar away with him.

"Pleased to meet you, Theo," she said, over her shoulder. "And he means it about having a nice day."

Theo watched her walk down the street and turn in toward the park.

She was tall and slender with long dark hair that swung in a shiny ponytail from one shoulder to the other, her dress swirling beneath her cinched waist.

He thought suddenly of watermelon. It was hard to come by back in Scotland but even before he'd ever tasted one in the flesh it had reminded him of summer (which was also hard to come by back in Scotland).

He knew what watermelon tasted like now; it was one of his favorite things. He could almost feel it in his mouth as he stood there, that cold sweet powerful explosion of almost nothing.

He needed to find a slice as soon as possible.

His phone rang and jolted him back to life, but it didn't seem like the same old one.

"You have been away from home too long, Jay," Sugar said, as they walked back to find the van. "There's never any need to be rude, remember? Plus I don't think George is pond scum. He had such nice manners—better than yours, some might say—and he smelled of Old Spice. Should pond scum smell of Old Spice?"

"Nothing should smell of Old Spice. Oh, look at that, Sugar. I just stepped in the same dog poop again!"

Why couldn't Sugar have stayed in Weetamoo Woods? Jay berated her as they drove jerkily back to Flores Street. "Or go back someplace small like Mendocino or that cute little redneck town in Colorado? Or come to Virginia and be closer to me. New York's too big. And it floods. Plus it's filthy. You'll never be able to wear white. I hope you can live with that."

"Jay, honey, I tend to steer clear of white as a rule anyway."

"Oh, shit, I mean shoot. I'm sorry, Sugar. I just worry about you, is all. Every year moving someplace new, starting from scratch."

"I've got my bees, Jay. That's not starting from scratch. That's more than most people have. Look, there's a space right outside my building. A big one. You could fit three of these old jalopies in there. Come on, you can do it."

In Sugar's book, moving someplace new was infinitely preferable to going back someplace she had been before. "New York," she said to the bees on her knees. "New York!"

2ND

Ruby Portman nibbled on an eighth of a rice cracker as she watched the guy in the white florist's van park it awkwardly outside her apartment. She'd seen him lose his shit earlier on, when he couldn't fit into a space across the road and had bunny-hopped to the end of Flores Street. But now he was back and the woman in the passenger seat was looking up at the building again, smiling.

She looks sort of like a nurse, Ruby thought. Or a nun, but a movie star nun, not a real one, and an old-fashioned rescuing-the-orphans sort of movie star nun, not the comedy sort. It was her face. It was open and fresh and happy and she had shiny dark hair pulled back in a ponytail.

Ruby watched as the woman got out of the van. She was wearing a pink sundress and flat, red lace-up brogues and she had a red ribbon tied around the ponytail. Nuns probably don't wear ribbons and red shoes and have long, slim bare legs, she thought.

She pulled back from the window and looked down at her own legs. She was wearing an expensive pair of jeans and a sweater her mother had bought her and neither fit her very well. Even her ballet flats looked funny on her feet.

Ruby bit her lip and scraped her fine blond hair up, piling it on the top of her head with a clasp. Her whole body was a joke, actually. A complete joke.

She put the sliver of cracker carefully back on the plate next to the other slivers so that it formed almost an entire cracker again. She no longer wanted the sliver. It was distracting her. Besides, if she didn't eat it then, she could look forward to having it later. Or later still.

She dragged her chair closer to the window, tucking herself behind the burgundy velvet drapes with their gold fringe. Ruby couldn't stand those drapes. She couldn't stand any of the overpriced furniture in her apartment, all chosen by her mom: the rolled-arm sofa with matching armchairs, the writing desk, the dining table with its six chairs. Six chairs! Not one of them had ever been sat on.

The pictures on the wall were not to her taste either. She didn't even want pictures on the wall. She would have all white walls with nothing on them if it was up to her, not these dark reds and greens and uptown library hues.

It was all the same stuff that filled her mother's apartment on the Upper East Side, so why she'd wanted to re-create it here, Ruby couldn't imagine. It was not as though she wanted Ruby to think she was still at home. She liked having Ruby away from the Upper East Side as much as Ruby liked not being there.

Ruby had found the apartment herself about a year ago after seeing a sign advertising it on the noticeboard at the greenmarket around the corner. She'd been out walking after a fight with her mom that was so vicious she had gone from East Eighty-Second Street to Tompkins Square Park before she even noticed where she was.

She'd rung up straightaway about the apartment, and loony Lola, who lived upstairs, had ended up showing her the place half an hour later.

Then she'd walked all the way home again and begged her mom to let her move there. She couldn't pay the rent herself, of course—she'd never even managed to hold down a job for more than a month or two—but her mother was tired of her, Ruby knew that. Why wouldn't she be? Ruby was tired of herself. And if it wasn't quite independence when someone else paid the bills, at least it meant they could get out of each other's hair for a while.

Of course, her mother had been horrified that she was living in Alphabet City. Back when she was Ruby's age, the area had been full of drug addicts and pimps and thieves and murderers. But what had eventually won her over was the insanely cheap rent and the apartment itself, which was solid and roomy. And available.

It had taken a while to adjust to nothing but her own company but Ruby now felt she was almost ready, almost well enough, to start looking for a job and standing on her own two feet. Almost.

Outside, the van driver and the woman were unloading things from the back of the van. The woman was holding some sort of a cooler, and the driver was carrying a stack of brightly colored square wooden boxes. He did not look like the sort of guy who normally carried stacks of boxes. He had creases in his jeans, as if he'd ironed them.

The couple came right over to the building so Ruby drew back from the window again, pulling her long sleeves right down over her hands. She was cold, although it looked like a nice enough day outside. She was always cold.

15

One of the tiny "penthouse" apartments had been empty a while now, she knew, so she should not have been so surprised that someone was moving in. But, even though it was an unreasonable thing to think, she had somehow assumed she would know when that was going to happen and that she would have a hand in it. Of course, with her mother paying the rent, she didn't even know who the landlord was. Ruby had a hand in absolutely nothing.

Still, she did not know if she wanted a nun and a guy who ironed his jeans living in her building. She'd only just got used to the beefy redhead living in the other tiny rooftop apartment and he'd been there more than six months. Not that she'd ever spoken to him or anything, but she still saw him every now and then and, even though it did not annoy her as much as in the beginning, it still annoyed her.

She pulled closer to the window again as some skanky kid on a skateboard whipped past the woman in the pink dress so close and so fast it spun her around. The woman just clung to her cooler and laughed. Closer, Ruby could see how pretty she was, how delicate her features in that open face, how wide and clear her eyes. She looks nice, Ruby surprised herself by thinking. She hardly ever thought that about anyone.

Now the woman was laughing again and looking all soppy over loony Lola's ridiculous balloons, as though Flores Street wasn't the worst place in the world to find such a collection, and loony Lola wasn't the worst person in the world to have it.

Well, she'll find out soon enough exactly how much those balloons are begging for an attack of the knitting-needle variety if she's moving in, Ruby thought.

She wondered if the bad box carrier was the woman's boyfriend. They didn't really match each other, although they both looked about the same age, older than her, but younger than her mom. Midthirties, maybe? They'd better not have a baby in that van, that was for sure. Loony Lola had put all of Alphabet City off babies, possibly forever, with her toddler son who never stopped his squawking. If there was going to be another one of those in the building, Ruby would have to shoot someone. Or herself.

She took her plate of cracker slivers and covered them in three layers of plastic wrap, then put them on the top shelf in the kitchen cabinet, standing on tippy toe and pushing the plate as far back as she could. She would come back to the crackers later. She had stomach crunches to do. And maybe she would do her arm weight routine today since she'd only done it once the day before. And then maybe today she would walk to the Whole Foods Market on East Houston to get some quinoa because she'd read on the Internet that it was the new superfood, although actually she thought the Chelsea Whole Foods had a better layout so she might walk there instead, depending on how long her exercises took.

Maybe the van driver and the happy woman had met over a bunch of flowers, she thought. Maybe the woman's first husband had died and the driver had delivered flowers to her, then fallen in love with her. Or maybe the woman worked in the store and he was the delivery boy and after years of not telling each other how they felt, they were trapped together in the flower cooler one night and it all came out and now here they were.

Stupider things had happened.

3RD

Sugar paused at the iron railing leading down to the basement where the motley balloons bobbed sadly in the faint spring breeze. One of them was a world globe, its Northern Hemisphere seriously dented, another was a somewhat flaccid superhero, and the rest were a forlorn collection of ordinary shapes in washed-out colors and various stages of deflation.

The same boisterous ivy from the stoop spilled down the stairs like a feather boa and had thrown itself around a dusty window bearing a sign that read, if only just: LOLA'S BALLOONS.

Through the dirty glass Sugar could also see part of an inflated zebra, half of a giraffe, and the face of a blow-up monkey floating on the inside, but a large handwritten sign hanging crookedly from the rather imposing black door read CLOSED.

"Well, how about that," she said. "I guess it's a store."

"Yeah, it looks real inviting," said Jay, hitching up the empty hive boxes he was carrying.

"I know what you mean," Sugar agreed. "A balloon shop should always be open, just like a garden should always have flowers and a hive should always have bees. *Closed* is simply not a word that should be associated with something as bright and beautiful as balloons."

"These balloons are not bright and beautiful," Jay said, resting on the railing. "These balloons are pale and pitiful. In fact, unless 'Lola' is tying those things to herself and jumping out of cakes at bachelor parties she should probably rethink her business strategy."

"How you get from an innocent child's plaything to a girl jumping out of a cake, I just cannot fathom," Sugar said. "Are you sure they even do that at bachelor parties these days?"

"Not the bachelor parties I go to," Jay admitted. "Come on now, can we get going?"

They climbed the stoop to the apartment building's weathered outer door, heavy and difficult to open, which led to a tiny stifling space where the mailboxes were, with a second door squeaking moodily before letting them into the lobby. This was dark and had seen better days, but the worn red-and-green tiled floor was clean, and the place smelled better than many of the ones Sugar had moved into over the past few years.

The somber gray door to the only first-floor apartment had five locks on it, though, causing Jay to raise his eyes to the heavens instantly. "Please tell me this isn't you."

"Of course not, sweetie pie. I can't keep bees on the first floor!"

Jay looked up the narrow stairwell. "Can you keep them on the second?"

"No, I cannot. And not the third or fourth either. It's a climb, I admit it, but I do believe that when we get up there, there'll be a lovely surprise for my girls." She held up her bee box. "They'll be so happy, they'll make honey you will cry just thinking about."

"Is this your way of telling me there's no elevator?"

"This is my way of telling you that nine out of ten health professionals say climbing stairs is the best way to maintain your cardiovascular fitness."

Jay owned a florist shop in Middleburg, Virginia, and usually maintained his cardiovascular fitness in an air-conditioned gym under the tutelage of a personal trainer with a beautiful body and a magnetic mean streak. It was testament to his love for Sugar that he was hauling heavy boxes up countless stairs and driving his assistant's cruddy van, not his own spotless Miata. "You go on up, check the place out and find me the smelling salts," he said. "I'll keep unloading."

"Aren't you glad I have movers bringing the rest of my stock tomorrow?"

"I'm glad you trust me with your precious essentials, sweetie, but one year it would be nice to see you without pulling a groin muscle."

Up on the fifth floor, Sugar unlocked the door of her new home and stepped inside.

This was the fifteenth threshold she had stepped across in as many years and always she felt the thrill of the new, even if she sometimes felt the icy blast of a drafty window or the hot breath of a lecherous landlord as well.

Apartment 5B, 33 Flores Street had neither.

It was a 600-square-foot studio, with a bed in the middle of the far wall, although *far* was hardly the right word as nothing in a place that size was really far from anything else in it.

But what Sugar had been promised by the landlady when she had called after finding the listing on a beekeepers' website, what she could barely believe existed in the world, let alone in New York

City, let alone that it was to be hers for the next year, was the terrace that ran the length of the apartment outside the French doors.

From wherever she stood inside the tiny space she could see out across the neighboring rooftops; north to the treetops of Tompkins Square Park, south to the taller towers of the Lower East Side and east to the gritty glitz of the Alphabet City skyscape and beyond.

This wasn't the ordinary Empire State or Chrysler building vista that she'd seen sprouting up above the other skyscrapers in television shows and movie opening credits. This was a distinctly downtown horizon spiked with water towers, sprinkled with satellite dishes, scarred with spindly staircases and squat air-conditioning units, the occasional rooftop garden greenery dazzling for all the world like scattered emeralds.

It was a secret, suspended in the air, and she was now in on it.

In other words, it was perfect.

She had not loved a room so much since her brothers, Ben and Troy, had made over her bedroom at home when she was eleven years old. They'd painted it powder blue when she was spending the weekend with her grandfather and, although she didn't even like powder blue (which she had told her mother, who had clearly never passed it on), she'd loved that room anyway because they'd done it just for her.

Not that she was going to go thinking about that now.

Thankfully there was nothing powder blue in her new Manhattan home but that was not to say it lacked color. The wall behind the bed was particularly orange, the color of almost-burned marmalade, and the tiles in the neat little kitchen tucked against the right-hand wall were a brilliant turquoise.

A tired but not-dead-yet sofa in a faded eggplant color provided the only seating in the room, a jauntily tiled coffee table nudging one arm.

And outside through the French doors was the city, that big silver city with its slashes of blue spring sky and its rooftops turned to the heavens like sunflowers in a crowded crop of squared-off stalks.

Sugar placed her bees gently on the kitchen counter and rested both hands on top of the box, feeling the gentle hum of her colony-in-waiting beneath her palms.

"It's going to be a good year," she told them. "Just you wait and see."

"Talking to those damn things again?" Jay said coming in behind her, setting down a load of honey-filled cartons. "One of these days I'm going to show up to move you and you'll be all black and gold and fuzzy yourself."

"I wouldn't mind," said Sugar. "There are worse things to be than a honeybee."

"Yeah, you could be a homeless bum or the crazy-haired Smurf of a neighbor I just passed with her screaming kid on the stairway. Or you could be someone else's honeybee, just the regular kind, that gets ignored or eaten by birds or stood on, not treated like next of kin."

It was true. Sugar did treat her bees like next of kin but then again, they were.

Along with her manners, the accent she tried so hard to soften, a single china cup covered in blue daisies and a weathered box of essential oils, they were all she carried with her from her past. Her bees relied on her for shelter and food but she relied on them too. She made her living from their honey, not just the healthful liquid itself but from the salves and gels and tinctures and remedies she created and sold at farm stands or farmers' markets wherever she lived.

It was the most symbiotic of relationships.

"I treat everyone like next of kin," she told Jay. "Including bums and crazies and my oldest dearest friend in the whole wide world."

Jay looked at her, standing there like Holly Golightly in her vintage dress with the spikes of the city rising and falling behind her.

"Don't look at me like that," she said, with a smile that had barely changed since they first became friends in grade school. "You thought Weetamoo Woods was the badlands, remember? I can look after myself, Jay. I've had a lot of practice."

"I know, Sugar, and that's exactly what I worry about. Don't you get tired of it? Don't you want to put down roots?"

"I do put them down, Jay, wherever I go. I just pull them up again every spring and plant myself somewhere else is all."

"Well, those bees of yours must be some confused critters, crisscrossing the country at your every whim and fancy. Don't you want a significant other?" Jay persisted. "A family? You know, of your own, not your neighbor's or your hairdresser's or whomsoever you happen to be rescuing? I don't want to say the words 'tick tock' but still . . ."

"I don't rescue people, Jay; that is so sappy. I just help my friends when they need helping and give them a jar or two of honey."

"Sugar, you are a one-woman detox center stroke guidance counselor stroke bank teller stroke babysitter stroke you name it. I've met these people, remember?"

"What nonsense. I just do what any neighbor would do and then I'm on my way."

"That's my point. You're always on your way. Don't you want to actually arrive? I think of my life before I met Paul and we got the house and the dogs and matching chenille bathrobes and it's so much better than it was before. I want that for you too."

Maybe her smile hadn't changed but Jay was sure the light did not quite shine in her eyes the way it once had and was dimming further right now in front of him.

"I'm happy for you, sweetie, you know I am," she said. "And so grateful to have you in my life, even if it's only once a year, in fact especially if it's only once a year because if I wanted someone to make me feel bad about my life on a regular basis I would have stayed at home with . . ."

"Your mother? Ouch! That is one low blow, Cherie-Lynn Wallace!"

"And is that you shirking football practice again, Jason Llewellyn Winthrop the Third?"

They looked at each other for a moment, then laughed, and Jay stepped into her open arms for a hug, the way old friends who have been through a lot together do.

"You do realize there are prison cells bigger than this apartment," he said, over her shoulder.

Sugar grabbed his hand, opened the doors to the terrace, and pulled him outside. "But look at this!"

His eyes skimmed over the floating crop of neighboring rooftops and landed on one bland empty space with nothing but a large sculpture of what looked like a reclining nude in the middle.

"Who would just put a fat naked lady on their rooftop?" he asked, pointing it out.

"You would spot the only blot on the landscape. Look, we can see the Williamsburg Bridge from here and that's Brooklyn sprawled out behind it."

"Hard to believe you can see quite so much sky in a city this size," he admitted.

"It's a different world up here, isn't it? Like we're floating, or part of a beautiful hat."

Not for Sugar the out-of-place rooftop artworks or the everyday detritus at street level, thought Jay. She saw the world with different eyes. It had helped her get over the complications of her past, he knew that, but it was her future that worried him. "Are you happy though?" he asked. "Truly? That's all I want to know."

Sugar felt the buzz of the metropolis humming in her bones as she stood there with the city at her feet. All she could think of was her queen bee waking herself up, shaking herself off and laying herself a great big new happy family in the crazy electric air on this perfect Manhattan rooftop.

"Of course I am," she said. "I'm in New York! Now let's find a place to put the hive then I'll give you an iced tea and a slice of honey loaf and you can get off home."

For most bees, life was short and sweet and pretty uncomplicated. There was certainly no debating any mysterious twists and turns, no choices to make, no wondering how it might all end up. It would end up in a puddle, or against a windscreen, or without wings in a brisk northerly after a busy life of about six weeks, most of it spent hunting for nectar.

But a queen was different and Sugar's queen, Elizabeth the Sixth, was more different than most.

She had known the instant she first emerged from her birth-week diet of nothing but the finest royal jelly that there was more to her life than backing her regal rear into a million empty honeycomb cells and making baby bees.

For she had a special purpose: one passed down in her DNA from Elizabeth the Fifth and before her, the Fourth. In fact, it had been in all Sugar's queens, right back to the one raised by her granddaddy fifteen years before beneath the Belle of Georgia peach trees in his leafy backyard in Summerville, South Carolina.

As to the exact nature of that purpose? None of Sugar's queens had ever been entirely clear about that, but they assumed that when the time was right, they would know what to do.

When Sugar met Theo on Avenue B, even from inside her Styrofoam box Elizabeth the Sixth felt something so powerful reverberating in the air that it was as obvious as the odorant receptors on her face that the time was suddenly right.

4TH

Theo could not get Sugar off his mind.

Every time there was an empty space in his thinking, there she was filling it, floating in and asking him if he was OK, looking up at him with those wide brown eyes.

It had all happened so quickly: the old man knocking him down; the crucial phone connection nearly lost; and the extraordinary woman coming to their aid.

"Sugar." He'd said it out loud in a meeting and his secretary had passed him a Sweet'N Low.

What modern woman was even called Sugar? What modern woman would help pick a crumpled old stranger up off the street? Would worry about cursing? Would call it "cursing"? Would suddenly appear in his life just when he was starting to think it was lacking someone exactly like her?

And then there was the crackle of electricity that had run through his body when their hands touched. Theo had never felt anything like that ever before.

She'd gazed at him with those dark eyes in that astonishing face and all of a sudden everything else had just melted away and he'd all but forgotten his own name.

28

Theodore Lewis Fitzgerald, of Barlanark, Glasgow, Scotland. Sugar.

She haunted him all morning as he racked his brain trying to remember her surname so he could Google her. The exact line of her jaw he could recall, the curve of the tiny dip in the middle of her top lip—he knew that too.

"Sugar, Sugar, Sugar," Marlena, his secretary, caught him repeating as she came into his office later in the day carrying a stack of documents.

"What are you? Trying not to swear or diabetic? Sign this."

The word *ethereal* kept drifting into his thoughts until he looked that up only to find it meant delicate, which wasn't quite right.

She was slim but not insubstantial. Her dress was pink. Her shoes were red. And there was a ribbon in her hair. A ribbon? Could that be right? His niece had grown out of ribbons years before and she was still only ten. Yet Sugar was in her thirties, he figured, and still wearing one and what's more, it suited her. Red. Was it red? Or pink?

He could still see her lovely collarbones, the exquisite dimple at the base of her throat, the gentle pressure of her full breasts rising and falling beneath the fabric of her dress. He could not stop seeing that.

"You are acting very strangely today, Theo," Marlena said when she got back from her late-afternoon cupcake run. "Are you OK?"

"Never better," he answered.

"That's what I mean. You're almost chirpy. A bit dreamy. And then chirpy. Did you win the lottery?"

"Would I be sitting here if I had won the lottery?"

"Knowing you," she said. "Yes."

"It's not true what they say about Scotsmen being cheap," he said. "And anyway I'm always chirpy and did I mention you look particularly bonnie today, Marlena?"

"Get your own cupcake," she said. "I queued ten minutes for mine. And it is true about Scotsmen being cheap and you are not always chirpy."

Marlena reminded Theo of his mother, Shona, who had passed away ten years before on the opposite side of the Atlantic without Theo even knowing she was sick.

He never went a day without missing her, without wishing she was there on the other end of the phone, dispensing advice, her thick Glaswegian brogue coarsened by a lifetime of smoking forty Silk Cuts a day. She'd loved him unflinchingly but she'd been tough, like all Barlanark mothers, and relentlessly straight to the point. Marlena was like that too. It was why he had hired her, but he was surprised to find out she didn't think he was chirpy.

"Not even a wee bit of chirp?"

"No," she said. "Not usually. Until today. Did something happen?"

"Yes, actually," he said. "It did. I met someone."

Marlena put her cupcake down, midbite. "Well, it's about time," she said. "Do you think she is the one?"

Theo's mother had also believed in "the one." "You'll know her when you find her," Shona had told him, time and time again. "Without a shadow of a doubt."

"She's definitely something," Theo told Marlena. "But how do I know if she's the one?"

"You just know, I guess." She shrugged. "Let's start with her name."

"Sugar."

"Sounds fabulous," said Marlena. "You should marry her."

He was never quite sure when Marlena was joking, another quirk she shared with his mother.

"I'm not even sure I'll ever see her again," he said. "I just met her on the street and now I can't remember her last name so I can't find her on Facebook or LinkedIn and I didn't think to get her number."

"You're always telling me what a smart guy you are, Theo. You'll figure it out. Which street did you meet her on?"

"Avenue B."

"Well, that's a start, isn't it?" said Marlena. "And it's just around the corner."

5TH

Sugar woke after the first night in her new apartment, looked out at the jagged peaks of downtown Manhattan wavering behind the floating muslin curtains over the French doors, and wondered why she had dreamed of Theo Fitzgerald.

True, she'd been unnerved by the shock of his touch, by her body's physical reaction to him, but she'd quickly swept that under the rug of her past where she'd long stashed all romantic notions.

She had certainly not expected to think of him again, especially not in a way that continued to chase a shiver up her spine.

Sugar did not want a boyfriend, no matter what Jay thought, no matter what anyone thought. Not all romances were fairy tales; she knew that. She'd long ago decided handsome princes did not always mean happy endings, and she *was* happy—she made it her business to be.

She might no longer have a lot of what she started out with—her family for one—but she refused to mourn that. And her clock was not tick-tocking, despite her being thirty-six. Or if it was, she could not hear it.

Besides, she had her bees. And they were not confused critters at all. What Jay did not know was that Sugar's whim and fancy had nothing to do with where she ended up each year: it was her queen who chose.

At the end of every winter, when the sap started rising in the trees and the flowers and plants began to think about blooming, Sugar would coax a sleepy Elizabeth out of the hive where she'd been huddled for the winter. She'd place her carefully on an old map of her granddaddy's, let her crawl all over it, and wherever she finally stopped was their next destination.

Actually, it wasn't entirely true that she let her crawl all over. Sugar put up barricades, usually made with drinking straws, to steer the queen away from places she didn't want to go back to, which was anywhere she'd already been or the middle of the ocean.

The very first time she'd done it, after she'd fled South Carolina all those years ago, she'd deliberately set up the straws so they led out of the South like a trumpet, nudging Elizabeth the First north of the Mason-Dixon and away from the Atlantic.

That first year, her queen took her to Half Moon Bay in California, clear across the country. The following year she moved inland to the Napa Valley, then back to the coast and Mendocino (one of her favorite stops).

A new queen, Elizabeth the Second, had taken her to Truckee near Lake Tahoe next, then up to Jacksonville, and her successor, the Third, another gentle soul but a little dizzy, led them to Puget Sound, then north Idaho and back down to Santa Fe, while the Fourth chose Colorado and Pennsylvania, before the cantankerous but geographically unadventurous Fifth crawled to Vermont, Maine, New Hampshire and finally Rhode Island before slipping off to queen-bee heaven: five years being a particularly good innings for a queen.

Privately, Sugar had hoped the Sixth might take them elsewhere in California, where the weather suited her own circulation a little better. But if there was any proof that her queens had minds of their own and could not be pushed around like an upturned glass on a high school Ouija board, that confident new queen crawling purposefully toward the tiny overpopulated island of Manhattan was it.

And now here they were.

Sugar got up, drew back the curtains, and stepped out onto her terrace. The bees were parked, for the moment, still in the Styrofoam cooler but in front of the hive, which was currently sitting a few yards out from the exterior wall of neighboring 5A, an apartment that seemed from the outside only marginally bigger than a walk-in closet. It had no direct access to the rooftop as her 5B did, but rather two deep windows that faced out onto it, each one planted with the most exquisite window boxes. One was thick with parsley, sage, chives and coriander and the other with mint, lemon balm, chervil and a miniature pepper.

The perfect spot for her bees, in terms of sun and shelter, was right between those window boxes, but it was rude to put them there without asking whoever lived in 5A. And whoever lived in 5A had been mulching the garden boxes overnight but had not so far pulled back the curtains. However, one of the windows was open a smidge and Sugar could smell something delightfully spicy and buttery wafting from it.

She could not wait to meet such a dab hand in the baking department but people could be a little iffy about living next to bees, she had learned. And a person who gardened at night and blocked the world out during the day was likely more iffy than most.

She'd play that one by ear.

In the meantime, the hive, painted in rainbow stripes by a neighbor's six-year-old twins in some long-ago backyard, was sitting in the middle of the terrace with two gardenias acting as scented sentry guards on either side.

Sugar lugged the gardenias with her wherever she went to help guide the bees back to their new home while they were getting used to their surroundings.

She lugged an electric blue mosaic birdbath too, so they always knew where their drinking water was.

The hive and its accoutrements certainly added a little extra color to her terrace, which, for all its staggering backdrop of Manhattan's downtown alps, was otherwise empty but for a weathered teak table, a matching bench and a couple of slatted foldaway chairs.

"The things we can do here," Sugar said, crouching down close to the handful of bees buzzing around the cooler. "Then there's the park just around the corner, and the East River Park about three blocks that way plus there's Washington Square Park to the west and, not that much farther, Union Square. I mean, can you believe it, Elizabeth? Union Square!"

She always talked to her bees but it was more important than ever when they were in a new home because they needed to know that the air might smell different but Sugar was there, same as the gardenias, same as the birdbath, same as always.

She lifted the top two empty boxes off the beehive, leaving just the bottom brood box containing ten empty honeycomb frames hanging like files in a cabinet drawer.

This is where Elizabeth the Sixth would start laying her new kingdom.

"Sorry, girls, I know this isn't your favorite part," she said, taking the miniature frames the bees were clinging to out of the cooler and gently shaking them down into the larger honeycomb files.

"You go, Betty. Tell them it's business as usual. Just a little higher off the ground is all."

She replaced the top stacks, which held more empty frames waiting for the season's honey deposits, and put the lid back on. Then she swiped a leaf from the gardenia and wedged it carefully in front of the hive's opening on the bottom level, so that the bees could still get in and out but would have to think twice about it, giving them more time to get their bearings.

"Theo Fitzgerald," she said, still trying to shake off the night's uninvited visitor. "I mean, really!" The shake turned into yet another shiver, the sort usually inspired by a particularly wicked mouthful of very rich, supersmooth, utterly sinful ice cream.

6TH

The next day there was still no sign of Sugar's 5A neighbor, although the window boxes had been rearranged overnight, the mint harvested and Thai basil planted in its place. Again, the window was open and the heavenly scent of something deliciously cakelike was swirling around the rooftop.

"Sure smells good out here this morning," Sugar said louder than strictly necessary.

It was making her hungry. And the bees too, by the look of things. They'd eaten all the sugar syrup she'd put in their hive-top feeder the day before to give them some get-up-and-go while their numbers were building up.

And now she was out of sugar.

There was a big glossy market only a few blocks away, and a smaller convenience store closer by, but Sugar had made a lifetime of friends by *not* going to glossy markets or nearby convenience stores. She still got letters from them every single day.

And she might be in New York now, but that was no excuse not to do the exact same thing she would do if she were in Pittston or Truckee: knock on a door and ask for a cup of something.

She knew 5A must have sugar because of the tantalizing baking smells emanating from within, and she thought she heard someone shuffling on the other side of the door when she knocked, but no one answered.

Iffy, she thought again. Definitely iffy.

The door of Apartment 4 was painted bright green and was opened by a stocky little man of around seventy bearing an alarming shock of dyed orange hair.

"Whatever you're selling I won't be buying any," he said, "so you can feck right off."

"Good morning to you too, sir, I'm not selling a single thing," Sugar said, unfazed. "My name is Sugar Wallace and I've just moved in upstairs. I know it's an imposition but I wonder if you could spare a cup of sugar?"

The stocky little man peered at her, a deep suspicion rippling across his wrinkled face. "Did she put you up to this, that poxy feckin' she-devil? Did she?"

"No, sir, no one put me up to anything. I'm just after a cup of sugar is all. Simple as that."

"Sugar asking for sugar? You must think *I'm* simple. Damn the both of you!" He stepped back into his apartment and slammed the door shut so hard it rattled in its frame.

Had he been her only neighbor, Sugar might have been put out, but there were three more floors to go, so down she went to the next level where the faded green-red-and-white-striped door of Apartment 3 opened before she even had a chance to knock, and a similarly irritated woman emerged.

"He giving you trouble? Old McNally?" She looked older than the man upstairs, and her flowery smock looked older still, but a pair of delicate ruby earrings echoed some distant glamour from her past. "He gives you trouble," she said, "and I'll kill him."

"I'm not looking for trouble," Sugar said. "Just a cup of sugar if you have any to spare."

"Did McNally give you sugar?" the old woman asked.

"Maybe he didn't have any," Sugar said, shaking her head. "Anyway, I'm new to the building, just settling in up on the fifth floor and found myself short so—I'm sorry, look at me, standing here rambling on and I didn't even catch your name."

"I didn't throw it," the old woman said. "But it's Mrs. Keschl. You say McNally didn't give you sugar? I say I would give you sugar, if I had any, only I don't." She shrugged again and shut the door, not as strenuously as her upstairs neighbor but vigorously enough all the same.

Sugar dropped down another flight of stairs.

Apartment 2's door was beautiful: it had been painted in bright colors with a Polynesian dancer in the middle and tiny landscape vignettes at the sides like speech bubbles.

A pretty woman with tired eyes, long blue dreadlocks and a crying toddler on her hip opened it. "What do you want?"

"Why, I love your skirt," Sugar said. It was bright orange leather and blindingly short.

The compliment took the wearer of the skirt by surprise. "What?"

"Your skirt, I love it. You have the perfect legs for it." Indeed, her legs were long and slim and encased in holey fishnet pantyhose, which disappeared into tattered biker boots. It was not a look Sugar herself would go for but she appreciated that someone else could pull it off so well.

"Yeah, well, whatever."

"Hey, little man," Sugar said to the toddler, who started sucking his thumb and hiccuping instead of crying. "What's your name?"

"This is Ethan," said his mom. "And I'm Lola, OK? What do you want?"

"It's a pleasure to meet you Ethan and Lola. Are you Lola of Lola's Balloons?"

"Don't talk to me about those fucking balloons!" Lola's scowl deepened, snatching the prettiness from her face.

"Oh, I'm sorry, I was just admiring the store and—"

"Yeah, well, I don't want people to admire it, or stand here and talk to me about it, I want them to come in and buy the fucking balloons."

Sugar suddenly understood how a deflated balloon might feel. But she also knew that if a balloon had a choice, it would rather be full of air.

"Why, I would love to buy some balloons!" she said. "Just tell me what your opening hours are. And in the meantime, I was wondering if you have a cup of sugar I could borrow?"

Lola looked at her as if she was out of her mind. "What are you, like, a Walton?"

"A Wallace," Sugar answered. "We hand out cups of sugar left, right and center where I come from although I guess it doesn't happen so much here."

"Here in the twenty-first century? No," said Lola. Ethan took his thumb out of his mouth and started to cry again. "Look, I have agave syrup, but it's for him. No sugar. I'm running late. I have to go." And yet another door briskly closed in Sugar's face.

Still not put off, she descended the last flight of stairs and knocked politely, but for a good length of time, on the last apartment door, the dark gray one with five locks, each of which she eventually heard being slowly released.

The door was then opened by just about the thinnest girl Sugar had ever seen. She was wearing jeans that hung off her childlike hips, and two sweaters whose necklines revealed bones so close to the skin Sugar was amazed they hadn't broken through. She had blond hair that was tied up in a knot on her head, and lovely pale green eyes fringed with dark lashes.

"What are you looking at?" she asked.

"Why, I'm looking at you," Sugar replied.

"Well, don't," the girl said, but she didn't close the door.

"Please excuse my rudeness," Sugar said, reaching out her hand. "I'm Sugar Wallace."

"Sugar? What a stupid name," said the girl, looking at her hand for a moment before her eyes rolled back in her head and she fainted, dropping like a silk scarf onto the floor.

7TH

Mr. McNally limped back to his favorite chair and sank into it. His hip was killing him, just not quickly enough for his liking. He settled back into the worn cushions and reached for the remote.

Television was all he lived for these days even though there was nothing decent to watch apart from the classic movie channels. He figured he must have seen every movie at least a dozen times and none of them was improving with age but at least they weren't total shite to begin with like all the modern films.

His television was the only new item in an apartment otherwise untouched since the eighties. It was enormous, a flat screen, his pride and joy—or his pride, anyway.

Joy? He had forgotten how to feel that. He'd forgotten how to feel anything except anger: anger at making so many mistakes in his life and anger at not knowing how to fix even one of them. All his sixty-seven years had been a total waste of time except for a few years closer to the start than the finish where he'd found happiness and then thrown it away. And that made him even angrier: the fact that he had messed up his life himself. In fact, that made him so angry that he couldn't think straight—he hadn't thought straight in decades. He'd turned into the sort of grumpy old bastard he'd been terrified of as a boy.

Of course he had sugar. He had loads of the stuff, sitting in a faded striped canister in his empty kitchen. He didn't eat much these days but he still liked a cup of tea so strong you could stand a spoon up in it and half a pound of sugar too, thank you very much.

She was a looker, the new tenant, and he didn't know why he felt the way he did when he opened the door and saw her there; why he got angry before he got anything else. It was that poxy whore's-melt downstairs who was to blame. It must be.

Below him Mrs. Keschl had shuffled back to her kitchen where she'd been in the middle of making something but couldn't remember what. There was an onion on the kitchen counter, and a bay leaf, and a stick of butter and a ball of yarn.

She hadn't knitted anything for twenty-four years and she didn't have a kitten so she was hard-pressed to imagine what the ball of yarn was for. The kitchen was dark and put her in a bad mood, which wasn't far to go. That old fink McNally! Not letting the new tenant have a cup of sugar when she knew the miserable toad practically lived on the stuff.

She shuffled back into the living room and over to her favorite spot in front of the dresser crammed full of her mother's china, brought from Hungary decades before and never used, or admired, but in prime position anyway. Her ankles were swollen and her back hurt and she felt like reading a good book except that she didn't have one and her glasses had broken during the Clinton administration and she hadn't bothered to get them fixed.

43

"This is old age," she said as she sat down. "I ask myself—what's the point?" She asked herself a lot of things these days and couldn't always remember the answers.

Her moods were worse, she knew that. She was not always a nice person to be around but that was just her way of avoiding the sadness that filtered its way into her like rainwater into a dry mountain creek.

There was still goodness in her, even though it might not be obvious to others. But she knew it for a fact and she clung to it. Then she heard the kid start caterwauling in the apartment below and wondered just how long she could keep hold.

Downstairs, Lola was gluing butterflies on to a bright pink lampshade that spun and sang "Send in the Clowns" when she turned it on. It was one of the few things that stopped Ethan's crying. Her son was her most prized possession but his crying exhausted her so life was being boiled down to a string of things that shut him up. All she wanted was to be a good mother but it was harder than anything else she had ever done.

When she wasn't painting the walls to give him more color, adding a sapphire blue sofa there, a scarlet toy box here, a cobalt throw there, she was trying to make a living, but sometimes she struggled to see how she would ever have fun again.

There was never enough money, enough time, enough customers, enough vodka, enough good-looking men who had even half a clue what to do with an amenable female—that's if she could ever get a sitter.

There was a way forward, that was becoming clear, but she didn't want to taint the life of her perfect, pure, sweet-smelling son the way she had once tainted her own.

She looked at her boy on the rug, his sad little face crumpled, tears collecting in the corners of his eyes like dewdrops. Then he lifted his fat little arms up to her, hands opening and closing, and she scooped him from the floor and hugged him close.

He was still crying, but the way he burrowed into her she knew he felt better.

8TH

At the touch of Sugar's soft hand on her cold brow, Ruby's eyes flickered open and she stared up, trying to work out what had happened.

Sugar just let her stare, then gently helped her back to her feet.

Whether people tended to need more helping to their feet when Sugar was around or whether she just noticed them being on the ground more than others in the first place, she could never quite say. But either way she seemed to help people to their feet a lot. They were the people who still wrote her letters.

Most of them took more out of her than Ruby. She weighed next to nothing; it was like herding a cloud.

"The name my mother gave me is Cherie-Lynn," Sugar said, as the fragile girl wobbled on her spindly legs like a newborn foal. "But I'm not sure it's any less stupid."

"It isn't," said Ruby. "I'm Ruby." She was seeing stars. She loved seeing stars, although it meant that the hospital was not far away and she did not love the hospital.

"You know I could really use a glass of water," Sugar said. "Would it be OK if I came in?"

Without waiting for an answer, she stepped forward and shut the door behind her, then took Ruby by one bony elbow and navigated her to a big red wingback armchair over by the window.

The apartment was roughly twice as big as Sugar's and furnished expensively, but not in a way she thought a young woman like Ruby would go for. The colors were dark and a wall of books, mostly fairly weighty reading from what she could see, lent it an aristocratic library feel. With the drapes pulled all but closed, the apartment had a sour, stale feeling to it, as though the windows were never opened.

"I'll just sit you down here and if it's all right with you I'll get us each a drink."

Ruby's gaze followed her into the kitchen. She was kind, this Sugar woman, but Ruby knew where such kindness usually led: to food.

Ruby was down to sixteen one-eighths of a cracker, three wedges of orange, a whole stick of celery, which she did not even like, a small jar of baby food for vitamins and minerals, and half a diet soda each day and she felt good at that level although she thought that perhaps she could cut back to two wedges of orange. Of course, if the hospital was just around the corner, she should probably consider raising her quota to four wedges of orange and even maybe add a carrot but it was just that she felt so good the way things were at the moment with three and just the celery.

"Now is there anyone I should call for you?" Sugar called from the kitchen, a beautifully equipped gourmet setup of which she doubted Ruby used even a fraction. "I could do that if you need me to; otherwise I'm quite happy to sit with you until you get your equilibrium back." She took in the neatly displayed boxes of cereal, the array of artisan pastas, the selection of oils, the preserves, the shelves heaving with cookbooks. "Equilibrium is very important," she continued, checking out the refrigerator, packed with unopened cheeses, meats, a cooked chicken, a box of whoopie pies—none of it touched. "Nobody tells you that when you're young. Always yakking on about the birds and the bees and vocational guidance but let me tell you, equilibrium is right up there with breathing."

She carried the two glasses of water into the living room and handed one to Ruby. "I learned that myself some years ago but I learned it the hard way. It comes naturally to some but I'm sorry to say I wasn't one of them."

"I'm fine," Ruby said.

"I'll just sit here and finish my glass of water and then I'll be on my way. I have a lot to get done today. What about you?"

Ruby had thought about walking up to the Whole Foods at Columbus Circle because they most likely had the biggest selection of quinoa, but now she wasn't so sure. She tried to remember how long it had been last time between the stars and the hospital. She had a horrible feeling it had been not that long. Maybe she should just think about going to the smaller Tribeca Whole Foods. Or the Chelsea one.

Actually, now she came to think about it, she was pretty sure that it was a couple of weeks between the stars and the hospital. Possibly even a month. It had been OK until the nurses had called her mother. Then there'd been a scene that she didn't care to revisit. She should have the extra bit of orange and the carrot. And some quinoa.

She couldn't remember how her daily intake had been whittled down to so little. She was sure she had been trying harder, had been doing better. Where had she gone wrong?

"I don't need you to call anyone," she said. "You can go now if you want. I'm fine."

"All right then," said Sugar, not moving. "You know I always wanted to be named after a jewel. In fact, I wanted to be called Jewel but the best I could get away with was Sugar, which is what my granddaddy called me, or Sugar Honey to be exact, which sounded OK the way he said it but otherwise I guess it is a bit much."

"Your water is finished," Ruby said.

"So it is," Sugar agreed. "But I still have a terrible thirst so would you mind if I help myself to another glass before I go? It's hot up there on the rooftop—I live up there, did I mention that? And a person can get dehydrated climbing all those stairs. Or just walking on the flat for that matter. I'll get you another glass while I'm at it."

Ruby was too exhausted to object. She would wait until she felt better, perhaps do a few more sit-ups. Then she would walk down to Tribeca and maybe get a diet soda and take it to Battery Park if it was such a nice day that people were getting dehydrated everywhere. They had one of those fountains that spurted up from the ground down there and if you found the right seat, you could watch the children play in it and see past them to the Statue of Liberty in the distance. Ruby liked that. She felt the farthest away from the Upper East Side at the very bottom tip of Manhattan.

"Oh, you keep a scrapbook," Sugar said, noticing the leather-bound book sitting on the coffee table near Ruby's chair when she came back with two more full glasses.

49

Ruby picked up the book, and held it to her chest, blushing. "It's private," she said.

"I kept a scrapbook when I was younger," Sugar told her. "For years, I put all sorts of things in it. I wanted to keep a diary but I knew my mama would read it so I just collected bits and pieces to remind me of things instead of writing it all down."

"Mine isn't that sort of a scrapbook," Ruby said. "It isn't about me."

"So who's it about?"

"Other people."

"Other people you know or other people you don't?"

It occurred to Ruby that it had been quite a long time since she had talked to anyone. It felt foreign, like Dutch. She couldn't now work out how Sugar had gotten in to her apartment and started a conversation. Had Ruby invited her? Had Sugar invited herself? It all seemed hazy somehow, but familiar too, in a good way, like she was always talking with people, which she wasn't unless they were people her mother paid to tell her she should eat and she didn't do that anymore. Talk to the people that is.

Sugar hadn't mentioned eating. Not once.

"I remember my scrapbook had a birthday card from my oldest brother Troy," she was saying, "who told me I was the sweetest sixteen the whole city had ever seen, and it had a dried red rose from my prom date, Charlie Harrison, who turned out to have thirty-three warts on one hand and eleven on the other. And I had a photo of Grampa Boone—on my mother's side, the one who called me Sugar Honey—getting married to my grandmother and I even had a tiny little piece of lace from her wedding veil."

Ruby looked down at the leather-bound folder. "Oh," she said. "Mine is a little bit like that."

Sugar smiled and pointed at the scrapbook. "Go on then, honey. Let's take a look."

To her own surprise, Ruby found herself opening it, smoothing the pages with her small bony fingers as she slowly started to turn them.

"Goodness," Sugar said. "I wasn't expecting that."

Far from being the record of a single city girl's misspent youth or a collection of aspirational skeletons as she had suspected, each page bore a neatly glued *New York Times* clipping of a newly married couple beaming into each other's eyes, or at the camera, or twirling on a dance floor.

"Weddings," said Ruby. "Every weekend they have all these lame stories about people getting married. It's such a crock. I mean they just come out with all this ridiculous stuff about falling in love and all that. And they talk about how they met and what they first thought and how it all went wrong but then they met again and realized it was meant to be and so they got married."

"They do?"

"Yeah, no one just says, 'We met in a bar and didn't hate each other and my ovaries were about to shrivel up and die so we hooked up.' There's always some big story."

"Is that so?"

"I just started putting some of the really weird ones together and then it kind of turned into a scrapbook. The world's most stupid scrapbook."

"So, are you in college?" Sugar asked.

"Look at this one," Ruby said. "Katie Sheehan and Adam O'Neill met in some dorks' online support group for *Jeopardy!* fans. Can you believe that?"

"People sure do meet in the strangest places these days," said Sugar. "You don't even have to be anywhere."

Ruby flicked over the page. "And Trey Tenforde and Genevieve Ford? A bird shat on his ice cream on their first date and that made her fall in love with him. Bird shit! Can you believe it? And these two—look, two men—lived together for twenty years but then one got cancer so they went to Iowa and got married. That's before they changed the law here so the same sexes could get married at home."

"Well, looks like you're quite the romantic, Ruby."

"No, I'm not." Ruby bristled. "I'm just someone who likes stories with bird shit in them." She slapped the book shut. "That's why it's private. That's why I never show it to anyone. It's not about me. It's about all the losers out there and their stupid lame stories."

"They're definitely better to collect than stories about murder and mayhem," Sugar said.

"Or stamps," Ruby added. "I hate stamps."

A pale pink hue had snuck into her cheeks. Sugar didn't know what had done it, looking at all that marital bliss or having someone to talk to about it. One thing she was sure of was that this girl was starved of more than just food. She was lonely.

And Sugar was good with lonely.

9TH

Theo was at Gramercy Park Hotel on a second date with Anita, a sophisticated blond advertising executive with whom his former brother-in-law had set him up.

She was halfway through a story about a photo shoot she'd just been on with a celebrity whose famous rock-star husband had terrible body odor issues when Theo thought he saw Sugar walk past outside.

"I'm so sorry; can you excuse me a moment?" he interrupted, not waiting for a reply as he jumped up and raced out onto the street, on the trail of the shiny swinging ponytail. But then the ponytail turned the corner and he saw its owner was of Asian heritage—and pregnant.

It was not Sugar at all.

He breathed out, long and slow, the crushing ache of disappointment sitting on his chest like a Glaswegian smog as he walked back to the bar to apologize to Anita. She was very pretty. Smart, and good company too.

"Do you want to try that new Spanish place around the corner?" she asked when he sat down again. "It just got three stars."

Usually Theo would have said yes, even though he knew he did not feel anywhere near enough for Anita to take it much further (and he thought tapas were bad value for the money). Usually, he would go on a third date before letting her down gently, saying he just wasn't ready for anything serious and did not want to pretend otherwise. Usually that would be the truth. But suddenly he had the feeling he was ready for something serious. Just not with Anita.

And what his wreck of a marriage, subsequent divorce and years of therapy had reminded him was that honesty was always the best policy. His mother had taught him that too, but somewhere along the line he had forgotten. Never again.

"This is going to sound terrible," he said. "But I just saw someone I thought I knew and it made me realize I'm just not in the right space to pursue anything here, Anita, so I should really pass on the Spanish place. I'm so sorry."

"Is this because you think tapas are too small?" she said. "Sam told me you were cheap."

What would Sugar be doing in Gramercy anyway? Theo thought, after he'd paid the check. Marlena was right. He needed to spend more time on Avenue B.

10TH

Tompkins Square Park did not quite have the polish of its uptown cousins like Madison Square or Washington Square, but it had an eclectic charm that appealed to Sugar nonetheless. The street frontages around the park housed a mixture of cafés, bars and convenience stores in varying stages of gentrification, a state that seemed to be reflected by the park's occupants.

The dog owners congregated in one corner, the moms and playing children in another, the vocal but otherwise harmless homeless took up a line of bench seating over by Avenue A and a group of Hare Krishnas were generally found praying at the foot of a tree on the south side.

One clear morning not long after she'd moved onto Flores Street, Sugar was sitting on a sun-soaked bench listening to a blind saxophonist softly channeling Louis Armstrong by the temperance fountain in the middle. As she watched a trio of bees happily fly from leaf to flower to somewhere in the distance she thought that it was, indeed, a beautiful world.

"You go on and fill your boots now," she told the bees, wondering if they were hers as they flew over her head. Lord knew she loved the creatures but she could still not tell hers from anyone else's.

"You talking to me or the insects?" It was George Wainwright, wearing the same coat as he had the day she met him, though it looked as though it had been dry-cleaned. The buttons shone, as did his shoes, and he had a pair of near-new black trousers on too. Without the flotsam of the curb stuck to him, he looked a world away from the tattered souls arguing with each other or no one in particular on the other side of the park.

He was no more homeless than she was.

"Well hello, George. What a pleasure to see you again."

"The pleasure is all mine, Miss Sugar. Mind if I join you?"

"It would save me from the pain of having everyone else think I'm crazy sitting here on my own talking to the bug world."

"Oh, I don't think too many people would mind that here," said George. "This park is kind of known for its crazy."

"It sure has a certain color to it," Sugar said.

"Always has had. They say this used to be the most populated two square miles on the planet. First stop in the new world for most folk. Although by and large they couldn't get away from it quickly enough." He winced as he shifted his weight on the bench seat.

"That leg still giving you trouble?" Sugar asked.

George flapped his hand in front of his face. "It's nothing," he said. "Just another sign of being old and decrepitated and at eighty-two years of age I've already had my fill of those. But who wants to hear about an old man getting older? Tell me something about yourself, Miss Sugar. Where are you from?"

"I'm from just around the corner on Flores Street," she

answered. "You know the building with the balloon shop in the basement?"

"No, Miss Sugar, that's where you're *at*," George said, with great indignation. "I mean where are you from? You know, *from*."

Sugar sighed, a sorry little flutter of air that she barely noticed but that told George more than she could have imagined. "I guess I'm not really from there anymore," she said, watching another bee hover around George's head as if something were about to bloom out of his ear. "I haven't been from there for a long time."

George's eyes followed the bee to a pale yellow rosebush in the garden opposite them.

"Bees love yellow," Sugar said. "And blue. But not red. Isn't that strange?"

"I find red a little tacky myself," said George. "Although yellow doesn't do much for my complexion either, now I come to think on it."

"Nothing worse than tacky," Sugar said, and they smiled at each other. "And you, George? Where are you from?"

"The place you haven't been from for such a long time, I think I haven't been from somewhere nearby for even longer."

Now that he said that, now that she recognized the rhythm of his words, Sugar realized she must have known that all along, although usually she steered clear of anyone with a southern twang, wary of treading too close to the deep roots of her past.

"Do you ever come to the greenmarket here on a Sunday?" she asked. "I'm hoping I can get a spot."

"Occasionally I do." George nodded. "It's small but there's a mighty fine baker and a cheese man from upstate and there's ice cream too, I think. And lavender. Leastways, it always smells of lavender. And what would you be selling at a greenmarket, Miss Sugar?"

"Honey, mostly, which is why I was communing with the bees here. I need to keep on the right side of them."

"You strike me as the type to keep on the right side of most things if you don't mind me saying so."

Sugar did not mind him saying so. He reminded her of her grandfather was the thing, so he could say just about whatever he wanted.

She felt tears collect in the corner of her mind, which was as far as she usually allowed them to go. "Do you miss it?" she asked, even though she hardly dared ask herself the same question. "The place you used to come from?"

"Oh, there's no 'used to' about it, Miss Sugar. Where you're from is where you're from and a person will always miss it. There's no getting away from that. But that's not the end of the world. You just get familiar with the missing, is all."

He was right, of course, although he said it like it was an easy thing to do when she knew that wasn't the case. "Did you ever go back?" she asked.

"No, ma'am, I did not."

"Did you ever want to?"

It was George's turn to sigh now, but his flutter of air had a more resigned impression to it than Sugar's; his reason for sighing had been around a lot longer. "Truth is, I did a terrible thing," he said. "Hurt a lot of people back there, back then, so I was not welcome back. Wanting never came into it."

"I'm sorry to hear that, George."

"Me too, sorrier than most anyone will ever know, but that doesn't change things."

"Well, I'm sorry about that too."

"So what about you, Miss Sugar? You ever going back?"

"I did a terrible thing too," she answered. "Just like you."

"Whatever you did, I bet you it wasn't just like me," George said.

"I hurt people, just like you, and I'm not welcome back, just like you."

George reared back and took a funny look at her. "You don't look like you would hurt a flea."

"And you look like the guy who drove Miss Daisy."

He laughed. "Nice of you to say so," he said. "I appreciate that. And that other business, well, that was a long time ago and the truth is, I wouldn't have it any other way."

"You don't have to tell me any more," said Sugar. "I understand secrets."

"It's not so much a secret, just something that doesn't sound so good when you say it out loud. But I guess if you put it plainly, I stole my brother's wife right out from under his nose. And while it was a terrible thing to do and caused more heartache than you could ever imagine, truth was, she was with the wrong man and she wasn't going to get the happiness she deserved with him. And I knew she could get it with me, and as the good Lord knows, so indeed she did. I loved that sweet woman with all my heart and soul every moment of every day until she passed away three years ago this July."

"Oh, George, I'm so sorry for your loss."

"Thank you, Miss Sugar."

They sat companionably in the sun giving their thoughts a little breathing space as they watched the bees zoom in and out of the elms.

"So where are you at, George?" Sugar eventually asked.

"I live with my great-nephew and his family up in Harlem," he said. "They're wonderful people and I'm very welcome there but his wife doesn't need me getting in her hair all day long so I come down here, where Eliza and I, that's my wife, had some of our happiest times. We lived over on Avenue C most our lives and I stayed there for a time after she passed but then I lost my job—replaced by a camera. Strange old world we live in. Slippery, as you said the day we met."

"What was your job?"

"I'm a doorman," he said. "Yes, ma'am, I have farewelled and welcomed some of the best this city has ever seen in my time. But modernization got me in the end and now I like to sit around down here, remembering better times."

"I'll bet you were the perfect doorman," Sugar said. "Manners like yours are hard to come by."

"Funny thing is, I always felt like the perfect doorman. Got interviewed for a magazine article once and the young fella writing the story asked me if it was demeaning, opening and closing doors for people, but I never felt that way about it at all. I felt honored to be in a position of such trust, to have people depend on me, even if it was only for little things. I liked that I could start someone's morning in a way that might fix their mood a little better, or make them feel good about coming home at the end of a long day. That's not demeaning where I come from. That's the bread of life. And I miss it. In fact, too much of my day is spent missing things, which does a person's spirit no good in the long run."

He shook his head. "Listen to me, whining on like the world owes me a living. It's a beautiful day and I'm sitting right here in it. I'm more blessed than most. And the pleasure of your company is a blessing on its own. But I'm going to head over to the river now, sit and look at the Williamsburg Bridge a little while before the wind comes up."

He stood up, but almost buckled under his own weight.

"That leg of yours does not look like nothing to me," Sugar said.

"It's giving me trouble," George admitted.

"You mind if I take a look?"

"Are you a doctor?"

"No, but I can sometimes fix things, just the same."

"Nothing to lose." George sat back down and lifted his trouser cuff to reveal the open sore on his shin.

"Did you do this falling on the curb the other day?"

"Reckon this is why I fell on the curb the other day. Been there for months. Just can't get rid of the darn thing."

"And you've been to the ER?"

George raised one distinguished eyebrow. "It might seem like I have nothing better to do than sit around a hospital all day but something always comes along."

Sugar stood up. "I have a remedy at my apartment that's going to clean this up real quick," she said. "Want to come by and let me see what I can do?"

He smiled and held out his arm. "Miss Sugar Wallace, it would be rude not to."

11TH

Lola tied a new balloon to the railing—a dinosaur, good sized but with a slightly surprised expression on its face and not quite the same shade of brilliant green she had imagined when she ordered it.

She looked up Flores Street and saw Mrs. Keschl scuttling like a crab down one side and Mr. McNally studiously ignoring her, dyed orange hair glinting in the sunlight, on the other.

The crazy guy who always dressed in a purple glittery cloak was crossing up at Avenue B and the actress converting an entire building at the other end of the street was being driven past in her limo.

None of them were balloon buyers.

Lola flicked at the dinosaur with her multicolored nails just as her phone vibrated in her pocket. It was another text from Rollo, a friend, sort of, from the bad old days before Ethan. She'd bumped into him in the square recently but he still ran with the old crowd and she was not interested in running with him.

U LOOKD SO GUD THE OTHER DAY, the text said. SURE U DONT WAN2 MAKE SUM $$? CALL ME.

She did not want to call him. She really did not. But she needed $$.

She looked up and down Flores Street again. It was empty. She punched the dinosaur in the head and stomped down the stairs to the store, slamming the door closed behind her without flipping the CLOSED sign to OPEN.

Moments later, Sugar and George came around the corner. The dinosaur was still looking surprised and bobbing from Lola's punch but it was far perkier than the other balloons. The world globe now looked like a peach pit, and the superhero had aged a further decade.

"I'd buy some balloons to help her out if I could ever get in the place," Sugar said. "Or at least help her blow them up a little better. But she keeps closing the store."

"Some folk just don't want helping," George said.

"Speaking of which, we have four flights of stairs to climb. Are you going to be all right with that?"

"My leg will do fine but my head might suffer," he said examining the building's entrance. "I'm not much of a one for heights. This door is an original, did you know that? It sticks, I bet, and it'll be heavy to push too, but still, that's one fine-looking door."

Sugar thought this through as George opened the second door and then slowly followed her up the stairs.

Once they reached her apartment he stuck to the wall like a limpet and Sugar had to prize him away and lead him, eyes closed, to the sofa.

"Up off the ground and in a lady's boudoir," he said. "This does not feel right."

"It's my kitchen and my living room as well," Sugar assured him. "And if you open your eyes and look outside, it's my rooftop terrace too."

George opened one eye enough to confirm that he was too high off the ground.

"Just let me look at that leg of yours and I'll have you on your way back down to ground level in no time," Sugar assured him.

His eyes stayed closed while she bathed the wound but he opened them to watch her apply pure honey with a drop of tea tree oil in it.

"You think honey can really fix this?" he asked.

"I think honey can fix anything," she said. "I know most people just want to eat it but there's a heck of a lot more you can do with a little honey. It's practically magic."

"Is that so?"

"It's all antiseptic," she said. "Every last drop. But there's a type of tree over in New Zealand called manuka. It's not so pretty to look at, kind of dark and scraggy with a tiny white flower. Anyway, the bees love it like nothing else and the ones who feed on it make the best healing honey in the whole world. I tasted it once; it's real strong and woody, with a hint of lemon." She showed him the label on the jar of honey she'd used on his leg. "This New Hampshire amber is pretty good too, but it might take a week or so. Still, you'll be opening and closing doors before you know it."

"If only I had any doors to open and close."

"About that," Sugar said. "I was wondering . . . You know, it seems to me that you are a doorman without a door and that is not a good state of affairs, yet right here at 33 Flores Street we have a door—and, as you have already pointed out, a very unobliging one at that—which seems to me to be seriously short of a doorman."

"Indeed you do and indeed it is," said George.

"I would even go as far as saying that opening and closing that door all day long is just wearing me and the other tenants of this building out. They're for the most part not in the best shape to begin with, it has to be said. So what I was thinking was maybe you could act as an honorary doorman for a while. Then you'd be helping us all out and you'd be handy for me to keep an eye on while your leg heals too."

"You think that would be all right with the others?"

"Who in their right mind would complain about having a free doorman?"

"I knew it the moment I laid eyes on you," George said. "You are an angel."

"I most certainly am not," Sugar said, "and I think you'll find that neither is anyone else who lives here. I've met all but one of them and I'm sure they are sweethearts, really, deep down. But on the surface . . ."

"Manners are somewhat lacking?"

"Yes," Sugar agreed. "Manners are somewhat lacking. But I'm sure we can do something about that. Just give me a chance to run you up the flagpole, so to speak. Come back Monday and hopefully we can put you to work."

12TH

Marlena bought Theo a cupcake, which had never happened before. He was more of a shortbread person, as it happened, but he would rather face three inches of putrid pale pink frosting than risk hurting her feelings. He would rather face three feet of it.

Plus it was truly difficult for a Scotsman to look a gift horse in the mouth. It hardly ever happened.

"I see from the time of night you've been sending e-mails this week that your dating has come to a standstill," Marlena said. "What's up with that?"

"I thought I saw her," Theo said. "Sugar, I mean. The one I told you about. And even though it turned out not to be her, it got me thinking."

"Oh, thinking," Marlena said. "Yeah, sure, like you haven't done enough of *that* since your divorce."

"As you're clearly taking such a close interest, you might like to know then that I'm also doing a wee bit of stalking."

"OK," said Marlena. "Now we're getting somewhere."

Marlena had worked within eyeshot of Theo ever since he first arrived in New York so knew all about his meteoric rise in fortune, his catastrophic marriage to a society blonde and his subsequent descent into misery. She'd also played a bigger role than she knew in his salvation.

Theo had been fully aware how much his mother would have despised the person he turned into after marrying Carolyn. And the one he turned into after Carolyn left him for their Amagansett gardener, Joe. But every time Marlena brought him an aspirin after a big night out or walked in on an unsavory phone conversation or laid a reassuring hand on his shoulder just when he most ached for a gentle touch, he was reminded how much he once wanted to be a man of whom his mother would be proud.

And with Marlena's stoic support he eventually turned back into that person.

He'd changed so much since those days. He had a different job, a different haircut, he wore different clothes. He was just plain different. And he was much better at being different than he was at trying to fit in, which was what he'd attempted in the first few years after he moved to New York.

"You just have to accept that you have old-fashioned values," his therapist had told him when they both agreed he was no longer likely to rip the heads off flowers or beat up people called Joe, which meant he could stop coming. "I guess it's a Scottish thing. But it can put you at odds with the modern world so you must always trust your instincts, Theo. You have really good instincts."

His instincts were now telling him that his mother might no longer be around to counsel him while sipping on a Rusty Nail and sucking on a cigarette, but he could hear her voice ringing in his ears all the same. He would know the one when he found her, she'd said. Without a shadow of a doubt. The problem was that he now thought he had found her but he'd lost her before the shadow of a doubt could either make itself obvious or be discounted. His instincts clearly weren't *that* good—they hadn't even kicked in enough at the time to do anything sensible like nudge him to ask Sugar for her number. But they were still suggesting that if he kept looking for her, he would find her.

He'd practically made a nuisance of himself hanging around Alphabet City since the aborted date with Anita, asking after Sugar at the Tibetan handicrafts store, the Indian spice shop and even at the dive bar on the corner of Sixth Street, where he was pretty sure they thought he was a cop.

His instincts told him to get the hell out of there before he got his arse kicked. They also told him that the coffee at Ninth Street Espresso was better than the coffee at the bar next door but he couldn't see enough of Avenue B from there.

13TH

If there was one place Sugar had come to feel truly comfortable, it was among a crowd of people yet to discover the joy of good manners.

When she first fled the South, full of shame and remorse at her own unforgivable rudeness, she had been totally overwhelmed by the lack of courtesy shown in the world outside the one she knew. On the leafy peninsula of Charleston, South Carolina, where she'd been born and bred, folks still said "please" and "thank you" and "excuse me" even if they were hopped up on goofballs, pointing a shotgun at you and demanding the contents of your purse. But farther north, it had been the first of many rude shocks—rude being the operative word—to discover that courtesy counted for far less.

Until she found herself adrift from her family, her future, her home and her friends, Sugar had not known how important common courtesy was to her. In fact, she had not known what was important to her at all. In those first few dark months, however, she'd had plenty of time to take a good hard look at herself and she had seen, stripped of all her history, what was left of her, what lay at her core. There wasn't much there. So what there was counted for a lot.

She had her manners. And she had her bees.

Both of these she had inherited from her grandfather: the most important fixture in her past and a devoted beekeeper who cared about manners more than most. "Doesn't matter if no one else has them," he'd once told her, "just so long as you do. That's how good manners work. Do unto others as you would have done unto you. Manners aren't anything but a polite person being nice, no matter what everyone else is doing. But they make the world a better place, Sugar Honey, you can trust me on that. So don't you ever go forgetting yours, you promise?"

She had promised, and she had broken that promise, but only once; and as she traveled across the country year after year, tending her bees and harvesting her honey, she tried to spread her manners around as much as she could to make up for that single transgression.

It was what her grandfather would have wanted, she figured. And it wasn't exactly hard to make improvements when the starting point was quite so low.

No matter where she went—California, Colorado, Washington, Pennsylvania, Vermont, wherever—pretty much nobody was as clued into manners as she was.

And 33 Flores Street was certainly no exception.

"I do believe that George can help make this world a better place," Sugar told Elizabeth the Sixth once she'd escorted him back downstairs and seen him on his way. "And I know just the way to get everyone to agree with me."

It was called brunch.

Very early the next morning, Sugar heard her 5A neighbor rustling in his window boxes. She slipped on her robe and scuffed over to the French doors, opening them enough to poke her nose out and pick up the scent of butter, flour, sugar, eggs and a hot oven working their indisputable magic.

The sun was coming up, casting its cotton candy colors on the skyline; the early-morning shadows fell across the surrounding rooftops like Dr. Seuss fingers on crooked piano keys.

She stood there for a while, breathing in the city, the baking, the good fortune of finding herself in such a delicious moment.

She could see someone behind 5A's curtains moving around the tiny apartment.

She slipped out onto the terrace, whispered a quick good morning to her bees, and faced the windows.

"Sugar Wallace from 5B right next door speaking," she said. "I've invited everyone else in the building for brunch and I just wanted to make sure you got the note I put under your door."

The figure stopped moving and sniffed loudly.

"I completely understand if you would rather keep to yourself but there is a small matter I need to discuss with you personally if you would be so kind."

The figure moved closer and sniffed again.

"The thing is, I need to introduce my bees; it's the polite thing to do, because they're living even closer to you than I am."

Sniff.

"This is my queen, Elizabeth the Sixth, and her subjects. There aren't too many of them just yet but she's building up her numbers and I'd like to move the hive a little closer to your window boxes if that's OK."

Sniff.

"Would you like a handkerchief? I have a whole drawer full of them inside."

The figure moved again, then the curtain drew back just enough for an arm to emerge, bearing a basket full of pastries.

"For me?" Sugar said. "Oh, you shouldn't have!" She took the basket and grasped the hand that had held it before it could be drawn back.

It was a solid young man's hand. A worker, she thought, possibly redheaded.

"A pleasure to meet you, Mr. . . . ?"

"Nate," he said, sniffing again. "Just Nate."

He pulled back his arm and let the curtain fall.

"The bees are fine," he said from behind it. "I like bees."

"And brunch?"

"No."

"No you don't like it or no to the invitation?"

"I like it but no."

Not so much iffy as just plain shy, Sugar thought. She could deal with shy. "Well, you just sit tight," she said. "You should be able to hear everything from right there anyway."

She was not sure who, if any, of the other neighbors would show up although she had slipped invitations under each of their doors the previous evening, promising food and goodie bags to take home. "Everyone likes a goodie bag," she told her bees.

Mrs. Keschl, as it turned out, was particularly fond of them. She arrived an hour early.

"I don't want that old fink McNally making off with more than his fair share," she said, pushing past Sugar and looking around the apartment. "Plus I like to make sure the facilities are properly cleaned. Hospital corners on the bed. Good to see."

"Would you like coffee or tea?" Sugar asked.

"I suppose. So you like this color orange?"

"I do like this color orange, as it happens, although I'm not sure I would have chosen it myself. It strikes me every day as pleasantly surprising, I guess is how I would put it."

"Oh, you're one of those," said Mrs. Keschl, fixing her with a beady eye.

"One of what?"

"One of those glass-half-full types. I've met people like you before and let me tell you this; surprising is just another word for shocking. You think I don't do the crossword? And shocking is never good. That guy who moved you in, that your boyfriend?"

"No, I don't have a boyfriend."

"Girlfriend?"

"No, I don't have a girlfriend either. What about you?"

"What about me what?"

"Do you have a boyfriend? Or a girlfriend?"

"Are you kidding me? Girlfriends weren't invented when I was on the market and boyfriends in my experience are nothing but a ton of flesh and bone just sitting there waiting to turn themselves into deadbeat husbands who will squash the joy of living out of you as soon as look at you. I had one of those for twenty-three years and I won't be having another one."

"Oh, I'm sorry to hear you've had such a bad time," Sugar said, thinking that she needed to make sure Mrs. Keschl did not sit next to Ruby.

"We've been divorced twenty-seven years now," Mrs. Keschl said with a dismissive flap of her hand, following Sugar out onto the rooftop. "Although hardly a moment passes when I don't wish he was dead or, you know, permanently disfigured. Bees!" she said, clapping her eyes on the hive.

She seemed to be smiling.

"You like bees?" asked Sugar.

"My grandmother had them, back in Hungary. Talked about them like they were her children."

"Did she keep any here?"

"She didn't live in some fancy schmancy penthouse like this! Although I think her apartment was bigger. No, nobody kept bees in the city in those days. But I took her to the Brooklyn Botanic Garden one day—you been there?—and do you think she cared about the tulips or the roses or the flowering rhododendrons? No. All she cared about were the bees. Made her happy and God knows her glass was almost always completely empty."

The muffled rooftop air was pierced then by the approach of Lola and Ethan.

"Oh, crap," Mrs. Keschl said. "You had to ask the bad balloon seller?"

"I asked everyone in the building," Sugar said.

"You should can my coffee order then," snapped Mrs. Keschl. "I don't want to be awake for too much of this."

Lola looked tired and suspicious, yet seemed to relax when Sugar took Ethan straight out of her arms and led her out onto the terrace to sit with Mrs. Keschl at the table that she had laid with her honey loaf, Nate's pastries, fresh berries, cream and jugs of iced tea.

Sugar then took the little boy back inside and quickly checked his ears and throat. She wondered if his sinuses were inflamed because of allergies, and she got a piece of honeycomb out of the fridge for him.

"Hey, looks like she got the brat to shut up for once," said Mrs. Keschl, not altogether unkindly.

Lola opened her mouth to bite back but instead just reached for a pastry and flopped in her seat. Despite the warm morning sun, she was wearing a fluffy vest in fluorescent green, and her hair was up in bunches. She dressed like a much happier person.

"I gave him some honeycomb," Sugar said, bringing Ethan back to the table. "I hope you don't mind. It's a little sticky but otherwise delicious and it's my own so I know exactly what's in it, which is nothing but good old-fashioned bee stuff."

Ethan took the comb out of his mouth and smiled at them all.

Lola gaped. "You can give him whatever you like if it makes him do that."

"Kid's quite cute when it stops its caterwauling," said Mrs. Keschl.

A gentle knock at the door heralded the arrival of Ruby but when Sugar answered the door they were both almost bowled over by Mr. McNally, who thrust his way straight toward the terrace without even stopping to say hello.

"I should have known," he said to Mrs. Keschl, grabbing a pastry and taking a bite before he sat down, crumbs cascading. "Any chance of a free feed and there you are."

"Meanwhile you're sitting at home with your hand in your pocket," Mrs. Keschl returned.

"That sounds disgusting," said Lola.

"And who are you?" Mr. McNally asked Lola.

"I'm Lola, from the second floor."

"And this is Ruby from the first floor," said Sugar. "I'm sorry, I thought you would know each other already."

"I know him and that's one too many," Mrs. Keschl said.

"And I know her too, more's the pity."

"OK then," Sugar intervened, sensing blows were soon to be exchanged, "before I tell you the special reason I asked you all here today, these beautiful pastries were made by Nate, who lives in Apartment 5A but couldn't be with us this morning."

"Is that the big guy with the ginger hair?" Lola asked.

"All I know is that he's a real good baker and has a very nice voice. Don't you think these are delicious?"

Everyone, apart from Ruby who couldn't even look at the pastries, agreed.

"Also, I need to make sure that it's OK with you all for me to keep my bees up here."

Mr. McNally's eyes swiveled around the rooftop and alighted on the hive. His features seemed to soften and Sugar caught a glimpse of what he must have looked like before he was old and angry. "Honey on porridge oats. Now there's a feed."

"Are you allowed to keep bees up here?" Ruby asked.

"Of course I am, sweetie! Do I look like a rule breaker to you?"

"You look like Julie Andrews in *The Sound of Music*," said Mrs. Keschl. "But with better hair. I'm ready for my coffee now, by the way."

"So we're all good with the hive?" Sugar asked, and everyone nodded. "Coffee coming right up then." She smiled, just as there was another firm knock on the door. "Although first, there is someone else I would like to introduce."

Her neighbors looked at each other as Sugar opened the door. As far as they knew, they were all already there apart from Nate, who wasn't coming.

"This is George Wainwright," Sugar called from the doorway as they peered over and saw George standing there hanging on to the frame with both hands. "And he won't be staying as he suffers from vertigo and prefers it on the ground floor, which is where you will see him from now on." She gave George a pastry and introduced him to her other guests.

"Pleased to meet you," George said. "And thank you for having me. But if that will be all . . . ?"

"That will be, George. Just quickly, how's the leg?"

"It's a miracle, like you said."

"Well, we can all do with one of those," said Sugar. "See you downstairs?"

"Indeed. Good day."

She shut the door and turned back to her neighbors.

"And who the heck was that?" Mrs. Keschl demanded.

"That was our new doorman," Sugar explained, bringing out the coffeepot and pouring the coffee into mugs.

"Our doorman?" echoed Mr. McNally.

"Yes," Sugar said, offering him another pastry, which he took. "The poor man is a real natural when it comes to doors but is temporarily without one due to being replaced by a camera so I said he could have ours. I hope none of you mind. It's presumptuous of me I know, and I'm sorry for that, but it won't cost a thing. And we have two doors downstairs and they are both quite hard to open—had you noticed? Especially if you are carrying anything."

"You're a real whack job, you know that," Mrs. Keschl said. "This is Alphabet City—not Trump Towers. We don't have doormen down here."

"Well, why shouldn't we?" countered Mr. McNally. "We're as good as anyone on the Upper East Side."

"Better, in my opinion," said Ruby.

"And those doors are heavy," added Lola.

Mrs. Keschl blinked.

"He can help carry up your groceries," said Sugar. "Especially since you're on the third floor, which is closer to the ground."

"I vote yes," Ruby said.

"This is an apartment building not a democracy," snapped Mrs. Keschl.

"You would throw an old man out on the street," Mr. McNally said bitterly.

"I didn't say that. I just said an apartment building is not a democracy."

"So the doorman can stay?" Ruby asked.

"If the majority rules," said Mrs. Keschl, "then I suppose yes, the doorman can stay."

"OK, then, so it's settled," Sugar said, smiling around the table. "We have bees and we have George. Now, time for goodie bags. I've made you all your own special beeswax candles. Here, Mrs. Keschl, yours are rose scented; Mr. McNally, yours are rosemary; Lola, yours are chamomile . . ."

The two old people looked at her as though she'd lost her mind.

"Ruby and Lola, I have lip gloss for you too," Sugar continued, "and some hand cream, Mrs. Keschl, because I noticed what lovely nails you have."

Still she looked perplexed.

"And I've baked some of my favorite lemon honey cookies," Sugar added quickly, "in case anyone wants those too."

"You can keep the hand cream," said Mrs. Keschl, snatching up her bag. "But I want the cookies and I'll take McNally's candles, too. He'll only burn the place to the ground and then where will we be?"

"I made extra," Sugar told him after Mrs. Keschl had left.

"And I have cookies for you too, Lola," she said.

"I can't believe we have a doorman," Ruby said. "That's so cool."

After they had all gone, Sugar knocked on Nate's partly opened window. "Did you hear any of that?"

"Yes," he said. "We have a doorman."

He pulled back the curtain and sniffed.

He was of solid build with a round, pleasant face and thick, curly copper-colored hair. He couldn't quite meet her eyes but managed a shy smile.

"And they really liked my pastries."

"Yes, Nate, honey. They really did. Now you sure I can't get you a handkerchief?"

14TH

Two weeks after he first met her in the street, Theo saw her again, and this time it was so definitely Sugar that he couldn't believe he'd bothered to follow the pregnant Asian woman.

She was walking toward him along East Seventh Street: a slender goddess in a pale green floral dress on a sidewalk that suddenly seemed devoid of any other color. Her hair was loose and falling in a thick shiny swath behind her shoulders, swinging with each step. He instantly craved every detail about her: what she smelled like, what she ate for breakfast, what she sang in the shower, what her first pet was called, who was mean to her at school.

He wanted to tell her about his first tooth falling out, about his mother not wanting to worry him with her lung cancer, about his new favorite song, about how ready he suddenly was for the next chapter in his life.

He could feel her in his bones from twenty paces. His mother was right. His aunts were right. Marlena was right. She was the one and he just knew it. Ridiculous. But true. But ridiculous.

But true.

And while he was standing there, watching her, baffled by the strangeness of such inexplicable certainty, Sugar looked up and saw him.

She stopped in her tracks, one hand flying to the delicate gold necklace and pendant that rested neatly on her smooth pale skin.

Theo had continued to be a frequent visitor to her dreams but she'd swatted the memories of them away like flies, all but forgetting he existed in real life. Yet there he was, standing in another loud Hawaiian shirt on the sidewalk, impossible to deny. And he had such a funny look on his face; excited, but pained. He was jiggling on the spot—buzzing, almost, like a bee.

Sugar smiled. She didn't really want to but couldn't help herself. Her body seemed to have its own separate reaction to him; nothing to do with the rest of her. She never quite remembered what her dreams were about but woke up after them feeling not embarrassed, exactly, but—no, actually, she was embarrassed.

"Why, hello, Theo," she said, reverting to her default setting of politeness. It trumped embarrassment every time. "How nice to see you again. I'm Sugar Wallace. We met the other day on Avenue B with George, you know, the gentleman with the burger wrapper stuck to his coat?"

That was how she remembered George, Theo thought. Because of the burger wrapper? "Wallace," he said. "Of course. As if I could forget you, although the Wallace I did. So stupid. William Wallace, after all. *Braveheart!*"

"I'm sorry?"

"Famous Scotsman," he said. "No relation, I'm sure. Like the Amish." It occurred to Theo that he hadn't thought for even a moment about what he would say to Sugar when he found her.

"No, no relation to William Wallace," she said. "Although I did see Mel Gibson once, out in California. At least I think it was him."

"Was he short?"

"He was sitting down."

"Speaking of which," Theo said, rather artfully he thought. "Would you like to go for a drink? McSorley's is right across the street and it's one of New York's oldest bars."

It was just past eleven in the morning and, where Sugar came from, a girl did not start drinking till lunchtime and, even then, probably not with a man she'd met just the one time while scraping a potentially homeless person off the pavement.

"Oh," she said.

Theo had a meeting he was supposed to be at in ten minutes' time and didn't know himself about the sense in asking her for a drink at that hour, but McSorley's was right there. And there was no place like it outside of the backstreets of Edinburgh and possibly Dublin and, in a pinch, London.

Mostly though, he just could not bear to think of Sugar slipping through his fingers again.

"Would it help if I said please?" Theo asked.

It always did. "Well, all right then," she agreed.

But when he put his hand on her elbow to escort her across the street the rush of heat she felt radiating from his touch proved too much of a shock. She stopped short of an audible gasp and scurried into McSorley's unaided.

It was like stepping back in time. There was sawdust on the floor and faded sepia framed photos crowding the walls. An eight-foot-tall ice chest behind the battered bar was piled with old chamber pots and jugs and urns. Ancient horse paraphernalia hung from the ceiling; dusty knickknacks filled up every nook and cranny.

A black woodburner sat in the middle of the crooked tables and chairs and the dappled light cast a surreal sheen on the whole place—giving it the aura of a faded sepia photo itself.

There was no one else in there but Sugar would not have been surprised if a saloon girl had appeared from the back room or a cowboy fell in the door with a gunshot wound. However, it was a cranky-looking gray-haired barman wearing a garbage bag for an apron who sidled out from the shadows at the back of the room and slid behind the bar.

"Are you open?" Theo asked him.

"Did you break in?"

"No."

"Then we're open."

"All part of the service," Theo assured Sugar, showing her to a small round table near the window. The light danced in through the elm tree on the street outside.

She felt like she was asleep and dreaming again.

"Wait right here," Theo said. "I'll get you a drink."

She opened her mouth to say she pretty much always stuck to bourbon, no matter what the hour, but Theo had already turned to the barman and ordered.

Despite the fact he was wearing a loud shirt and horrifically mismatching checked Bermuda shorts, he looked good from the back, there was no denying it. He was tall with broad shoulders and hips that weren't too slim, and nice legs, she realized. The Theo she dreamed about looked exactly the same, but without the shirt and Bermuda shorts.

An unfamiliar heat leaked out from some long-forgotten place deep inside her, waking the butterflies that had been lying dormant for years from their slumber.

"I got you a double," Theo said, returning and putting two half-pints of beer in front of her. "Light ale and dark ale. I hope that's OK. It's the specialty of the house."

He had beautiful long fingers, like a piano player.

"They're both for me?"

"That's all they serve here. It's the tradition."

"Oh, all right then, thank you. And what are you having?"

"The same," said Theo, heading back to the bar for two more half-pints. "To your health."

Sugar took a sip of the light ale, which fizzed on her tongue, further unsettling the butterflies. She could almost see their wings uncrumpling and trying to spread out after so much time in hibernation. "I'm not usually much of a beer drinker," she said. "You should try a mint julep, maybe, made with good Kentucky bourbon. One afternoon. Or evening. The evenings are probably better. I'm more inclined to drink iced tea at this time of the day, to be perfectly honest." She took another sip, this time of the dark ale, as Theo's smile slid toward the sawdust.

"I guess iced tea would have been better," he said. Of course it would have been. "I don't usually drink beer in the morning myself. Or anything else. I'm so sorry. What an idiot."

"No need to feel too bad about it," said Sugar. "It's not like you've lured me into a cave and made me eat raw buffalo."

"That's happened to you?"

"No," she said, blushing as she wondered if a cave and perhaps a small amount of nonthreatening dragging had featured in one of her dreams. "I'm just trying to make you feel better."

"I do feel better," he said. "Not about that but about everything."

"Everything?"

"About you, actually. I've been thinking about you ever since we met the other day. I've been looking for you. Seriously. So to find you, it seems so . . . I don't know. I want to say miraculous but that's not quite what I mean although it's as close as I can come up with."

His eyes were such a transfixing color that she had to look away from them. She was drinking the beer too quickly. "Oh, well . . . I'm . . . all right then," she said. "That's good. So do you work around here?"

"Yes," he said. "Not far. And live too." Why could he not string a sentence together? "You?"

"I've just moved here," she said, keeping it deliberately vague. "But you're from Scotland, right?"

"Glasgow," he said. "Son of Shona Fitzgerald, deceased, and father unknown. By me, anyway. Obviously she knew him, but only briefly. Not that she was fast or anything. And she really did love him but there was always a shadow of doubt, so she said."

The shadow of doubt had been his father's occupation as a full-time burglar. It was the difference, his mother claimed, between a lifetime of happiness and a two-to-four stretch in Barlinnie. "He went away soon after they, you know . . . so that was pretty much that."

Sugar thought his eyes seemed more turquoise today, the lashes thick and dark, like a little boy's in a grown man's face.

"I'm sorry about your mother," she said. "And your father too, I guess."

"I don't know why I told you that," Theo said. "I'm making myself sound tragic and although we did live in a very small flat with my gran and four of my aunties, I actually thought it was the best. I didn't even notice I was short of a father until I was eighteen."

Sugar's butterflies had gotten their wings unfurled and were flapping, flapping, flapping.

"You certainly seem pretty cheerful about it."

"Oh, my mother would have loved you," said Theo.

Sugar nearly choked on her beer. "Excuse me?"

"It's true. I have very good instincts. Everyone says so."

She laughed and it was such a sweet sound, he relaxed. Though he wished he hadn't blathered on about his family like that. "So, do you like it here then?" he asked. "In New York?"

Her face lit up. "I think it's the most amazing place I've ever been. There's a balloon shop in my apartment building. Dmitri down the street teaches the accordion from his accordion repair store. And I can get a knish just about any time I want although actually that's not that often. Oh, and Chinese pancakes. Have you been to Vanessa's on Eldridge Street? The colors down there in Chinatown; I mean it's the opposite of coordinated, but talk about alive . . ."

The way she looked, sounded, smelled (like limes, mixed with something sweeter): everything struck him. There was no other word for it. She struck him. Sitting there in the dappled sunlight of the dusty saloon, Theo's whole life suddenly made sense. Everything that had happened to him up until that point, everything that he had made happen, it all led up to this very moment, sitting there with Sugar, the one, without a shadow of a doubt, he thought. The one. He just knew.

She smiled at him. "It's real pretty in here, isn't it? I mean for a gloomy old spit-on-the-floor barroom."

"Do you like children?" Theo asked.

"I'm only a godmother about twenty-two times over."

"Do you like oysters?"

"I'm from the South," she said. "It goes without saying."

"Per Se or Babbo?"

"The restaurants? I'm sure they're both great but, like I say, I prefer Vanessa's pancakes. And I cook. I like eating at home. Where are you going with this, exactly?"

"Sugar Wallace," he said, "this is going to sound really weird, but from the moment we met I just had this feeling about you . . . and I don't really know how to put this without totally giving you the creeps but on the other hand I know that this doesn't happen every day. George was supposed to fall on me, you were supposed to get me to help him up, we were supposed to meet on the sidewalk right outside here today because we are going to end up together, you and I, Sugar. I don't know what will happen next but I swear I can actually see us together in forty years, an old married couple, holding hands and hobbling down East Seventh Street toward Tompkins Square Park in the sunshine. I can see that right now."

The words hadn't even skimmed the surface of his thinking before they tumbled from his mouth. He just opened it and out they poured into a puddle on the table between them, unfiltered.

The look on Sugar's face left no doubt in his mind that filtered would have been better. Perhaps honesty was mostly the best policy, but not always.

"Too much? It sounds like too much. But I just know it, Sugar. I can't properly explain it but I know it. My mam always said I would know 'the one' when I found her and she was right, God rest her. I found you and I can feel it. Can't you feel it?"

"That we will be an old married couple, holding hands and hobbling down East Seventh Street in forty years' time because we both like oysters?" Sugar was not smiling anymore. "Where I come from," she said, "we don't joke about that kind of thing."

Where she came from, being married was definitely not a laughing matter.

"Where I come from it's exactly the same," Theo said, panicking. "I know this seems strange, and trust me I am not normally like this, but I just have this overwhelming certainty that we are going to spend the rest of our lives together."

Sugar put her near-empty beer tankard back on the table next to the other near-empty tankard. "You don't know the first thing about me," she said.

"But I do! You picked George up off the street! No one does that here. In Barlanark, yes. Most people in Barlanark end up on the street themselves at some stage so we're used to picking each other up. But not here. You're kind, Sugar. And you are smart and beautiful. You're really beautiful. Plus you came for a drink with me, doesn't that mean something?"

"I came for a drink with you to be polite. And I do know what is going to happen next," she said, gathering up her bag. "So I can help you out with that part of your little story."

"This is not turning out the way I imagined," Theo said. "I've scared you."

"I'm not scared. I'm—well, I don't know what I am but I met a man once before in a Walmart parking lot who wanted to take me to Norway. Of course, it was easier to tell he was crazy because he had shopping bags on his feet and was wearing a crown."

"I don't even own a hat, if that makes a difference."

Sugar stood up. "No, it doesn't. You shouldn't joke and you shouldn't go around telling perfect strangers you're going to end up with them!"

"You're right, of course, I can see that now. I'm so, so sorry, Sugar."

"I'm sorry too, Theo, but I think I really do prefer iced tea in the morning, so please excuse me. Thank you for the drink, for the drinks, and you take care. Oh, and I don't know if you were thinking of following me but I seriously hope you don't because that officially would give me the creeps."

She turned and picked her way around the bar tables, disappearing out through the saloon doors, the sunlight blinding Theo as he watched her dissolve into the street, his heart sinking into the sawdust beneath his feet as he fought the urge to do exactly what she had just asked him not to. How had he gotten it so horribly wrong?

Outside, Sugar's heart felt like it was pumping the blood of a thousand nations through her body.

Something deep and dark and complicated was battling to emerge. It had to do with the blowtorch on crème brûlée, with the butterflies, with the heat, the inexplicable pull she felt when she looked into Theo's eyes—and it was most unwelcome.

The gall of the man, talking about being married, of all things, and hand-holding and forty years together after he'd known her for all of twenty minutes!

She would not cry, she told herself, she absolutely would not. She would go home and maybe work on the syrup she was developing for Ethan and a cream for Mr. McNally's psoriasis.

She would not cry.

But if she did, she could not honestly deny as she fled home to Flores Street, it wouldn't be because a deranged stranger had talked about wanting to hold her hand in forty years' time.

If she did cry it would be because despite everything—and there was a lot of everything—in the split second before she decided Theo Fitzgerald was out of his mind, she too had seen them hobbling down East Seventh Street in their dotage, holding hands. Together.

Elizabeth the Sixth was graciously basking in reports from her foragers of a particularly fragrant wisteria vine climbing up a back garden wall not half a block away when she felt Sugar's approach.

She stopped what she was doing—which was backing her rear end into a cell to lay her 1,327th egg for the day—and alerted all her senses. She could not hear—she did not have ears—but she used her sight, her smell, her touch and 150 million years of evolution to keep her antennae on the pulse of the world around her, in particular Sugar's world.

In Elizabeth the Sixth's eyes (all five of them), Sugar had been changing color with each passing day since she first spoke Theo's name out loud, appearing extra-vibrant when she had dreamed of him at night, and even more so when she thought of him during the day.

This energy emanating from her keeper gave the queen considerable oomph, and she had been building hive numbers up with alacrity, proving a popular ruler whose house bees were keen to look after her and whose workers were desperate to feed her and get the honey stores going.

But when Sugar came home from McSorley's she radiated a powerful energy that the queen could not recall from her genetic memory file.

It wasn't just ale, this new influence. It was strong and unhappy.

Bamboozled by such complicated pheromonal activity, Elizabeth the Sixth started throwing in an extra waggle of her tush with every egg she laid, somewhat hindering her progress.

To begin with her handmaidens were ruffled, but as their queen didn't seem annoyed or sickly, they soon followed her lead and quickly adapted to the new, slower rhythm.

15TH

Nate opened the *New York Times*, no mean feat considering he lived in the smallest apartment in Manhattan. Opening the *Times* meant he had to close something else, or move it.

Apartment 5A might have had a spectacular view across the window boxes to the Alphabet City skyline and beyond but inside there was room for little more than a single bed, a table for one—which he used for bench space—a stove, a sink and a small refrigerator.

There was no pantry so he kept his herbs and spices in his tiny closet, his olive oils in the bathroom cabinet and his vegetables in a crate on the bed.

He sat beside them, his heart sinking as he read the Dining Section's latest restaurant review. Roland Morant's Upper West Side restaurant, Citroen, had been awarded three stars by the *Times*'s critic, which was the worst news Nate could ever hope for.

His boss, a bellowing bully who insisted on being called "Chef" even though that didn't go anywhere near describing what he did for a living, hated Morant with a vengeance. They'd worked together back in the Dark Ages but Morant had gone on to stardom working with kitchen gods Danny Meyer, Alfred

Portale and Jean-Georges Vongerichten, while Chef had spent the last decade slinging burgers at his father-in-law's Tribeca diner.

"That talentless back-stabbing bastard never had an original idea in his head," Chef had been known to thunder of his arch-enemy. "Asshole couldn't slice a carrot unless someone marked it with a pencil first and sharpened his knife for him while they were at it."

He'd been beyond furious when Citroen opened the year before, insisting that Morant's rightful place was at the bottom of the scrap heap with last week's chicken livers, not up on West Eighty-Fourth Street with all the numb-nuts who were stupid enough to throw away their money just for the pleasure of getting food poisoning.

And now Citroen had been awarded three stars.

Chef hated everyone, but particularly Nate, on a good day.

Today he would have his guts for garters.

Nate looked at his watch. He would just have enough time to get up to the Poseidon Bakery on Ninth Avenue for some finikias—soft madeleine-shaped cookies made of ground almonds and walnuts, moist with thick, sweet syrup. He'd been trying to make them himself but he was missing something and needed to work out what that was.

It was going to be a difficult day and he needed to start it with something really sweet.

Outside he saw the shadow of Sugar checking her hive and moving quietly around the terrace inspecting her growing garden. She'd done wonders with the place since she moved in and, if he hadn't felt so sick, he would have drawn back the curtains and told her.

16TH

Sugar had grown up in Charleston, South Carolina: possibly the most luscious of the world's garden cities. Behind every wrought-iron gate or exposed-brick wall in the picturesque peninsula blooming between the Ashley and Cooper Rivers lay a sweet-scented treasure trove of camellias, roses, gardenias, magnolias, tea olives, azaleas and jasmine, everywhere, jasmine.

With its lush greenery, opulent vines, sumptuous hedgerows and candy-colored window boxes, it was no wonder the city's native sons and daughters believed it to be the most beautiful place on earth.

In her first years of exile Sugar had tried to cultivate a reminder of the luxuriant garden delights she had left behind, struggling in sometimes hostile elements to train reluctant honeysuckle and sulky sweet potato vines or nurture creeping jenny and autumn stonecrop.

In the Napa Valley she'd had jasmine growing like a weed and her bees loved it, and so, she thought, did she. But a faint foreign cloud of regret seemed to lurk above her when the vine flowers started to bloom and, once she realized the beautiful sweet scent from her childhood was making her homesick, she pulled it out and never planted it again.

From that point on, she stuck to growing things that kept her looking on the bright side and made the most of her natural surroundings.

In Santa Fe her whole yard had been crowded with different-sized terra-cotta pots, out of which she grew everything from rosemary and lavender to ornamental pear and plum trees and even peppers, although they were not particularly popular with the bees.

In Colorado she'd created a fertile oasis out of old gas cans and cut-off oil drums. Her neighbors had been skeptical to begin with but once her creepers grew up and her flowers draped down and her shrubs fluffed out, the junkyard ugly duckling was transformed into the proverbial backyard swan.

For Flores Street, George had found some discarded cast-iron half-pipes on an East River building site and arranged for Ralph, a young friend of his great-nephew, and two of his buddies to help haul them up to 5B.

Sugar had tried to foist some money on Ralph for payment but he would not hear of it.

"Any friend of Mr. Wainwright is a friend of ours," he said. "My mom always says he saved her bacon when we were kids. I don't know how but I think it had something to do with my dad moving back home. Whatever, he's a pretty cool dude. And he really likes your door."

"And it likes him," Sugar said, sending him away with two jars of North Idaho clover.

Perched up on salvaged bricks, the half-pipes made perfect

planters with an industrial edge that oddly complemented Sugar's pretty favorites: pansies, lantana, verbena and heliotrope.

She laid two of them by the long wall of the taller building next door and planted a clematis vine at one end and a moonflower vine at the other: the clematis because the variety she picked had the prettiest purple bloom and the moonflower because it opened in the early evening and emanated a heavenly scent just when a person most felt like smelling one.

She made gingham covers in different colors for her eclectic collection of patio furniture and bought Chinese lanterns and a strand of bistro lights at the Hester Street flea market, then a couple of oversized outdoor candle holders with matching cracks from a closing-down sale on Essex Street. She even found a jardiniere for sale on a Chinatown corner for twenty dollars plus two jars of propolis. She planted a miniature magnolia tree that did not remind her of the ones in the garden at home at all because her mama took great pride in her magnolias being the biggest in the street and this little specimen was as petite as could be.

It took a few weeks, but with all her hard work and the city providing its own staggering backdrop, her rooftop garden was taking shape.

In the days after she slugged back her half-pints of dark and light ales at McSorley's, she had worked even harder. There was nothing like lugging twenty-pound bags of potting mix up four flights of stairs to keep a person's mind off anything so vexing as having a perfect stranger . . . Well, she wasn't sure what Theo had done, but it was wrong.

Still, she dreamed of him. Some mornings she could almost taste him, a sensation that seemed exquisite in her half-sleepy state, excruciating when fully awake. He was salty, with intense caramel notes that echoed in her taste buds well past breakfast.

"I need to get Theo Fitzgerald out of my head," she told Elizabeth the Sixth one morning, patting mulch around the base of the mini-magnolia to keep the moisture in. "He has no place there. Or anywhere else in my life for that matter."

Her gardening was interrupted by a knock on the door: it was Ruby, pale and tired-looking, clutching her scrapbook.

Sugar had been keeping an eye on her frail downstairs neighbor, dropping in on her every few days since the brunch, and while Ruby never slammed the door in her face the way Mr. McNally still liked to do, or threw her the stink eye the way Mrs. Keschl did, or pushed past her in the stairs like Lola, her reception was often closer to frosty than anything else. She generally thawed out soon enough but Sugar always felt like she was starting their friendship back at square one, so she was tickled that she'd taken it upon herself to drop by.

"I've got some new ones," Ruby said, holding up the scrapbook in her spindly arms. "Real creepy."

Weddings were the last thing on Sugar's mind. "I was just about to check my queen," she said, by way of a diversion. "Would you care to join me?"

Ruby screwed up her face. "What?"

"Excuse me?"

"I said 'What?'"

Sugar decided she'd work her gentle magic on Ruby's manners another day. "I was just about to look in on Elizabeth the Sixth," she said. "If you come on over here I'll introduce you."

Ruby moved closer and watched suspiciously as Sugar took the lid off the hive. "Aren't you supposed to wear a suit and smoke them all out or something?"

"I do have a suit inside if you'd like to wear it, but these bees are pretty tame," Sugar explained. "The smoking is just to calm them down but they're a pretty relaxed crowd to begin with so I don't bother. It can't be nice having your house all filled with smoke is what I think. If it happens to us we call the Fire Department. But you can stand inside and watch from there if you'd rather."

"I'm not scared of bees," Ruby said as Sugar pulled out a frame crawling with the insects.

"See they've covered all these little cubbyholes with wax," Sugar pointed out. "There's a little baby bee in each one."

"Where's the honey?"

"Well, they haven't made a whole lot yet. They're just getting up and running. When Elizabeth the Sixth, or Betty as I sometimes call her, has laid a few more eggs and they've all hatched and grown up, they'll start to fill the cubbyholes on the next floor up with nectar. Then they dry it out by beating their wings and, next thing you know, you have honey!"

But Ruby was not really interested in honey; she was checking out Nate's window boxes. "So, do you know him: the ginger-haired guy who's always red in the face?"

"He just blushes because he's shy, is all."

Ruby shrugged. "What's he got growing in these little garden things?"

"He's got just about everything," Sugar said. "And as soon as it's ready, he picks it and makes something delicious with it. He made this Moroccan lamb stew the other night—oh my goodness, just the smell of it drove me so crazy I had to knock on the window

99

and find out what it was. He cooked it in the cutest little dish with a funnel that came up out of the middle, served it with couscous, and was kind enough to share it with me. I had to go and look Morocco up on the map afterward just so I could be sure where such a heavenly thing came from."

"Are you, like, dating him or something?" Ruby asked.

"Heavens, no! He's too young for me. And I've only just met him."

"You don't have to know someone for long for them to be a boyfriend. Sometimes it's instant. It happens all the time in my scrapbook."

Sugar cleared her throat. "Well, I can hardly be considered an expert in that field because boyfriends and I don't traditionally work out real well."

Ruby looked at her. "Boyfriends and I don't traditionally work out real well either," she said. Indeed, she'd never had one. Not even come close.

"I've found bees to be far less complicated," said Sugar. "Now, where's my queen?" She pulled out another frame, this one laden with even more bees, and carefully turned it around in her hands, looking for Elizabeth the Sixth.

"How can you tell her from the other ones?"

"She's bigger than them, and she has an extra touch of class, just like a real queen. I usually have no trouble spotting her anyway but—oh, look, here she is." She pointed out Elizabeth the Sixth, who was perched half in and half out of a brood cell. "See, she's longer than the rest although it's hard to tell because of where she's sitting." She waited for Betty to lay her egg and move to the next cell, but Betty did not.

"Hm, that's strange," said Sugar. "She's taking a while on this one. Best I stop disturbing her, I suppose."

She slid the frame back into the hive and put the lid back on.

Ruby perched herself on one of the gingham cushions, holding her scrapbook in her arms, a sad but hopeful look on her face, like she wished she didn't want what she wanted. Bees were obviously not the tonic for her that they were for Sugar, and if Ruby needed anything, Sugar thought, it was a tonic. In the interests of being helpful, she was going to have to suck up some more marital bliss.

"Now what say I make us an iced tea," she suggested, "and you read me some of those stories of yours?"

"What's in iced tea?"

"Just tea and lemon, there's probably not even half a calorie in a whole jug."

"OK," Ruby said.

"Just OK?"

"What else would there be?"

"Sometimes it's nice to add a little sweetener."

"I'm not interested in sweetening anything," said Ruby.

Sugar left it at that, but when she made the tea, she put half a teaspoon of Jacksonville ocher in it because if Ruby needed anything it was sweetening. The honey was subtle yet slightly tart and Sugar knew the tannin from the tea and the spike of the lemon would camouflage its taste.

She was sure she saw Ruby's cheeks pick up a bit of color as she drank. It was like watching a wilted flower start to straighten and bloom after a summer rain shower.

17TH

The next time she saw Theo, Sugar was selling ice cream at the Ronnybrook Farm stand at Tompkins Square greenmarket. She'd volunteered at the market information booth three weeks in a row and the market manager had then recommended she spend a while working at someone else's stand before setting up her own.

Marcus Morretti from Ronnybrook had begrudgingly let her help him although he'd had volunteers offer to help out before and generally they went for coffee about nine A.M. and never came back. Tompkins Square did not have the glitz and glamour of Union Square greenmarket in the Flatiron District, where hordes of well-heeled Manhattanites picked over fresh courgette flowers as tourists snapped photos of golden raspberries stacked like boxed jewels next to plump strawberries and glistening blackberries. Crowds did not block Tompkins Square mulling over plump eggplants and vegan cookies or queuing for Quaker pretzels and vegetarian wraps. It was unlikely to feature in glossy magazines or popular guide books.

Instead an eclectic mixture of East Village locals ambled up to the half a dozen or so stallholders, who were a butcher, a baker, two vegetable producers, an apple farmer, a lavender grower, plus Marcus and his organic ice cream.

The vibe was laid-back, and most of the stallholders knew most of the shoppers. Further adding to the Alphabet City flavor was the colorful collection of homeless and addicted, who mostly minded their own businesses but, Sugar had been warned, had been known to spend an entire Sunday shouting—or worse, singing—at stallholders and passersby.

On this particular morning, however, no one was shouting at anyone. The daffodils were out in full force beneath the park's famous elms, sprinkled across the ground like gold dust. A group of ancient musicians played gypsy jazz on the benches over by the children's park, while mothers watched their kids and chatted to each other, feet tapping.

It was the sort of day that promised a perfect summer and, in such premium conditions, it took less than an hour for Marcus to work out that Sugar was a natural-born saleswoman. After two hours he did a quick count and realized he had doubled his normal profit. He decided she was just exactly the sort of person you wanted to buy an ice cream from first thing on a sunny morning: refreshingly lacking in tattoos or piercings but with a smile that suggested she could mix a little mischief in with her wholesomeness if she felt like it.

When it dawned on him that the customers were actually waiting for her to serve them even though he stood right there next to her, he gave Sugar full responsibility for the stall and ran off to meet his girlfriend for an early lunch. His girlfriend did not have a wholesome bone in her body, which was pretty much why he liked her.

Once Marcus left, Sugar hardly got to lift her head out of the ice-cream tubs, she was so busy serving people. They crowded in front of her, calling out their flavors, but when someone called out an order for ginger crème supreme in a certain sort of sing-song voice, she felt the hairs on the back of her neck stand to attention. She looked up to see Theo standing there.

"Oh, it's you," she said, her hand suddenly sweaty on the scoop. "Hello." There was still no point in being rude. There never was. And besides, she could hardly go anywhere.

Theo's eyes had nearly fallen out of his head when he had mooched around the corner and seen Sugar standing there in her pretty blue dress, doling out ice cream.

He'd spent the weeks since he'd scared her away from McSorley's patrolling East Seventh Street at every possible chance, lurking around all its corners in the hope he could find her again, explain himself, repair the damage he had done. He'd even rehearsed a little speech but now wished he had written it down because all he could think about was that faint sweet lime scent that lingered in the air, the curl of her fingers around a half-pint of beer, her teeth biting into her plump lower lip.

"Yes, it's me," he said.

"Would you like that ginger crème supreme in a cone?" she asked. "Or a tub to take home? Or perhaps you would prefer if I just hung on to it for forty years and gave it to you for our anniversary."

"Hey, join the queue, buster," snapped a young mom standing in front of him, jiggling her kid on her hip. "I'll take a pint of vanilla."

"Coming right up, ma'am," Sugar said to her, handing her the

104

ice cream. The mom stalked off and Theo moved closer to the counter.

"I know that pretty much everything that comes out of my mouth," he said, "would appear to be the ravings of a complete and utter lunatic—"

"Yes, it would," Sugar said, taking another order from behind him, riled that he was forcing her to consider that perhaps sometimes in special circumstances there was a point in being rude which went against everything in which she had long believed. "I'm sorry, but it would."

"No, I'm the one who is sorry," Theo said. "Trust me, I am really, really sorry for taking you to McSorley's for a beer when I'd really only known you so fleetingly and for everything else too. For the whole wanting to get married and hold hands thing. I'm so sorry about that too. I was wrong."

Sugar stopped what she was doing, her scoop raised in midair. "You were wrong about knowing that we were going to be together forever and walking down East Seventh Street in our old age?"

"No!" said Theo. "Not about that. I'm right about that."

"Then aren't we back to the whole ravings-of-a-complete-and-utter-lunatic thing? There you go, ma'am. Two double-scoop raspberry and white chocolate cones. Enjoy."

"No, I was wrong to spring it on you like that in a bar where people still spit on the floor," Theo said. "It was completely inappropriate but please don't for a moment think that I was in any way mocking the seriousness of relationships or marriage. I was married once myself and, even though that didn't work out, I still believe in the institution. I really do. I was just speaking without considering the consequences because, the truth is, you have this unbelievable effect on me and I just can't seem to help myself but if you gave me another chance I know I could prove myself to you. Honestly, please, trust me. I beg of you."

"You buying ice cream or auditioning for Shakespeare in the Park?" an elderly man agitating at his elbow interjected. "Gimme some of that mint lace, will you, sweetheart?"

"Are you crazy?" pitched in another customer, a plump woman of about Sugar's own age, dressed in sweats. "Chocolate chip, two pints." She leaned over to the elderly man. "The guy asks her to marry him after only just meeting her and means it? My husband waited fourteen years and even then he burped it out during an ad break." She waved her hand at Sugar. "Say yes, honey. Look at the guy. I'd marry him myself if I didn't have my in-laws coming for lunch. And he has that cute accent. Like Gerard Butler. Although what's with the shirt?"

"He looks like one of those West Coast bums who smokes pot and writes poetry," agreed the elderly man.

"I don't smoke pot. Or write poetry, not that there's anything wrong with that," Theo told them. "And I didn't ask her to marry me. I just said I could see us being married."

"Now you sound like a lawyer," the elderly man said.

"Are you a lawyer?" Sugar asked. "Because that would just completely take the cake if you were a lawyer."

"Never mind that, or being married, or—would you just have dinner with me, Sugar? Please?"

"What does she want with dinner?" the old man said. "You've already told her you're a loon."

"Any chance of getting some ice cream back here?" asked a man at the back with a baby in a stroller. "Chocolate. One pint."

"Hold your horses, we have a romance happening here," said the woman in sweats. "Are you already married?" she asked Sugar.

"You know I would really prefer to stick to the subject of ice cream, if that's all the same to you, ma'am."

"Got a boyfriend?"

"Regular chocolate or chocolate chip?" Sugar asked the man with the stroller.

"How could you not have a boyfriend?" asked the old man. "If I was twenty years younger, I'd ask you to marry me myself."

"Make that forty," snorted the stroller man.

"Go for dinner with Gerard Butler," the woman said.

"As long as he takes you somewhere nice," added the old man, "and there's no hanky-panky in the cab on the way home."

"And make him pay, honey," said the woman in sweats. "Enough with the going Dutch already. We hate that." Then she and the old man shuffled off together arguing pleasantly about mint versus chocolate chip.

"I'll just wait over there until you're not so busy, if that's OK," Theo said, and he retreated to a shady bench as other hot and hungry customers slipped into the space he left. But more than once Sugar felt his thoughtful gaze upon her.

In the meantime, she spotted Mrs. Keschl, who came to the greenmarket every Sunday pretty much just to hassle the apple guy for not having tart enough apples. "Can I get you an ice-cream cone, Mrs. Keschl?" she called.

The old lady shuffled over. "What's that black stuff in the back?"

"That's licorice, not the most popular flavor it would appear."

"I'll take one of those then," the old lady said. "And you'd better make it half price since I'm helping you get rid of it."

Not half an hour later Mr. McNally spied Sugar behind the makeshift counter and pushed his way to the front of the line, ignoring the complaints from those elbowed out of his path.

"So, you," he said.

"Sorry, y'all," Sugar told the other disgruntled customers. "This is my neighbor Mr. McNally and he has blood sugar issues." Sometimes a little white lie went a long way to avoiding a riot. "What can I get you, Mr. McNally?"

"What's that black stuff down the back?"

"That's licorice. Would you like some of that?"

"What do you think I'm waiting for?"

"That's Mrs. Keschl's favorite too," she said as she handed over a cone. For a moment she thought he was going to throw it back in her face. "Just taste it before you do anything rash," she said.

He did, and found it to his liking, so he grunted what might have been a thank you and elbowed his way back out of the crowd.

Finally, there was a lull in the queue and, taking the opportunity to catch Sugar on her own, Theo appeared in front of her again.

"Just consider this," he said. "If I hadn't already mentioned the whole marriage thing, it would not be so weird to be asking you out. It's just dinner, Sugar. Look at it that way. And if, after dinner, you still think I'm bonkers, I promise I will never ask you anything ever again. In fact, I promise you'll never even see me again."

Sugar had been on plenty of dinner dates since she left Charleston—she liked male company, she had grown up with it—but she restricted her dating to men in whom she was not seriously interested because it was easier to avoid complications that way. On occasion she'd allowed the odd dalliance to develop into something a little more substantial: she'd spent a wonderful winter with a ski instructor in Idaho; and a sizzling summer with a winemaker in Napa.

But she was not in the market for a heart-stopping, pulse-racing, knee-weakening, bone-shaking, jaw-dropping love affair. She'd had one of those once before. It had wrecked her life, and a few others besides, and she did not want another one.

Yet there she was standing in a beautiful park in the spring, in New York, ice-cream scoop in hand, her heart stopped, her pulse racing, her knees weak, her bones shook up and her jaw all but hanging on the ground.

She let the scoop fall back into the mint lace.

She thought she'd been so strong all these years, avoiding the vicious thrust of Cupid's arrow, yet, gazing across those rainbow pints of ice cream into the blue, blue eyes of Theo Fitzgerald she suddenly wasn't so sure. Maybe Cupid just hadn't been pointing in her direction all this time. Or he had been and was a terrible shot.

She hadn't been in love with the ski instructor—she'd been drawn by his grief at losing his wife to cancer and knew she could help him. And she hadn't felt anything close to a quiver for the winemaker either. He'd had hay fever, which she'd cured with her California honey, plus he had really nice hair.

All these years without a heart-stopping love affair she'd still been happy. Mrs. Keschl was right: Sugar's glass was always half full, more than half full. Plus she filled up everyone else's glass while she was at it. That was just what she did. And despite everything that had happened to her, despite what had gone so terribly wrong with that one big love affair all those years ago, she had never—apart from a few days when she first left Charleston and that was perfectly understandable—felt lacking.

She'd felt in control.

Until now.

Now, looking across the ice cream at Theo Fitzgerald with his pleading eyes and the thoughtful wrinkle between them, she felt what was missing, right there in the empty space in front of her. She couldn't see it but it nonetheless danced between them like bonfire flames, only twice as hot. She hadn't felt that heat in all these years, had barely registered its absence, but now it was here burning up the oxygen right under her nose, and she just couldn't ignore the yearning it thrust her way.

But she didn't want it.

What she had learned the first time was that this physical desire and the longing that came with it could not be trusted for anything other than to ensure a certain painful sort of torment, which she simply could not bear to suffer again. Theo might be good-looking and have a cute accent and make her laugh and have at least a modicum of gumption, but the way he made her feel scared the living daylights out of her. And her living daylights had long had their fill of being scared.

She liked the strong independent woman she'd turned into over the years. She'd created that woman more or less from dust and had come to take it for granted that she would be that woman forever. She could not let a crazy person like Theo turn her back into anything else.

"I'm sorry, Theo," she said. "Really, I am. But I think it would be better if we just skip to the part where we never see each other again. Thanks for coming by but I would be really grateful if you left the greenmarket alone on a Sunday from here on in. I don't mean to be rude and I'm sorry if it seems that way but I have to go now." A new wave of hot and hungry customers swallowed the space between them and Theo melted back into the park.

He was not going to remind her that he never got his ginger crème supreme. But nor was he going to give up. And she might not want him at Tompkins Square on a Sunday but he would find a way to win her heart, even if he couldn't come back to the greenmarket.

Ginger crème supreme was Sugar's favorite flavor too, as it happened, but the longer she sat beside the beehive on her roof terrace and continued to plow her way through a whole pint of it, the more perplexed Elizabeth the Sixth became.

The queen knew Theo Fitzgerald was what she had been waiting for: that certainty had emerged from the twisted rods of her DNA as definitely as the instinct to survive. What she didn't know was what to do next. Her DNA was telling her diddly-squat about that. She had assumed, inasmuch as a queen bee could, that Sugar would now take over. But all Sugar was taking were large spoonfuls of full-fat dairy products with a strong whiff of ginger, which was good for fending off colds and easing constipation but not a great favorite with bees.

Something had to change, that was for sure, and as nothing but great waves of angst continued to emanate from Sugar, Elizabeth the Sixth decided that the something would have to be her. She backed her rear into the closest baby-making cell and stayed there.

Her go-slow had just turned into a tools-down.

Initially, her handmaidens panicked. A hive could not survive if its queen stopped laying. They started to clamber over her, desperate for guidance, fearful that she was weakening and that they needed to start feeding a new queen. But, to the contrary, the signals Elizabeth the Sixth was sending out were only getting stronger.

Trust me, she told them. And although they were bewildered, they trusted her.

18TH

Mrs. Keschl arrived at Sugar's door the following afternoon asking for more candles. She'd been burning them all day every day since the brunch and had grown used to the smell of rose oil. "Usually my place smells of onions," she told Sugar. "Usually I like the smell of onions. But now I like the smell of candles."

"They're supposed to be uplifting, Mrs. Keschl. Have you felt uplifted?"

"You don't get uplifted at my age," Mrs. Keschl said. "It's all downhill from about twenty years ago."

She looked over Sugar's shoulder at the kaleidoscope of foliage blooming out on the terrace. "So. Green fingers," she said, pushing past and stepping outside. "It's like the Garden of Eden up here. Good work. Coffee, if you're making it. Milk. Two sugars."

Sugar obliged and went to make the coffee, watching Mrs. Keschl through the window as she gently lifted the moonflower to her nose to smell it, then closely inspected the magnolia.

Actually, she was happy to have the company. She'd had a terrible night's sleep and had woken with an uncustomary headache. Usually a cup of mint tea and a few quiet moments spent lingering on the skyline and she couldn't wait to get on with her day, but this morning had been different. She'd had to fight the urge to stay in bed and pull the sheets up over her head. Worse, she'd felt on the verge of tears ever since and it was not a verge she cared for.

"I have some lemon honey tarts," she said, as she delivered the coffee. "Nate made the shells, and the bees and I did the rest. Speaking of which, are you OK to sit here while I do my hive check?"

"I'm OK to sit here till Thanksgiving if you keep bringing food," Mrs. Keschl said.

"Have you lived on Flores Street long?" Sugar asked as she lifted the lid off the hive, then removed the top super, which was already filling with capped honey.

"Forever," Mrs. Keschl said. "Although the neighborhood didn't always look like this. There used to be more dead people."

"Dead people?" Sugar pulled out the most populated frame of bees to look for Elizabeth the Sixth.

"Junkies and hos and that," explained Mrs. Keschl. "Then they made *The Godfather Part II* around the corner and the neighborhood started to come alive."

"Well, that's strange," said Sugar.

"I know. You would expect more dead people after a Mafia movie, not fewer, am I right?"

"No, I mean, yes, I mean what's strange is Elizabeth the Sixth, my queen. She doesn't seem to be laying."

There was no fresh brood pattern, no change in the frame around Elizabeth the Sixth since Sugar had last checked the hive. But her queen was alive, she was being fed, she looked healthy.

She just wasn't working.

Sugar slid the frame back into the brood box and put the hive back together again.

"You look like you swallowed some of those bees," said Mrs. Keschl. "Got any more little cakes?"

"It's never happened before," Sugar told George out on the stoop the following day.

"It's not colony collapse disorder because the bees just disappear with that, and it's not the varroa mite because you can actually see varroa mites and my bees have never had them. And it can't be foulbrood either because that's obvious in the hive and yet there's no sign of it. It's none of those things, George."

"Sorry to hear that, Miss Sugar," he said.

He'd never seen her so agitated. She was missing her rosy glow, had dark rings under her eyes and her smile lacked its usual warmth.

In his weeks on the stoop of the orange brick building on Flores Street, he had closely observed all its inhabitants—that was a doorman's job—but he had paid particular attention to Sugar of whom he was of course especially fond. She was a rare thing in his opinion: a modern city dweller who put stock in caring for those around her. She was treating everyone in the building one way or another with her honey, and her time, and it did his heart a world of good to see.

Plus, 33 Flores Street clearly wasn't the first place where Sugar had worked her particular brand of magic. George had never known anyone to get so much mail from so many different corners of the country. She might get two dozen letters or cards in a single week—and that wasn't all. One day she might show him the copy of a report card some proud mom had sent her from California; the next it could be a needlework sampler hand stitched by a former landlady in Idaho; the day after she might be unwrapping a wonky clay pin-tray sent by some seven-year-old from Santa Fe.

But George worried that Sugar's caring was something of a one-way street. She put her heart and soul into helping fix up everyone else but didn't let anyone do the same for her. A person could only do that for so long.

"Oh, look at Lola's world," she said, pointing at the sad balloon. "It's gotten so small. That's not a good advertisement at all."

"You sure have to wonder about that woman's career advice," George agreed. "Although Ethan seems to be doing better—you wouldn't have anything to do with that I suppose?"

"Ambrosia," Sugar said, brightening. "I make it with honey, propolis and royal jelly and it works wonders."

"Well, I couldn't guarantee it but I thought I saw his mama actually smile yesterday," George said. "And what are you doing to Mrs. Keschl? She was singing last night and that woman has a much sweeter voice than you would ever imagine."

"I'm keeping her stocked up with rose oil candles," Sugar admitted. "Burning them is supposed to reduce irritation."

"She certainly seems to have a plentiful supply of that."

"I'm starting to gather quite a supply myself," said Sugar. "I just don't understand why Elizabeth the Sixth would stop laying like that, George. I'm doing all I can to make her happy but it's like she's just choosing not to be and that's not like her at all."

"You know, I have a place I go to when the problems of the world need my special attention. I don't suppose you would care to join me there, Miss Sugar, talk things through a little?"

"Is it a bar? Because I'm not a real big drinker at this time of the day."

"I'm not a drinker at all, Miss Sugar. This is nature I'm talking about: that's why I know you will like it. And the best thing about being an honorary doorman is I don't need to ask my boss if I can leave my post because I don't have a boss. And look at that, it's near enough to lunchtime."

He offered Sugar his arm and she took it.

Just a couple of blocks away, on a tiny slice of East Sixth Street, sandwiched between two apartment buildings, was an uninviting gate hanging half off its hinges in the middle of a rusted fence.

George led her through and, to Sugar's astonishment, they emerged into a thriving vibrant garden anchored at the rear by a giant oak and crammed with flowering shrubs and teenage trees beneath which nestled an eccentric collection of garden sculptures, chipped gnomes, lurking ceramic toads and moldy cherubs.

"Grace's Garden," George said. "Been here since the seventies when the building on this site burned to the ground, and in those days nobody round here was in a hurry to build anything back up again. No one can remember who Grace was but the locals have been keeping the garden going all these years just so the likes of you and me and anyone else who cares to open the gate can come in and check out of the rat race for a while."

"It's beautiful," Sugar said. Brilliant blue hydrangeas posed like frosting on the plump greenery of their bushy bodies, crowding the base of the ivy-covered wall belonging to the apartment building next door. Quirky mismatching tables and chairs were scattered about the small space, as though waiting for an eccentric ladies' tea party to arrive, but George led her over to a pair of wooden benches hidden in the shrubbery. They looked onto a row of little red-and-white birdhouses perched on a piece of picket fencing planted on its own in the middle of a flower bed.

There they sat, catching a complicated modern dance of sunlight through the leaves of the oak tree and a neighboring willow, as George pulled a wax-paper package out of his bag. He carefully unwrapped it and offered Sugar half of the bagel sitting inside.

"Norwegian smoked salmon with cream cheese, capers and onion from Russ & Daughters on East Houston," he said. "I've been buying my bagels from them since 1969 and they just keep getting better and better, which is just as well because they sure ain't getting cheaper."

"I couldn't, George! That's your lunch."

"And have I ever turned down your honey, or your tea, or your ointment for my leg, or that cake you made that I ate four pieces of?"

"No, but—"

"No, but nothing, Miss Sugar."

"I can't take your lunch, George. I just can't."

George started wrapping it up again. "Well, I'm not sitting here eating it all by myself so either you take half or the birds get the whole thing. That's the deal."

"You drive a hard bargain."

"You're a tough customer."

Reluctantly, she accepted half the bagel. "Thank you," she said, taking a bite. "Oh, this is really good."

"You see?" George said. "All you had to do was allow me to share it with you."

Sugar stopped chewing. "I was just worried that you wouldn't get enough yourself," she said.

"And here's me worrying the same thing about you."

"I eat like a horse, George. You don't need to worry about me."

"I'm not talking about food, Miss Sugar."

"You're not?"

"I'm not."

"Oh." Sugar put the bagel down and wiped delicately at the corners of her mouth. "Then what are you talking about?"

"Since you asked," George said, "I'm old, and getting older, Miss Sugar, and not much in the mood for wasting time, so if you don't mind, I'll just get on with it."

"Oh!"

"There's something bothering you, I can see that, and you would probably prefer to keep it to yourself, because that's your way, but I happen to know that troubles disappear a heck of a lot quicker if you share them with someone who cares about you, which I do."

"But it's my bees," said Sugar. "I have shared that."

"Your bees might be acting up, Miss Sugar, but I don't think they're at the heart of the matter. I think your heart is at the heart of the matter. And matters of the heart happen to be my specialty so if there's anything I can do to help, I'm sitting here waiting, just hoping I haven't offended you by being so forward, but like I said, I'm not getting any younger. And keep in mind that when you finally agreed to help me eat that bagel, it worked out pretty well."

He was right about that: Sugar had already finished her half. But it was just a bagel. She felt sudden palpitations in her chest that didn't seem entirely bagel related. "Whatever makes you think my heart's got anything to do with anything, George?"

"Hearts are all that matter in the end, one way or another," he said. "And you are just about the best-looking young woman in Alphabet City plus you are smart and kind and concerned for your fellow human beings and you seem to have everything a person could possibly wish for—except someone else to share all that with."

"Well, goodness gracious me, not everybody needs someone to share it with. It's not a crime to be single! Some of us are just fine on our own, George. It's a perfectly respectable way to be these days. Better than being stuck in a terrible relationship with someone who doesn't love you."

"Or the same, if it's just fear that's stopping you from moving on. Either way you're stuck."

Sugar was stunned. "That is quite forward," she said.

"I know, and I'm sorry. But it could be that what you're refusing is every bit as bad for the soul as refusing food is for poor little Miss Ruby. And I know you're doing everything you can to help her so now I am going to do everything I can to help you."

"But why would you, George?"

"Because everybody needs an angel some time or other, Miss Sugar. You were mine and I guess I might be yours."

A bluebird flew over the wooden fence from the backyard next door and perched on the platform outside one of the birdhouses, fixing Sugar with its gaze. She opened her mouth to protest, to politely fob George off, to laugh away the ridiculousness of his concerns but nothing came out. Instead she felt a peculiar sense of something approaching calm spread slowly through her, like syrup on a hotcake, starting from the top of her head and traveling south, chasing away her palpitations.

George was right. Of course he was right. Not about being an angel but about her heart.

It wasn't just Elizabeth the Sixth.

It was Theo.

He had shaken up something inside her that had long been buried and did not seem to want to stay that way, no matter how deep a hole she kept trying to dig for it. She was stuck. She was stuck because she was still running away from the sins of her past, scared of making the same mistake again. She didn't move towns every year because she was brave or adventurous or because her queen bee told her to. She moved because she was afraid of feeling about someone the way she currently felt about Theo.

"His name was Grady," she said. "Grady Parkes."

19TH

They'd met at the Carolina Yacht Club when she was twenty. Sugar did not sail herself, but her mother, Etta, had sent her down to the club to deliver a message to her brother Troy. She found him sitting up in the clubhouse that overlooked the sparkling water of the Cooper River, having a beer with a law school friend: Grady Parkes.

She knew of Grady. Every woman in Charleston knew of Grady.

A few years older than the other young men Sugar mixed with at the time, he was beyond handsome, with blond hair, gray eyes, a sportsman's tan and an electrifying charisma that pulled every man, woman and child in his direction as though he were a magnet and they just poor hapless lead shavings.

Grady looked her in the eye, smiled his ridiculous smile and insisted she sit down and that she stay sitting down when Troy left half an hour later.

Things like that, people like him, didn't usually happen to her. Indeed, she'd assumed the Grady Parkeses of this world were made for more sophisticated souls than hers. But within minutes of having his attention all to herself he had her feeling like she was as sophisticated a soul as he had ever met. Within an hour she thought—as she looked in those clever gray eyes, the river twinkling behind him—that if he didn't ask her out, she would die, she would just die.

She'd heard other girls say such things in the past and privately thought they seemed hysterical. But that's what wanting Grady felt like: hysteria.

He took her breath away, literally. Her heart, she felt, was beating in her cheeks.

And she could tell from the expression on Etta's face when she found them still chatting together under an umbrella some time later that this was something of which her mother thoroughly approved. She didn't know then that the whole thing was a setup, although she should have guessed because she was supposed to be going with her mother to the Garden Club that afternoon. Etta was very particular about her club commitments, and about Sugar's too, but when Sugar started to excuse herself her mother suddenly would not hear of it.

"Y'all just look so cute, the two of you, sitting there like that," she said. "You never mind about the Garden Club, Cherie-Lynn. I can take care of that myself. Just relax and enjoy yourself. Go on! So nice to see you, Grady. And make sure to say hello to that handsome devil of a daddy of yours now, won't you?" And she was gone in a swirl of primrose and mauve, her hips swinging as she walked away from them, knowing Grady's eyes would be on her.

Seeing her mama wiggle and swagger like that always reminded Sugar of her own shortcomings in this department. She knew the sort of daughter Etta wished she had—another wiggler and swaggerer—but that flirtatious behavior just didn't come naturally to Sugar. She wasn't a tomboy, exactly. Her mother would have shot her rather than let that happen, but Sugar didn't particularly like parties or shopping trips or lengthy visits to the beauty parlor, all of which her mother adored.

She preferred helping her grandfather with his bees on his orchard farther up the Ashley River; she always had. She liked reading books on her own or walking the family dog, Miss Pickles. Worse, she couldn't manage high heels no matter how hard she tried, which was an utter disgrace to her southern roots. The pretty only daughter of a well-known beauty married to one of the city's wealthier sons should by rights follow directly in her mother's footsteps: in nothing less than three-inch stilettos, as far as Etta was concerned.

But she and Sugar were cut from different cloth.

"The girl just doesn't have your spunk, Etta," Sugar once overheard her father, Blake, saying. "But that doesn't mean there's something wrong with her. Heaven knows you have enough spunk for the whole goddamned family. She just takes after your daddy, is all. That's what riles you."

Until that point, Sugar hadn't known that she riled her mother but it certainly explained the undercurrent she often felt herself caught in, or swimming against.

"You're such an odd girl," Etta once said, looking at her as though she was something the cat had just dragged in. "Why I couldn't have a daughter like Treena Murray or Melissa Knowles, I'll never know. Melissa and her mama are having golf lessons together, she told me at church on Sunday, and they have a spa weekend planned on Kiawah Island."

Melissa Knowles was a fashionable socialite who would not give Sugar the time of day if her life depended on it. And Sugar was no good at golf. Or tennis. She wasn't sporty at all, or musical, or particularly academic, or remotely interested in spa weekends on Kiawah Island.

But she didn't want to seem odd, and she certainly didn't want to keep upsetting her mama, so she tried to do the right thing. She spent time on her hair, her nails, her skin and her looks in general, even though she could just have easily spent every day inside a beekeeper's suit, which Etta knew, and which drove her crazy.

"Did Mama help you with the bees when she was my age?" Sugar once asked Grampa Boone when she was in high school and struggling to feign interest in cheerleading tryouts and horse-riding lessons.

"Your mama never had much time for bees at any age, Sugar Honey," he answered. "Not interested in much outside her own hive. Not that there's anything wrong with that. Just a different way of looking at the world, is all. She came out that way—always wanting to be somewhere else, be something else. You, Sugar child, on the other hand, take after me, and your grandmother. We got all the time in the world when it comes to bees."

"And honey," added Sugar.

"Well, you particularly take after your grandmother in that regard," he said. "She fixed more people than any doctor you could find around here, that's for sure. Couldn't cross the street without stopping to help someone."

Sugar had inherited this do-gooder spirit, as her mama called it. Even back then she would make up lotions and potions using her grandmother's supply of precious oils mixed with her grandfather's honey and use them on Miss Pickles, or her music teacher or the man outside the Piggly Wiggly who was always begging for change.

"It's polite to help people out once in a while, Cherie-Lynn," Etta said. "But do you have to make such an honest-to-goodness career out of it?"

Indeed Sugar did want to make an honest-to-goodness career out of it. After vocational counseling during her senior year of high school, she decided she wanted to become a nurse, but her parents would not hear of it.

"Wallaces don't clean up other people's mess," her father said. "It's not what we do. You don't need to be a nurse, honey. You don't need to be anything. There's no shame in getting married and starting a family when you're still young. That's what your mama did and look how happy she is."

There was absolutely no doubt in Sugar's mind that Etta was happy. She envied her mother's ability to derive such pleasure from flower arranging or upholstery or lunching with her friends but she couldn't quite manage it herself. She enrolled at the College of Charleston majoring in biology, which felt like nursing once or twice removed. She even glimpsed something of a future where biology and honey could combine and take her somewhere.

She did want a husband, a man like her grandfather, who adored his wife, took care of his family and kept bees, of course, but until Grady it was more of a distant dream than a distinct possibility. Watching an afternoon regatta over lemonade on the clubhouse deck, it all suddenly got a lot more distinct. Biology took her somewhere that day all right.

Grady's cool fingers on her arm, his lips firm on her cheek, his strong, salty scent wafting in the air as they parted that first afternoon woke a fire in her belly—and beyond—that she didn't know could burn.

"Bethany Towers says girls your age line up just to be ignored by Grady Parkes," Etta told her daughter after their third date. "Play your cards right with this one, Cherie-Lynn, because I'm telling you, Grady is as good as it gets."

Sugar didn't need to be told that. She was just as much of a lead shaving as the next pretty southern belle waiting for a handsome man with acceptable genes and blinding prospects to sweep her off her feet. Not that she cared about his genes or his prospects; she just fell head over heels in love with him: the flesh and bones and skin and smile and eyes and magnetism of him. Until then, she hadn't known that falling in love really was like falling: fast and uncontrollable with no way of knowing how soft or otherwise the landing would be. It wasn't sweet or safe, as she had imagined. It was frightening. There was a big black empty space growing inside her and only Grady could fill it with his voice, his touch, his attention. When she didn't have any of those things she felt like she was drowning. When she did have them, the thrill of finding that everything she had assumed was out of her reach was right there in front of her was almost as suffocating, but blissfully so.

The more she saw of him, the more she could think of little other than his lips on her neck, his hands on her naked body.

Not that his hands had been on her naked body. He was nothing but a gentleman on that front although the longer they dated the more she thrashed around in her linen sheets at night dreaming of the day when he would be thrashing around in them with her.

In the meantime, just saying his name gave her goose bumps.

"Grady and I thought we might go to the beach tomorrow," she would say and feel the delicious shiver run down her spine. "Grady and I are having lunch with his sister at McCrady's on Sunday." "Grady and I are going to Savannah for the weekend." "Grady and I, Grady and I, Grady and I . . ."

Etta was so happy she all but floated a foot off the ground. And Sugar's father and brothers were encouraging of the romance too. Grady Parkes Senior owned a shipping company that was a major client of the Port Authority, and to get his business in the tough economic times everyone seemed to be going through—even the Wallaces—would be more than beneficial.

But Sugar did not need to be talked into loving Grady. Chemistry had taken care of that and, after a lifetime of feeling out of step, she suddenly saw the myriad benefits of falling in line.

She dropped out of college ('Good riddance," sniffed Etta), she stopped reading books, she stopped walking the dog, she stopped hanging out with her grandfather and helping with the hives. She did whatever Grady wanted her to do whenever Grady wanted her to do it. But it didn't feel like a sacrifice—she just couldn't get enough of him and the way he made her feel. This was what everyone was talking about. This was love and she was in it and not thinking twice.

When Grady came to the house to ask for Sugar's hand in marriage just four months after that first day at the Yacht Club, Sugar thought her daddy was even happier than she was and that was saying something, because Sugar herself was impossibly happy. And because she'd never loved anyone like that before she assumed that it was a state in which she would stay forever.

About that, of course, she was entirely wrong.

It started the night of their engagement party, which was held in the ballroom of the Wallaces' Legare Street mansion, where two hundred and fifty of the happy couple's nearest and dearest gathered to toast their future.

Sugar had enjoyed herself so much, dancing with Grady and his brothers and her brothers and anyone else who asked her; she was loving the limelight for once, delighting in being the belle of the ball.

The only glitch was Grampa Boone, who had been invited but didn't want to come. He wasn't feeling well, he said, which was unlike him, but he rarely came to the parties at the Wallace mansion anyway. He said they made him itchy. He said they used to make Sugar itchy too but she just laughed and told him Grady had cured her of that. Still, she felt bad about her granddaddy because he and her fiancé had never even met. Grady didn't much care for the countryside, he said, but kept promising to go to Summerville with her as soon as they had a free weekend.

He looked so handsome the night of the party, and he was so gracious and charming. He paid as much attention to Sugar's whiskery great-aunt Emmerline as he did to Meredith Burrows who was a model in New York and drop-dead gorgeous although, according to Grady, too bony for his liking.

They'd been to other balls and grand parties before, the two of them, during their brief courtship. Grady loved to socialize and on his arm Sugar truly didn't find it quite the chore she always had before. But did he always drink that much? she wondered halfway through the night. She hadn't noticed him being drunk any other time, and it wasn't as though he was falling down or embarrassing himself or anything. Charleston men were known for being able to hold their liquor. But despite that grace and charm of his, she recalled afterward seeing a gleam in his eye that she hadn't noticed before. She hadn't thought at the time that it was dangerous but then why would she? She was at her engagement party with the man of her dreams.

But after their two proud daddies made their speeches and their two proud mamas cried delicate tears (Etta's didn't even smear her mascara), Grady pulled Sugar outside, down the stairs at the back of the house and into the room that her mother referred to as her "decoupage studio."

"You are so beautiful," Grady said, pressing her up against the wall. "You are so fucking beautiful. God, I love you. You're amazing. Do you know that? I love you so much, so fucking much. You are perfect. Fucking perfect."

He'd been such a gentleman up until then; she'd just assumed they would wait. She was embarrassingly old-fashioned like that, despite dreaming over and over of their first time together, the lingering kisses, the slow removal of clothes in the half-light of their first shared bedroom, the exquisite tenderness of two people exploring each other's bodies, knowing they had a lifetime to get to know each other's pleasures and pain. But hearing him say how much he loved her, as though he meant it so much it was tearing him in two, despite the cursing, which usually made her flinch, Sugar suddenly didn't feel quite so old-fashioned after all.

She'd waited for this particular pleasure for long enough: every part of her cried out right now for every part of him.

She lifted up the layers of her skirt.

"You're the best thing that ever happened to me," Grady said, roughly kissing her neck, biting her ear, pushing his knee between her legs. "I mean it, CeeLee." That was his pet name for her. "God, how I mean it."

But before she could even offer him her plump and desperate lips to kiss, he had undone his pants and was thrusting into her, grunting, his eyes closed, his head down, his body heaving.

It was as though she wasn't even there.

Then, one brief searing pain and it was all over. Grady fell back against the wall next to her, his eyes still closed, sweat pouring off him as he did up his zipper. "Talk about worth the fucking wait," he said. "Come on, we should get back inside before they miss us."

Sugar fixed her hair back up in its loosened pins with shaking hands, bewildered by what had just happened.

Grady saw her expression and mistook it for regret at caving in to her desire. "It's OK, sweetheart," he said. "I was going to pop your cherry anyhow. Does it really matter when?"

Inside, someone had turned up the music and she heard one of Grady's friends calling his name. "I fucking love this song," he said. "Come on, CeeLee. Let's party."

In the ballroom, the guests were too drunk or tired or both to notice that the bride-to-be had lost some of her glow. Her eyes still twinkled, but it was no longer the unbridled joy sort of twinkling.

On the night of her engagement party, Sugar saw something in Grady that didn't fit her dream of the adoring husband-to-be, the charming son-in-law, the charismatic lawyer. She saw a sweaty drunk who popped her cherry. On the night of her engagement party, it occurred to Sugar that while there was no denying the powerful and intoxicating physical chemistry between them, there was also no denying that something else was missing.

20TH

The bluebird had hopped on top of an antique clock that hung from a tree bough, but was still looking at Sugar, its head cocked as if it too were listening.

"Love hurts, Miss Sugar," George said. "Even more so when you're young and don't know that it can be any other way."

"It was a long time ago," Sugar said, her eyes following the bird as it moved to a higher branch of the oak. "And it's not like I think about him much these days. I've spent the last fifteen years trying not to think of him at all, but then along comes Ruby, God bless what's left of her, and she has this thing for romance. She acts like she hates it but the poor little thing is addicted to weddings and it seems to make her happy to talk about them but all the same, it has me churned up inside like you would not believe. Plus . . ."

"Plus what, Miss Sugar?"

"Well, it may have nothing to do with anything."

"Or something to do with everything."

"It's what you said before about the fear of moving on. Oh, I can't believe that I'm even contemplating such a thing!"

"Contemplating what, Miss Sugar?"

"I met someone, George."

"You did?"

"I did."

"And what all is happening there?"

"Nothing all is happening but I'm sick to my stomach just thinking about it."

"Sounds like I'm onto something with this matter of the heart situation then."

"I don't even know him and he doesn't know me and besides, he is a total fruit loop."

"All the best people are total fruit loops, Miss Sugar. Didn't you notice that yet?"

"The whole business just scares me half to death."

"You need to get rid of all that scared."

"I need to get rid of my past, is what I need to do."

"That can't be done. You must know that by now. But with a little help, you could most certainly reduce its influence."

"Do you really believe that?"

"Miss Sugar, I'm living proof of that."

Grady was so sweet and charming after the engagement party that Sugar put her disappointment in the decoupage studio aside and with it any other doubts.

The first time was always a disaster, she knew that, and she was coming to it later than most. She knew a couple of other girls her age who were still saving themselves for their husbands, but most were carefully glossing over what they had carelessly already spent.

"Did you and Daddy, before you were married . . . ?" she asked Etta one morning, trying not to sound as awkward as she felt.

Etta was bent over her writing desk and Sugar saw a familiar blotchy rash creep up her neck. "Grady is a gentleman," she said. "He wouldn't ask for anything it's not right to give."

"Even if it's—"

"Even nothing, Cherie-Lynn! Men have needs. It's not just something people say; it's true. Marrying Grady Parkes is the best thing that could ever possibly happen to you so please don't do anything to ruin it or, so help me, Jesus, I will never forgive you, never. And neither will your father."

And with that she started to talk about how to seat her old friend Louisa at the wedding so she couldn't see or hear her ex-husband Hank, which was going to be pretty hard since you could hear him from where they were sitting now and he lived in Texas.

There had been another encounter the week after the party, snatched in the car outside a clam shack on Folly Island. Again it had been over almost before it started. Again Grady had not even looked at her, let alone kissed her. Again, he had been nice as pie afterward.

She tried to suggest that they go to a hotel, or sneak into her room, or at least lead up to it nicely somehow but she was embarrassed and Grady was offended by the merest suggestion that his lovemaking—quick, rough and almost public—was anything other than ideal.

"Never had any complaints before," he said. "And I'm not new to this, baby."

It wasn't as though Sugar thought for a moment that she was his first, but something about the way he smiled when he said that pulled at her heart. Privately she thought he could have spared her the obvious insinuation.

Then, after a couple more weeks of putting it off, he redeemed himself by keeping his promise to meet Grampa Boone. They arrived out at Summerville on a sunny Sunday afternoon just as he was taking the lid off the beehive at the side of the porch to check on his house supply of honey.

Sugar couldn't wait to go help, but Grady grabbed her arm as she started to get out of the car. "What's he doing?"

"He's cleaning his beehive. Come on, Grady, let's give him a hand."

"To clean a beehive? I don't think so."

"Grady, honey, let go, you're hurting my arm. I've been helping Grampa clean out his hives and raise his bees since I was a little girl. My very first memory is tasting honey fresh off the comb. Honestly. Whatever's the matter?"

"With me? Absolutely nothing. It's you I'm worried about. You're the one who wants to go rooting around in some scrappy backyard with a bunch of insects like some second-rate farm hand."

"It's not scrappy, Grady. And Grampa expects me to help. I always do. It's our thing."

"Not anymore, it isn't," Grady said, but she pulled her arm out of his grasp, the red mark where he had gripped it burning her flesh as she walked toward the house.

Her grandfather watched this exchange from behind the veil of his bee helmet and to save his granddaughter any shame he just put the lid back on the hive, walked to the front of the porch and started to take off his suit, like he was finished with his chores already.

Sugar hugged him tight and if he felt thinner than usual or seemed frail or unwell in any way, she didn't notice.

"Grady, I would like you to meet the other man in my life."

"Pleased to meet you, sir," Grady said, holding out his hand for Grampa Boone to shake. But he wasn't radiating his usual charm. "Mind if we move away from those bees?" he said, going to the opposite end of the porch. "Never did much care for the things."

Sugar busied herself moving the chairs around and then chattered away as she fetched Grady and her grandfather a bourbon and got an iced tea for herself.

Her grandfather told them all about his day, keeping bee talk to a minimum out of courtesy to her fiancé, and asked politely about the family business and the engagement party and the wedding plans.

But when they went to leave, he held her back a moment and maneuvered her toward the bees while Grady kept heading for the car. "This queen has to be my best one yet, Sugar," he said when they were standing next to the hive. "I call her Elizabeth and you should see the way she's laying eggs, all neat and even and quicker than any other one I've had. Never seen a brood pattern like it. I reckon we'll get more honey out of her than we've ever seen before."

"She certainly has her workers going at fever pitch," Sugar said, looking at the wild concentration of bees going in and out of the hive entrance. "I can't believe I missed her arrival into the world."

"You've been busy, Sugar Honey."

"But I should never get too busy for you or the bees. You're two of my favorite things. I sure hope Elizabeth forgives me."

"There's no need for that but if there was, she'd be up for it," her grandfather said. "She's real strong, Sugar. Just like you."

"Me?" Sugar laughed. "What makes you think I'm strong?"

"Knowing you for the past twenty years," he said. "You're not a drone, Sugar. You're a queen. Don't you forget that."

"Oh, Grampa, what a sweet thing to say."

"I don't mean for it to be sweet. I mean for it to help you if you need help."

They looked at each other.

"You are strong, Sugar child," he said again. "Never forget it. And never let anybody make you feel like you are not. Promise me?"

"I don't know what you mean," Sugar said, but she blushed and couldn't meet his eyes.

"Just promise me."

"OK, OK, Grampa, if it makes you feel better, I promise, of course I do, but honestly . . ."

"You're too good for him," her grandfather said. "And not Charleston good either, just ordinary good."

"You mean Grady?"

"Sugar Honey, the man doesn't like bees."

"A lot of people don't like bees!"

"Yes, but you're not one of them."

She wanted to protest, to defend the man she loved and was about to marry, but instead glimpsed her opportunity to talk to the one person who most understood her about her creeping doubts. The truth was that the closer she got to the wedding, the less she felt like her old self. And in the absence of the romantic intimacy about which she had so often dreamed since falling under Grady's spell, the novelty of fitting in was wearing thin.

He wanted her to get gold streaks put in her hair, he liked it worn down not up, he preferred her in heels even though he knew they hurt, and he called her CeeLee, which actually she did not care for. None of these things on their own amounted to much, she would feel silly even talking about them, but together they were combining to wake her up in the middle of the night with a panicky feeling that she was about to make a big mistake.

And now he didn't want her to help out with her grandfather's bees.

That amounted to something.

But then he tooted the horn and revved up the car and she thought of her parents and her brothers and the wedding plans and the house they were decorating on Church Street and the honeymoon in France and her doubts slithered away. "Don't worry about me, Grampa," she said, stepping in to give him a kiss goodbye, the bees buzzing around the two of them as she did. "I'm right as rain."

"I love you, Sugar Honey," he said, as she walked away from him.

"I know you do, Grampa," she said, turning around to wave. "And I love you too."

It was the last time she ever saw him.

Sugar's grandfather died peacefully in his sleep four days after she and Grady visited him in Summerville, leaving her inconsolable.

"But he was old, CeeLee," Grady said, quickly bored by her despair. "What were you expecting?"

A week after the funeral she still couldn't keep from crying and her mother, tired of such "histrionics," told her to pull herself together.

"Your eyes look like sea creatures," she snapped. "Time to dry your tears, Cherie-Lynn. We have a wedding to plan."

But it was Etta's own eyes that bulged and blinked when her father's will was read and Sugar was named the major beneficiary. It wasn't that Etta cared about the money—thanks to Blake she hadn't had to care about that in a long time—she was just astonished there was any. Thea and Jim Boone had always lived such a modest life, way too modest for her liking. She'd started plotting her escape from what she considered their rural backwater when she was just a little girl after seeing Grace Kelly on the cover of a magazine. Beautiful blondes deserved handsome princes and lavish palaces, Etta realized, and she was not going to find either in Summerville.

But her father had died a wealthy man. He had done well, the lawyer said, selling off bits of land Etta didn't even know he had, and he'd been clever with his stocks and shares.

"You're a rich woman, honey," Etta told Sugar when she got back from the lawyer's office. "You and Grady will be able to do whatever you want, wherever you want. Although you could have anyway, but it doesn't hurt to have a little nest egg of your own. Who knows when you might want to redecorate the carriage house or go shopping in London?"

"I don't want to go shopping in London," Sugar said, starting to cry again. "I don't want his money, I want him."

"Cherie-Lynn, listen to me, you have to snap out of this. You think he would want you acting so disgraceful? All upset and red-faced and driving everybody including your husband-to-be around the bend with your amateur dramatics?"

"But what will happen to the cabin? And who will look after his bees?"

"You don't need to worry about any of that. That's all taken care of. Your brothers will sort out the house and the land. And the bees are going to some friend of your grandfather," her mother said. "He had it all organized. Apart from . . . oh, how infuriating that old man could be!"

"Apart from what?"

"I don't want you to worry about it, honey. You have enough on your plate right now."

"Apart from what, Mama?"

Her mother rolled her eyes. "Apart from one stupid hive that he left to you, crazy old coot. What he was thinking, I can't imagine. You're not going to be keeping bees over at the Church Street place—"

"Which hive, Mama?"

"Does it really matter? You won't be taking those bees."

"It matters! He left them to me. They're mine."

"Well, he left you that stinky old pickup truck too and you're not going to take that, are you?"

"Is it the hive at the cabin? Did he leave me his house bees?"

"Yes, I believe he did. The lawyer said your granddaddy just added that to the will a few days before he died. Lord knows what for."

Sugar and Grady argued that night about those bees. She wanted to go and get them and take them to the house they would move into after they were married. He would not hear of it.

"If I say you're not keeping any damn bees, then you're not keeping any damn bees," he raged. "You're not some hillbilly going to grow corn, make moonshine and spend your life smoking a pipe on a porch, CeeLee."

"I could give honey to the church fair," she suggested. "Or to our friends at Christmas. It's not bootleg, Grady, it's food. And the bees won't bother you at all, I'll make sure of it. They're just bees."

"You will not bring them anywhere near our house," Grady said, in an unmistakably threatening tone.

"Or what?" she said as pleasantly as she could manage.

"Jesus, I don't need this shit from you. I don't need it from anyone. Let it go or one day when Meredith Burrows calls me begging me to reconsider my future I might just take her up on it."

"Meredith calls you?"

He looked at her, one eyebrow raised, a curious smile on his face, and her heart sank down to the tips of the high heels that felt like permanent crabs latched on to her toes.

"I'm just saying," Grady said.

Saying what?

Sugar thought of the queen bee abandoned out at the cabin waiting for her, and she thought of her grandfather, telling her she was strong, and that no one should ever make her feel otherwise, and that he loved her, and she thought she would never miss anybody in her life as much as she missed that man right then.

She looked at Grady, who could flatten the breath out of her with just one smile, who still gave her butterflies in her stomach every time he walked into a room, and who she realized could not fill even a fifth of her granddaddy's bee suit. Maybe there wasn't a man alive who could. But still, it shook her to think that about the man she was so in love with, the man she was set to marry, build an entire life with.

She'd happily given up her career, her hairstyle, some of her friends and even the comfort of her feet for him. But her grandfather's bees? The ones she'd been helping raise since she was knee-high to a grasshopper? It felt like too much.

Grady sensed something then, something that could hurt him, and his anger blew out like a candle in a spring gust. He took her in his arms and held her, told her it would be all right, that he would look after her forever, that she had nothing to worry about, that he loved her and needed her and he was just kidding about Meredith. He'd already told her, Meredith was too bony for him.

The tender side of him made Sugar want to believe every word.

But awake in the night, panic clutching at her stomach, she felt happily-ever-after sliding through her fingers.

"Why, you're wasting away to nothing, Cherie-Lynn," Etta told her daughter disapprovingly a few days later.

They were at the dressmaker's for her final fitting and the sumptuous gown that Charleston's most sought-after designer had created for her was hanging from her shoulders like a bird net over an apple tree in the winter.

"What happened to the rest of you, child?" asked the dressmaker. "I mean it looks a million dollars but I'm running out of pins trying to take the thing in."

Sugar looked at herself in the mirror, barely recognizing the face looking back at her. "Just nerves, I guess," she said.

"You have nothing to be nervous about," Etta said.

"And you are going to make a beautiful bride," the dressmaker said with a sigh, standing back and looking at her handiwork. "I just can't wait to see you walk up that aisle."

"Let's hope her expression is a little more cheerful, shall we?" Etta said. "We're talking about the happiest day of your life, for heaven's sake, Cherie-Lynn. You're going to have to cheer up if you want to keep that man of yours happy."

The weekend before the wedding, they went out for dinner with both sets of parents and Sugar watched with horror as Grady drank more than usual and got that look in his eyes that turned him into a stranger.

"Grady, please, can't we wait?" she suggested when he stopped his car in the street just up from her house and pushed back the seat, fumbling with his belt.

"And why would I want to do that?" he said.

"I just thought we could make it special," Sugar insisted. "You know, on our wedding night. At the hotel, with champagne and candles and music. To turn it into something we'll always remember."

"Suit yourself," Grady said, pulling his seat back up. "But just so we're clear, CeeLee, a man like me shouldn't rightfully have to wait for anything," he said. "Or anyone."

"And I would really prefer it if you didn't call me that," she said.

"I'll call you whatever the hell I want," Grady said. "Jesus, what's got into you?"

In her room at home, afterward, she picked up the photo of her grandfather that she kept in a silver frame on her dressing table.

She felt so far removed from the girl who spent hours helping him move bees from one hive to another, who mixed honey with lavender oil, who concocted special tinctures to ward off winter chills, that for once she was glad that he wasn't there because she knew it would break his heart to see her like this.

"You are strong," she told herself and, saying it out loud, it actually had something of a kick. "You are strong," she said again, only louder, this time, and louder again until eventually she could look at the woman staring back at her in the mirror and see someone she knew.

The next morning she drove out to her grandfather's cabin to pick up the beehive he had left her. The place looked overgrown already. In the weeks since her grandfather had died, her brothers had not taken care of it at all. But his pickup was still parked out back as though he'd only just driven up in it, the keys still in the ignition.

The house bees were nearly out of water and antsy with it, although a quick check of the queen revealed she was laying her derriere off in the steady, even patterns her grandfather had talked about.

"Hey, Elizabeth," she said. "Sorry it's taken me so long to get out here but there have been complications."

She cleaned up the hive as best she could, putting the supers laden with honey in the trunk of her car, and the brood box containing the queen in the backseat.

Usually the bees traveled on the deck of the old pickup, and they didn't seem happy about being in Sugar's Volvo. Grady had bought it for her and it still smelled new and leathery, which she suspected was the problem. They buzzed around the interior of the car in such an agitated fashion, she decided it would be safer to don her grandfather's bee suit for the drive into the city.

Visibility proved to be something of an issue with the veil casting a muted pall over the world as she drove cautiously away from Summerville. Her grandfather's oversized gloves had a job keeping hold of the steering wheel, but Sugar liked the feeling of her fingerprints resting just where his had.

In her grandfather's suit, his familiar scent still mingling with the sweet honey smells of the thousands of bees buzzing behind her, she felt happier than she had in weeks, the outside world little more than a passing blur.

"It feels like flying," she said out loud, as she sped down Ashley River Road beneath a canopy of live oaks bordering vast plantation gardens on either side, the Spanish moss stirring in the breeze overhead, waving her on.

It felt like freedom.

As she approached the city and the new house on Church Street, however, she felt the rattle of gathering shackles. Grady had made his feelings about the bees perfectly plain and the strength that she'd gathered in bringing them there faltered when she pulled up opposite their new house. But as she sat there in her bee suit wondering what to do next, the landscapers Grady's mother had employed to create the formal garden at the side of the house climbed in their truck and drove off on their lunch break, which she could only take as a sign to move right on in.

She found the perfect spot for the hive in a corner of the garden between a purple lilac and a collection of azaleas. It faced southeast, which was good for sun, and looked out on the water feature Sugar's mother-in-law-to-be had modeled on the much bigger one in her own vast grounds over on East Battery. Sugar had never liked it until then—even the smaller version seemed showy—but its shallow outer ledge would provide the bees with all the water they needed, plus a magnolia on the opposite side of it meant the hive was not visible from the house itself.

By the time Grady realized it was there, she would have proved the bees were not a nuisance.

But the bees had other plans.

Just days later, Grady turned up to pay the contractors and got stung, right on the neck, after which all hell broke loose. When Sugar arrived to pick him up and take him to their rehearsal dinner, he was in a rage, storming around the yard, kicking the ground, holding his neck where the sting was swelling under his fingers.

"You must have done something to rile them," she said. "They don't just sting for no reason."

"Fuck that! I told you I didn't want you messing around with any goddamn bees," he raged. "I told you that and you went and got them anyway."

"My granddaddy left them to me, Grady. It's not right to leave them to die out at the cabin. It's disrespectful. And worse than that, it's cruel."

"I'll tell you what's right and what's not," he said. "I'll tell you what's disrespectful."

"But having them here will make me happy. Don't you want me to be happy?"

"A fucking bee is not going to make you happy, CeeLee. I

am going to. And I will do it my way, right here, in my house, without those fucking pests. Do you hear me?"

She wanted to tell him that it wasn't his house, it was their house, that they weren't pests, that he was behaving rudely and he wore too much aftershave. The bees hated aftershave.

But her strength had faded.

"Come here and let me have a look at that," she said instead, reaching to pry his hand away from his bee sting, but he slapped her arm away with such force she twisted an ankle, tripped over a spade and fell backward onto the ground.

There was a moment—just a split second—when she looked up at his face and thought he was going to kick her. There was some sort of rage bubbling beneath his surface: she could almost see his skin stretch over it to contain it. But then he seemed to register what had happened and scrambled to help her up.

"I'm sorry, darlin', I didn't mean to . . . Oh, shit. Are you OK? I didn't mean anything by that; I just didn't want you poking at me. Are you all right, honey?"

"I'm fine," she said, dusting herself down. "I just need to go inside and sponge this dirt off the back of my dress."

"Baby, I'm sorry. You know that, right? I didn't mean to hurt you."

The way he looked then took her back to the Grady she had first fallen for. She felt the exquisite warmth where his hand touched hers, the thump of her heart beating more quickly under his gaze.

But she also felt something else now that was neither warm nor thrilling. She felt fear.

"I'll find a good home for the bees, I promise," he said. "I'll get the landscapers to take care of it. I'm not a monster, CeeLee, and I don't mean to be disrespectful. I'm goddamn crazy about you. You know that, right?"

"Of course," she said, forcing a smile. "We're getting married tomorrow, aren't we?"

It was far too late to even think about doing otherwise.

21ST

The bluebird flew off into the backyards of East Sixth Street as Sugar stood up and offered George a helping hand.

"That's enough for one day," she said. "Lord knows it's more than I've said about it in fifteen years."

"You feel any better for it?" George asked.

"I feel like I've woken up in the middle of a busy street wearing my nightdress and no makeup," she answered.

"Well, at least you've woken up."

"Thank you, George," she said, because although she didn't entirely agree with him, she knew that his heart was in the right place.

"No trouble at all, Miss Sugar. No trouble at all."

Back at number 33 Flores Street they were just in time to catch a tall skinny man dressed in black slinking out of the balloon shop.

"You're cool," the guy said to Lola over his shoulder as he left. "Rollo was right. And cheap too."

Lola shut the door, failing to see Sugar's hopeful face at the top of the stairs. There was no point in keeping the store open. Nobody would come.

She looked around the tiny space and sighed. The walls were lined with boxes of different colored uninflated balloons, arranged in blocks like a Rubik's cube. Crowded behind the counter was an eclectic family including Donald Duck, a giant strawberry, the Empire State Building, an elephant and even a human-sized cucumber. The elephant's trunk had gone soft. It had been faulty to begin with but Ethan could reach it and liked to tug on it so she had just left it there.

Her little boy was asleep in his stroller to the side of the counter, his dark eyelashes fluttering on his cheeks, his fat fists still holding the apple she had peeled for him, a little bubble blowing in and out of his mouth.

After nearly two years she still couldn't believe that a high school dropout and runaway like herself, famous for making bad choices, had created such a miracle. Ethan was the biggest mistake Lola had ever made—and she'd made some doozies—but he was also her savior.

She'd been wasted a lot back in the days when she fell pregnant, topless dancing for a living, doing whatever with whomever, not giving a shit either way. But Ethan was the result of a relatively sober two-night stand with a guitar player she met in a bar farther down on the Lower East Side. She didn't remember his name, but she remembered his sad brown eyes and his tender hands. He was Italian, she thought. Or Spanish. They shared two hot nights together and then she pretty much forgot about him until one of the other dancers asked if she'd been picking at the greasy fries in the slimy club where they were working because she was putting on weight.

The weight turned out to be Ethan.

The surprise was that she was so happy about it.

She fell in love with her son the first time she saw him. In fact, she felt like he'd somehow always been there, wafting in the air above her as a distant possibility, just waiting all those years to come along and give her something other than messing up to be good at.

And she was a good mom, she knew that. She got tired, and it was hard looking after him on her own, but she never resented him, or got angry with him, or lost patience with him. She'd given up dancing straightaway. She wanted Ethan to grow up to be proud of her, which was why she had moved out of the apartment she shared with a rotating collection of girls from the club and found the place on Flores Street.

There'd been a psychic in the basement storefront when she first moved in upstairs—an overweight blonde who wept loudly in between customers—but one day she disappeared and the store was empty. Around then, Ethan smiled for the first time when someone standing outside a new bar opening on the square handed her a balloon, which she tied to his pram. He was a colicky baby, his little body often racked with pain, and he cried a lot, so to see him smile was Lola's best moment ever.

Suddenly all the mistakes of her past melted away and she was still over the moon about being there to see that smile, chatting to him and smiling to herself, when she got back to 33 Flores Street and looked at the empty basement store.

What about a balloon shop? That was what she said to herself. If one balloon can make one little boy happy, imagine what a whole store full of balloons can do? It was a surefire hit.

That was her business plan.

Thanks to the recession the rent was dirt cheap, and she had been a good dancer: she'd saved enough money to buy stock and set the store up. For the first month she had sat down there playing with Ethan, blowing up the pandas and the Winnie-the-Poohs and the Mickey Mouses and the Guggenheims waiting for the customers. They came in trickles, often without opening their pocketbooks, and often not staying because, although Ethan was the love of her life, his bellow was nothing short of deafening.

She soon stopped going down every day and started hating balloons.

Then she got a job waitressing at a vegan café on Second Avenue. It paid the rent, but only just, plus she was allowed to keep her top on, but she was running out of friends to look after Ethan and sick of asking them to.

She needed money and Rollo had found a way for her to make it and had just sent his buddy to her for more of the same. She was scared, she had to admit to herself, as she bent down to kiss Ethan. But she was good at what Rollo and his buddy wanted, too.

"Mama!" Ethan cooed, as if surprised to find her there, her lips hovering over his downy little head. He smiled at her then reached for the elephant's droopy trunk. Whatever was in Sugar's syrup was working.

She flipped the CLOSED sign on the door to OPEN. But Sugar had already gone.

22ND

Mr. McNally heard Sugar coming up the stairs and opened his door to catch her as she passed. "Your woman on the first floor," he said. "The little stick? She was only in a dead faint in the lobby when I went down to check the mail."

It took a good few minutes before Ruby answered Sugar's persistent knocking and, when she did, her eyes were dull, her skin was gray, and she was even thinner than the last time Sugar had seen her, which she would not have thought possible.

"Oh, honey," was all she said, at which Ruby burst into tears.

"Don't say anything," she wept. "I've heard it all before. And I never end up liking the people who say those things, so don't you say them."

"OK then, I won't," Sugar said, stepping inside and taking Ruby's delicate frame in her arms, holding her as gently as she could, her thin shoulders quivering beneath her touch. She reminded Sugar of one of those dried leaf skeletons where nothing but the exquisite shape of the original leaf remained, just an intricate whisper of what once had been. Beautiful to look at, but too fragile to hold.

She didn't want to tell Ruby to eat. The girl had food in the house, after all, so she could eat if she wanted to, but she obviously didn't, or couldn't. And telling her to was going to get them both nowhere so she needed to park that for the moment and just work out what else she could do to help.

"You know I'm pretty close to having a fit of the vapors myself," she said. "My bees are out of sorts and I swear I'm right there with them so I'm going to make us both a cup of lemon tea and then you know what we're going to do?"

She wiped the tears from Ruby's hollow cheeks. "We're going to lie on that great big bed of yours and look at your scrapbook."

If there was a simple way to fix a problem quickly, her grampa had always said, you're a fool not to try it. Sugar didn't know how to get Ruby to eat more, but she did know how to make her feel better, so she would take it from there.

In the kitchen, she added to Ruby's tea a spoonful of the bee pollen she had in her pocket. Bee pollen, in her opinion, was one of the world's unsung superfoods and, while it would hardly restore Ruby to health the way eating three good meals a day could, it would at least give the starving girl a smidgeon of energy to help get her through the next few hours. Actually, Sugar needed a little oomph of her own so added a few grains to her tea too, then carried both cups into Ruby's room where she was nestling like a tiny twig into the many overstuffed pillows of her vast sleigh bed, the scrapbook open on her lap.

"It was a good week," Ruby said. "Will you read them to me?"

She was now down to one one-eighth of a cracker, two wedges of orange, a stick of celery, half a jar of baby food and a carrot but she had nixed the diet soda. She was not going to go back to the hospital, she was not going to even try quinoa; she just wanted to hear nice things about happy people.

Sugar slipped off her shoes, nestled back against the pillows herself, and picked up the scrapbook.

"*Brenda Lord and Victor Hamilton were married yesterday at Immaculate Conception Roman Catholic Church in Westhampton Beach, N.Y.,*" she read.

'*I knew from the moment I first saw him that we would end up getting married,' said the bride, who is taking her husband's name. 'It just took a couple of years for him to see it the same way.*'"

"That happens quite a lot," said Ruby. "With the taking a while to see it that way."

"Well, according to Mr. Hamilton, '*Brenda knows exactly what she wants and once I got used to that, I saw how handy it could be.*' Sugar continued.

'*Our fate was sealed the first time he told me not to worry, that everything would be all right,' said Mrs. Hamilton. 'He had no way of knowing that it would be, but I loved that he said that anyway.*'"

"He sounds pretty cool," Ruby said. "But she sounds bossy. Read me another one."

"You want to add a little please or thank you to that?"

"Please or thank you," Ruby obliged.

"*Benjamin Fielding and Gail Greenberg were married Sunday evening at Beth El Congregation in New York,*" Sugar read. "*The couple were introduced by their fathers, who met at Mr. Greenberg's synagogue and decided their children would be perfect for each other.*

'*Naturally I did not believe that this would be the case,' Mr. Fielding said, 'so I did not call Gail after my father gave me her number.*'

'*And I wouldn't have gone out with him even if he had called,' added Ms. Greenberg. 'Getting set up by your parents is not usually a recipe for success.*'"

"I happen to know that Ms. Greenberg is right about that," said Sugar.

"Continue, *please*," instructed Ruby.

"*However, a few months later the pair met by coincidence at a dinner party being hosted by a mutual friend and, to their great amusement, they got on extremely well.*

'*She was as smart and funny as she was beautiful,' said Mr. Fielding. 'That was a pretty big night, actually, to discover my soul mate—and that my parents were right!'*"

"You see?" Ruby said. "It took a while for them to see it but it worked out in the end."

"It was nice what he said about her being smart and funny and beautiful," Sugar admitted.

"Has anybody ever said that about you?"

"Not recently," Sugar said, "but my mama did fix me up once, although I didn't know it at the time."

"And what happened?"

"It didn't work out," Sugar said. "In the end."

"But in the beginning?"

"In the beginning? It's funny you should ask me that. I hadn't thought much about the beginning until today."

"And?"

"And now I have thought about it I would have to say that in the beginning it was pretty good but the beginning is only the beginning and it's kind of the middle and the end that really matter."

"What made it so good to start out with?"

"I guess I was just crazy in love with him and I thought that was all you had to be for everything to work out OK."

"What did it feel like to be crazy in love?"

Sugar lay back on the pillows. What a question. What did it feel like? "You know, being in love is not as much fun as they make it look in the movies. Most the time you feel like you ate a bowlful of bad shrimp. Your head tries to tell you one thing but your body has a whole different take on it. It's like being on a runaway roller coaster with a belly full of barbecue."

"I imagined that about the roller coaster," Ruby said. "But not with all the food. You make it sound scary."

"It is scary, sweetie, because one person never truly knows what is going on in another person's head. So your heart might be at the front of the roller coaster but your other body parts are at the back and the person you're crazy in love with might be on a whole different ride, plus there are twists and turns. It's complicated."

"What happened in the end?"

Sugar closed her eyes and pictured Grady the last time she had seen him. "I'm not sure that I want to talk about that right now."

"Did he break your heart?"

"I don't know about that."

"You must know if your heart is broken, Sugar. You must be able to feel it and it hurts, like everything inside you is black and hard and not dead, exactly, but pretty close."

"OK, well, I suppose he did break my heart then," Sugar said. "But it didn't happen the way I thought hearts got broken. It didn't mean I wasn't in love with him anymore, which was kind of strange. And it wasn't sudden. I guess it broke slowly, and it was a whole lot of little heartbreaks that one day joined up to make one big one, and then—well that was sudden, and it did not come at a good time, not for anyone, which only made it worse."

"Is it still broken?" Ruby asked.

"No, honey, hearts don't stay broken. That's the good thing. Just like everything else, they can be mended. And anyway that was a long time ago."

Ruby turned her head away from Sugar and reached out to stroke the dark green brocade drapes framing the view of the building next door.

"I don't think anyone will ever love me like Mr. Fielding loves Ms. Greenberg," she said.

"Oh, but someone will," Sugar protested. "Someone definitely will. Someone might be loving you like that right now and you don't even know it."

"I'd know it," Ruby said. "I know I'd know it."

"Well that's the thing about love, Ruby. You *don't* know. Mr. Fielding and Ms. Greenberg are a perfect example. They particularly didn't want to find love with each other—and then they met and whammo, there it was, love in all her glory, nothing to do with them at all."

She thought of Theo, of how she'd felt when their hands touched on the street the day they met, of how her insides quivered just at the very thought of him, of how one part of her—the part that wasn't scarred by her past—had melted at the thought of a handsome stranger with beautiful blue eyes and a bewitching certainty saying he saw their future together.

"But I'm the last person who has any business talking about love," she said. "You ought to talk to George. He seems to have a pretty good take on it."

"Will you stay here for a while?" Ruby asked her. "Till I go to sleep?"

"Of course, honey. Of course."

She looked so young, lying in that giant empty sea of a bed. Too young to know about feeling black and hard and almost dead inside. But she'd certainly nailed the feeling; Sugar had known it well. In fact, she knew it still. And she'd been wrong to tell Ruby that hearts did not stay broken. They did. It was just that until she met Theo Fitzgerald, she didn't know hers was one of them.

23RD

N ate slid in the diner's kitchen door just as the clock beside the extractor fan showed it was fifteen seconds after his start time. Everyone knew the clock was seven minutes fast but that made no difference to Chef.

"So pleased you could join us, Your Majesty," he called, his gravelly voice dripping with sarcasm. "Up all night banging your boyfriend? So dee-lighted for you. Oh no, wait a minute, that's right, I'm not. No, turns out I don't give a crap about your night or your day or who or what you bang and how often or how little or anything that goes on in your miserable little pissant world outside of this kitchen. Now move your fat sorry ass and get to work."

Nate shuffled in behind the grill, his cheeks aflame, thankful at least for the usual clatter and clang, the noisy bustle and hiss of the busy kitchen. Silence would only make it worse.

"Shouldn't let him treat you like that, dude," said LeBron, a nice kid who'd worked there for only a couple of months but already had the chef's number. "Douche has got a major bug up his ass today."

Douche's bug had traveled farther with each passing day since Citroen's three stars from what Nate could tell.

"I'm not letting him do anything," he said as quietly as he could while he scraped the grill plate clean.

"You two girls quit your gossiping and flip some fricking burgers," Chef roared.

"Flipping as we speak, Chef," LeBron said. "Under control. All orders cleared. Just keep 'em coming."

Nate looked at all the definitely uncleared orders clipped up above LeBron's head. LeBron could do that sort of thing. He possessed the easy sort of confidence that Nate would have given anything for. He had a buff body too. He worked out with his older brother six times a week, he told Nate, a little pointedly perhaps, but he was not being mean, and in fact had asked Nate if he wanted to join them, but he didn't.

Nate had been overweight for as long as he could remember but was far too self-conscious to go to a gym.

The girls who worked at the diner loved LeBron. He could have dated any one of them if he wanted but he told Nate they weren't his type, not even Tracy, the prettiest of all, whose thick blond hair fell in springy ringlets down her back. In his bravest moments, which he nonetheless kept to himself, Nate thought Tracy might have been his type. She'd picked up his apron the time Chef cut it off him in a fit of rage and threw it on the floor, and after that she had smiled at him at least once every shift.

But that was it.

This shift, LeBron was only working a half day so after attempting a series of complicated high fives, which Nate bungled, as usual, he sloped off.

Envying even the way he could slope, Nate sat in the doorway of the building next door with the lunch he'd brought from home.

He was halfway through his first sandwich when he realized that Tracy and her friends were having a smoke on the neighboring stoop—and they were talking about him.

"So Nate's gay, right?" Felicia asked.

"Chef certainly seems to think so," her friend Beatty answered.

"I don't know if he's gay, but he could be one of those nothings," Tracy suggested. "My cousin Lucas is like that. He just sits at my aunt's house fooling around on the Internet all day and eating Cheetos and shit. Doesn't even leave the house anymore."

"Probably looking at porn," said Beatty.

"No, my aunt checked his computer when he was in the bathroom a while back. Weirdo is looking at real estate. Like the dude doesn't even have a job and he thinks he can buy a house in Cape Cod or something."

They all laughed and started talking about some other loser they all knew while Nate pressed himself back against the doorway, hoping they wouldn't see him, his cheeks burning as he started on his second artichoke and sundried tomato on rye with fresh farm ham and mozzarella cheese. He wasn't gay and Chef would just as likely bully him for being straight, especially if he knew how bad he was at it. Tracy was not his type after all. How could she write him off as "one of those nothings"? How could anybody write anybody else off as a nothing? Nobody was nothing.

And her cousin Lucas might stay at home eating Cheetos but at least he dreamed of being somewhere else, of doing something else, and there was nothing wrong with that. Nate might be stuck down the grill line at a crappy diner flipping burgers for customers who didn't know their Wagyu beef from a hole in the ground but that didn't mean he always would be. He had graduated from culinary college with an excellent degree, after all, his tutors all agreeing that he was a man born to feed people, that he had a gift for it, that he would rise to great heights. And although his family upstate thought he was nuts to want to cook for a living—that was woman's work and in New York City? Please!—on campus Nate believed he had found his true place in the world.

Unfortunately, it wasn't the *real* world.

In the heat of your average working Manhattan kitchen it wasn't just a matter of feeding people, of taking a baby romaine and some parmigiano and a perfectly boiled egg and some Spanish anchovy and Italian oil and sourdough croutons and making the world's best Caesar salad. Well, it might be, if he was working for Mario Batali or Daniel Boulud or even Roland Morant.

But the truth of the matter was that having a gift for feeding people was only a small part of what was required. What was more important was the ability to remain supremely assertive in a hierarchy designed to suit the bold and boisterous and to swallow the quiet and fearful.

The nothings.

Yet somewhere deep down inside himself, buried beneath exquisite almond croissants, or exotic lunchtime bagels, or his homemade apple pie or three-layered coconut cake, Nate truly believed that he was good at what he did. The diner was crappy but the burgers he flipped were good. Even Chef knew that. (Which was why he treated him like dirt instead of firing him.)

And one day Nate would show him how talented he really was. One day he would show everyone.

Or that's what he told himself late at night when he pulled out his neat little gardening kit and lavished his precious window boxes with all the tenderness he had no one else to show.

24TH

Sugar had grown accustomed to hearing Nate digging in his garden in the middle of the night. Usually she found it oddly soothing enough to lull her back to sleep but tonight her mind was whirring with worry about Ruby, thoughts of Theo and echoes of George so when she heard the scrape of a trowel against soil, she got up, slipped on her robe, made two cups of tea with a slug of bourbon in each, and took them out onto the terrace.

It was a full moon and the light shimmered and bounced off the surrounding rooftops, casting eerie spiderweb shadows beneath water towers and behind fire escapes.

She could see the tops of the Tompkins Square Park elms moving beyond the buildings to the north and thought she could even hear them rustling.

"It's a different world up here, don't you think?" she said, handing a cup to Nate through the window. "Only ever seeing the tops of things. It's like we're truly the cream of the crop."

Nate sniffed loudly and kept digging.

"Bad day at the office?" she asked.

"I'm going to try heirloom cherry tomatoes this year," he said. "I just found this Greek recipe with feta cheese and shrimp. I think you'll really like it."

"Sounds delicious," agreed Sugar. "Although it's your pastries I dream about. Speaking of which, did you see the ad on JobFinder for a pastry chef at Citroen?"

Nate had told Sugar about Roland Morant, about what a genius he was supposed to be, about how mad it made Chef that Citroen had got three stars. Of course he had seen the ad—just when he thought his day could not get any worse. He'd seen it, felt sick about it, made a tiramisu, planted more basil, twice baked some pistachio biscotti, recalled every word of the conversation he had overheard with Tracy and wished he was dead.

"Is that something you would think of going for?" Sugar asked.

"No," he said, sniffing again, digging lemongrass roots into the soil.

"You don't want to get away from your situation at the diner?"

"It's not that bad," he said, but even in the moonlight she could see him color.

"Well, if you say so, but I've tasted your food, Nate, and I think you're wasted on a boss who doesn't appreciate you. Your place is with someone who will applaud your talent as will his customers so it's a win-win-win situation and everybody knows they are hands down the best kind."

"Every pastry chef in New York will be going for that Citroen job."

"But they won't all be as good as you! And if you have to do a trial, you could make some of your almond croissants or your finikias. You could use my honey. In fact, you know what? You could take a starter hive of bees and Roland Morant could keep them on his own rooftop. No other pastry chef would think of that! How about it?"

"I couldn't do a trial. I'm no good under pressure."

"You work with that bully at the diner every single day, Nate. You're always under pressure. You know, it's all very well to keep your light under a bushel—in fact it's a deeply endearing feature, one of many you exhibit if I may be so bold. But in the meantime the rest of us aren't eating as well as we could be."

Nate knew he just didn't have the cojones to pull off a stunt like that. He couldn't even imagine walking into the restaurant holding a starter hive of bees. How would he shake Morant's hand? How would he even open the door? He would be sweaty. What if the bees escaped?

No, he couldn't do it, and now he felt worse than he did before.

"I'm fine where I am," he said sniffing again.

"Would you like a handkerchief?" Sugar asked.

"Why are you always asking me that?"

"Because you're always sniffing, honey."

"No," he said. "I don't want a handkerchief." He closed the window and roughly pulled across the curtain.

Nate liked Sugar a lot, more than just about anyone else he could think of. But he got enough of being pushed around at work. He would get there, on his own, one day. Just not this one. Or the next.

He moved the crate of vegetables, tucked away his gardening tools and lay on his narrow bed. Still, today of all days it was nice that someone noticed he had a light, let alone mentioned the bushel hiding it. Sugar's intentions were good, if overwhelming, he knew that.

25TH

Cupid, awakened from his slumber, got his act together lickety-split and made up for all the time he'd lost shooting arrows into trees and stop signs. Just two days after ripping the scab off the wounds of her romantic past to reveal the tender heartbreak beneath, Sugar bumped into Theo over the last roast duck hanging in the window of a corner store in Chinatown.

"Hello," she said, the thrill of seeing him blooming on her skin like a sunset. He was wearing another Hawaiian shirt, a fuchsia one covered with turquoise waves and surfboards, making the color in his eyes pop even more than usual. "And here's me thinking we agreed never to see each other again."

"Without meaning to sound like a lawyer," said Theo, with a cautious smile, "you saying you didn't want to and me saying nothing in response does not actually qualify as an agreement. And I had absolutely nothing to do with this. It's kismet. There are eight million people in this city, Sugar, and yet the planets have aligned four times to bring us together."

"Didn't you hunt me down a little, the second and the third times?"

"Yes, but not the first time and not today. Doesn't that tell you something?"

"It tells me you can have the duck," she said. "I was half thinking of crab salad anyway. They have live crabs in the store two doors down. And shrimp that are still waving their tentacles around, if that's what tentacles are called when they're on a shrimp."

"I would not dream of forcing you to forage for waving tentacles," Theo said. "I wouldn't be able to eat the duck knowing I had snatched it out of anyone's hands, let alone yours."

"What were you planning on making?"

"Duck pancakes are the shining star in my otherwise limited gastronomic repertoire," said Theo. "Especially when I'm cooking for my niece. She is only ten but she is very critical of my culinary skills. It's like having a very small, female Gordon Ramsay in the house. He's Scottish too, did you know that? Although we're not so quick to claim him when he's throwing a wobbly in some poor wretch's kitchen."

"You're cooking for your niece?" Sugar's heart sank, not on Theo's account, but her own. She had nieces—four of them—for whom she would love to be cooking. But she'd never even met them.

"Once a fortnight my ex-sister-in-law gets a romantic night out with her husband," Theo was saying, "and I get the pleasure of being beaten at Scrabble, Monopoly, Mexican Train Game and, as of last month, poker. The kid takes no prisoners, let me tell you."

The elderly Chinese woman behind the counter clacked her tongs at them and said something to her husband.

"Who's taking?" the husband asked.

"Honestly, you take it," Sugar said to Theo. "I feel like crab salad after all."

"I couldn't." Theo shook his head.

"You or her or someone else. I don't care," said the man behind the counter as his wife rolled her eyes at him then made sarcastic kissy-kissy noises.

"Really, he can have it," Sugar said, panic rising in her stomach as she felt the unmistakable tilt of her equilibrium being challenged.

Was it talk of Theo's niece? The faint minty leathery scent she could detect from standing so close to him? The assumption of the duck sellers that there was kissy-kissy in the air? Or was it the insatiable longing she suddenly felt for the whisper of a Scottish burr in her ear, for arms to wrap around her, for lips to graze her, for gentle fingers to endlessly stroke her?

"Actually, you know what?" she said, her cheeks burning. "I have to run. I have to get the crab and a few other groceries so I am just going to leave you and your duck to live happily ever after and I'll be on my way. It was real nice to catch up again and good luck with the pancakes and have fun with your niece. Bye now."

She scuttled out into the street, heart thumping, then turned the wrong way down Grand Street and stopped at the Chrystie Street cross sign.

George was right: she was scared. Petrified. But knowing that wasn't as helpful as one might imagine. Maybe she should go back. Or cross. But what if she never saw him again? What if four times was all kismet and a bit of stalking would allow? What if four times was already four too many?

"Hang on a minute there," Theo said breathlessly behind her. "Please, Sugar, I know you don't want a lifelong commitment, or dinner, or a drink, but could we maybe just sit down and talk for a minute?"

She shouldn't. She absolutely one hundred percent shouldn't. Or should she?

But while she was dithering something rattled loose inside her disloyal body, which just turned her in Theo's direction and allowed him to guide her to a bench in Sara D. Roosevelt Park where a group of Brazilian boys were kicking a football around while three elderly ladies did tai chi moves at a glacial pace behind them.

"You've just got to love this city, don't you?" said Theo as they sat.

"I do," Sugar agreed. "That is, I do love New York. Not, you know, the other sort of I do, which I definitely don't. I mean I particularly don't."

Theo laughed. "Oh, it's so nice to see you," he said. "You've no idea. Look, I just wanted a chance to clear the air. But first, I shouldn't have accepted the duck. In fact," he thrust the bag at her, "it's yours. I couldn't swallow it now anyway and Frankie would tell straightaway that something was wrong and she would grill me as only the precocious child of two academics can do and before you know it I'll have told her about you and she'll tell Nina and then there will be two of us stalking you if not three."

Sugar looked at the duck.

"Who's Nina?"

"Of course! You don't know a thing about me. I keep forgetting that. OK, Nina is the closest I have to a sister but actually I was

173

married to *her* sister, Carolyn, for three years until she ran away with a gardener called Joe. They live in Italy now and they are very happy and I'm happy for them. Honestly."

"Honestly?"

"I've had therapy. I'm quite good at it. We should never have got married in the first place I think was the joint consensus. And I have not had a significant other since then. Not properly. I've been waiting and now, well, anyway, I am a lawyer. Sorry about that. I used to be a bad lawyer who earned lots of money, now I'm a good lawyer earning not very much but I like it that way. Shall I go on?"

Sugar nodded.

"I never knew my father, I think I told you that, but I had a wonderful mother so I didn't really mind. She died the day after I turned twenty-nine, which was the worst thing that has ever happened to me. And even though I'm forty now I still miss her every single day. Is that too namby-pamby?"

"Not namby-pamby at all. I miss my granddaddy every day too." Sugar missed the rest of her family as well, but she never liked to admit that, not even to herself.

"Anyway, I am one of the poor wretches Gordon Ramsay would throw a wobbly at. I'm a terrible cook, apart from duck pancakes. They're actually the only thing in my repertoire. What else? I hate radicchio. It's so bitter! I like Hawaiian shirts because they're the opposite of what I used to wear although Frankie says I look like I escaped from the circus and I hate the circus. And opera. Please don't make me go to the opera. I'm OK with cats but I prefer dogs, I'm thinking of getting a dog, and I'm allergic to—"

Sugar could not say what came over her at that point but she simply couldn't listen to another word. She just leaned over and silenced him with a kiss, long and tender, as though they kissed like that all the time.

She couldn't quite believe she was doing it, but she also couldn't quite believe she hadn't done it sooner. The scent of him, the taste, the faint bristles on his face against the smooth skin on hers. I should stop, she thought. I should stop before I get used to the taste of him, the feel of him, the possibility of him.

But it was too late. So instead she stopped thinking. She just let her body take the lead and it fell into Theo like she was a key and he was the door to home.

If Theo was surprised, she couldn't feel it. He drew her closer, one hand in the small of her back, the other beneath her hair, on her neck, gently behind her ears.

Actually he wanted to cry, but he also wanted to sing, and thank God, and his mother, and the universe, but mostly he wanted to keep Sugar wrapped up in his arms forever. Eventually, she drew back, but Theo kept her face in his hands. "I knew it," he said. "I just knew it."

She was afraid to look away from him, afraid the magic of what had just happened would disappear in a puff of smoke, taking with it the blissful wonder she was feeling.

"You have to trust it," he said. "I felt the same way. I feel the same way. From the moment I saw you. I'm just a few steps ahead."

He took her hands—which were gripping the duck as though it was still alive and about to jump off her lap—and she saw it again; the two of them, in forty years' time, walking up East Seventh Street together. She hadn't thought she would feel this way ever again. She'd been so wrong the first time, and so unwilling to risk her heart again since. But a kiss like that, lips like that, arms like that, a smile like that could undo a lot of damage.

"Say something," Theo said. "And please, please let it be something I want to hear."

"The duck is yours," she said, her teeth feeling wooden in her mouth, her lips aching.

Theo didn't move, just held his breath.

"And I was thinking of having a dinner party on Saturday," she continued. "It would be real nice if you would come."

"Yes," he said. "Yes, yes and yes. Just . . . Yes. And thank you. I'll be there. Of course I'll be there. I mean I would be there right now this minute if I didn't need to make duck pancakes for Frankie. But yes. Or we could meet tomorrow? Or the next day?"

"Saturday is good," Sugar said.

"You're right. We should wait. I should wait. But don't doubt me, Sugar. Time can do such strange things. Trust me, please. I know it's sudden, and foreign, and comfort zones are a distant memory but here's my number. If I don't turn up it will be because I'm dead and you will need to know that. That's the only thing that will keep me from you on Saturday. Death."

"If you talk like this to every girl you meet it may explain your recent lack of significant others."

"I haven't wanted one, Sugar. That's what I'm saying. It's just you. You are the one I've been waiting for."

She knew from reading Ruby's stories in the *New York Times* that people said these things to newspapers, but to each other?

Out in the open? With a woman dressed in blankets going through the garbage can next to them on one side and a Buddhist in saffron robes meditating on the other?

She took his card, wrote out her address on another one and explained that she did not have a cell phone.

He didn't want to go, didn't want to let her out of his sight but he had duck pancakes to make. He walked backward so that he could keep watching her until the last possible minute, then she crossed the road, feeling his eyes on her neck, her shoulders, her back, all over her body.

Again she felt a shiver, and it was delicious.

Elizabeth the Sixth could feel the change in Sugar as if it were a warm front sweeping in from the south. Finally, she told the kingdom when their keeper got back from her liaison with Theo in Sara D. Roosevelt Park. Finally.

She started laying again immediately, moving from cell to cell at a sprightly pace. She wouldn't make a top count of three thousand eggs but at least she was back on the job.

Then Ruby came to visit and Elizabeth the Sixth picked up the pace even more. She'd developed quite a soft spot for Ruby. Her aura was fragile, sickly, sad, yet she radiated a quiet strength from an open heart that never failed to make an impression on the queen.

Today, Ruby told Sugar about Patience Vincent and Ryan Ross, who had been married the previous weekend at the Four Seasons Hotel in Boston. Patience had been in love with Ryan in high school but never told him so didn't know that he'd also had a crush on her until twenty-five years later when they hooked up on Facebook.

Elizabeth the Sixth didn't know what Facebook was, but she sensed hope and excitement emanating in great crashing waves from Ruby. And when Sugar told Ruby about kissing Theo in Chinatown, the unbridled passion surging out of her practically blew the queen from one cell into the next.

Unbridled passion was exactly what had been missing.

Elizabeth the Sixth thought perhaps she might make three thousand eggs that day after all.

26TH

"You're looking mighty pleased with yourself this morning, Miss Sugar," George said on Saturday morning when Sugar headed out to shop for her dinner party. "Should I take it there's been an improvement up on the rooftop?"

"There has, George," Sugar replied. "Blow me down if Elizabeth the Sixth isn't laying her little patootie off again. All is right with the world it would seem, although I was hoping to buy some balloons for my dinner party tonight but I see Lola is not open."

The globe had completely deflated now and hung from the railing like a raisin, while all the superhero's limbs and his head had withered and just his torso remained blown up. The dinosaur leaned on what was left of the hero's caped shoulder.

"I'm not sure what she's selling down there but very few people come out with balloons," said George. "Now tell me, Miss Sugar, those bees the only reason for your smile today?"

"No, they are not, as it happens. Progress has been made, George. With, you know, the someone who might have nothing to do with anything."

"Or something to do with everything."

"He's coming, tonight, to my dinner party."

"Is that so? Well, I'll be on the lookout for a Prince Charming at around seven o'clock then."

"His shirt will possibly blind you before you get a chance, George. But you might even recognize him. You used him as a landing pad the day we met."

George raised his eyebrows. "How about that? Our friend with the cell phone from Avenue B. What a coincidence."

"I wish you would come tonight. You're sure I can't change your mind?"

"Thanks again for the invitation, Miss Sugar, but I take my meals at ground level. I will want to hear all about it tomorrow though."

"It's a date."

George beamed, and Sugar's heart swelled at the ease with which some people settled on happiness.

Even Mrs. Keschl seemed almost cheerful when she turned up just half an hour early at six-thirty.

"This is late for me," she said. "I'm usually in bed with the Sudoku by seven so I hope you cooked something decent."

"Would you like an iced tea while we wait for the rest of the guests to arrive?" Sugar asked.

"What are you, a Mormon? If I'm going to be up all night peeing it better be because I drank something more interesting than tea."

Indeed by the time Lola arrived with Ethan, Mrs. Keschl had two bourbon-fueled iced teas under her belt and was wreathed in smiles. "Give me the kid," she said, snatching him out of his mother's arms and dragging him outside to the terrace, where he seemed happy to go.

"Can I fix you a drink?" Sugar asked Lola, who was black eyed and pale faced and said, "Make it a double," before sloping out the French doors.

Mr. McNally again nearly bowled Ruby over in his haste to get to the honey-roasted peanuts when he spied them from the doorway.

"I'm not invisible," Ruby said. She carried a big cake box but in truth, she was getting more and more invisible with every passing meal.

"Excuse me," Nate said quietly behind her.

He had not said he would be coming, but Sugar had set a place for him all the same and now, there he was, bearing a wooden bowl full of fresh greens garnished with his window-box herbs and ringed with nasturtiums.

He couldn't look up, but Sugar herded him outside with Ruby then watched surreptitiously as the two of them shuffled to the far end of the table and sat next to each other without speaking or making eye contact.

"What's that growing up out of the pipe over there?" Mrs. Keschl asked when Sugar came out to freshen the drinks.

"I'm going to plant climbing roses," Sugar said. "Hybrid teas, I think, so I've been fixing the trelliswork."

"Roses? Some people get all the luck." Mrs. Keschl sniffed.

"What does luck have to do with it?" Mr. McNally snapped. "She's planting the feckin' things not conjuring them out of thin air."

"And what would you know about roses?" barked Mrs. Keschl. "Ouch, there goes my ulcer. When are we going to eat?"

"We're just waiting for one more," Sugar said.

"Not another new member of staff I hope," grouched Mr. McNally. "Because the doorman is about as far as I can go."

"No, it's not another staff member and you know George doesn't get paid so he's not really staff."

"We don't need any more volunteers either, if that's what you're thinking," said Mrs. Keschl. "Although I guess I could live with a maid."

"I would kill for a maid," said Lola.

"Is the one more *him*?" asked Ruby, her face lighting up when Sugar blushed and nodded.

"Who's him?" demanded Mrs. Keschl.

"Just a friend," Sugar said quickly. "No big deal. Really. Another cocktail, anyone?"

But it was a big deal and when seven-thirty came and went without Theo knocking at the door, Sugar started to feel sicker and sicker with every relentless tick of the heartless kitchen clock.

He had told her to trust him, to trust "it," that time did strange things; and she had trusted him although it hadn't been easy. She had bounced like a Ping-Pong ball from sinking into the memory of that delectable kiss to plotting her escape from New York silently in the night, never to return. But with every hollow rebound she'd repeated his words, over and over again, until eventually she arrived back at a delicate balance.

By eight she felt like she had a million Ping-Pong balls, all of them in her stomach. She would never listen to Theo or George or any man ever again. Her life was better without their empty promises and flimsy fairy tales.

"You should have a cell phone," Ruby said, sidling up to her in the kitchen. "Then he could call and tell you why he's running late."

"He shouldn't be running late," Sugar said. "Running late gives you brain cancer."

"No, cell phones give you brain cancer," Ruby said.

"You see! They're both terrible."

"I could call him on mine."

"And fry your precious brain? No, Ruby, I can't let you do that."

"It's almost like you sort of don't want him to come," Ruby said.

Sugar stirred her carrot soup a little more robustly than required. Right now, she did not. Right now, she would rather tear her heart out and feed it to the snow leopard at Central Park Zoo than put it through the gut-wrenching turmoil of love. It was so ... undignified.

"Looks like it will be just us," she said, ladling the soup into bowls. "Can you help carry these out onto the terrace?" But as she spoke a sharp crack in the air above them heralded the arrival of a summer thunderstorm.

A jagged streak of lightning ignited the sky, illuminating the beautifully laid table, the blooming garden, the surrounding rooftops, the bridge in the distance. Then thunder cracked again and Sugar rallied Nate and Mr. McNally to bring the table inside.

It was something of a squeeze with all of them and the table jammed between the bed and the French doors, but she stood and watched for a moment as the rain fell in luscious sheets that bounced off the terrace tiles, danced on top of the beehive, shook the leaves on the vines, pummeled the smaller plants and flowers.

Watching nature in all her spontaneous glory seemed to calm her nerves.

"It's kind of beautiful," she said. "And sad. Like a ballet."

Lola and Mrs. Keschl rolled their eyes.

Then Sugar pushed the sofa and coffee table up against the wall and the seven of them sat down, crammed into the bright little studio that flared up like a pinball machine with every strike of lightning.

"Again with the orange," Mrs. Keschl said looking balefully at her soup.

"Just eat it, woman," snapped Mr. McNally.

"Ethan might like it too," Sugar told Lola. "It's usually pretty popular with kids."

"He's not so good with a spoon," Lola warned, trying the soup herself. "It's good. What's it made of?"

"Would you care to have a guess, Nate?" Sugar asked.

Nate blushed just hearing her say his name, then tasted another mouthful and carefully considered it. "Carrots," he said softly. "Ginger. And honey, I guess."

Ethan took that opportunity to flick a spoonful of the thick, creamy soup across the table where it landed fair and square in the middle of Mrs. Keschl's wrinkled cleavage. "Most attention that's seen in a while," she said, barely pausing as she emptied her bowl.

"Jesus, Ethan, can't you just put it in your mouth?" Lola asked, her own spoon falling to the table as if the effort of holding it was suddenly too much.

"Give the little chap a break," said Mr. McNally.

"Let me," Mrs. Keschl said, dragging her chair over to Ethan, taking his spoon, and feeding him.

Lola left her to it.

185

"Can I help you clear the plates?" Ruby asked, getting up and starting to do so anyway.

Sugar knew this was a way of disguising that she had barely eaten anything, but she'd had half a glass of her drink, which had another sprinkling of bee pollen in it, providing at least a small spurt of energy.

Suddenly, Sugar was tired of worrying about Ruby, about Nate, about the balloons. Suddenly, she wanted everyone to go home so she could crawl into bed and sleep away her foolishness at believing, at trusting, at dreaming that she and Theo would one day be lying there together, their naked limbs entwined, their hearts beating in time, her wretched longing finally acknowledged and tenderly sated.

The room lit up again and the whole table jumped as thunder cracked right above them. It took a few moments after the boom faded away for Sugar to realize that someone was knocking at the door.

"Well, what are you waiting for?" Mr. McNally asked. "The butler?"

27TH

George stood in the doorway with Theo soaking wet beside him. His lime-green shirt was sodden, its giant bananas plastered to his body in bunches.

"Please pardon the intrusion, Miss Sugar," George said. "But I found something I thought you might be missing."

"I am so sorry," Theo said. "But I had to nip in to work and then I was so nervous about being late, which I wasn't going to be, but I was holding your address too tightly. The ink ran!" He held up the card she'd written on. It was nothing but a blur. "I couldn't find you. And then it rained."

Sugar's heart was banging so hard she could feel it in her ears. She was not sure how much more she could take of this particular roller coaster. "You do know this is the gentleman whose fall you broke that day," she said politely, indicating George.

"Yes, yes, I've already apologized for not being more . . . springy," Theo said.

"And I've accepted the apology," George offered. "A man who knows how to apologize is a man who knows how to get on in life."

"Did you hear that?" Mrs. Keschl said to Mr. McNally.

"Sugar, I know I seem to do nothing but apologize but I'm so sorry," Theo said again. "I knew it was Flores Street but I couldn't remember the number. I knew there were two of them and they were sort of fat like nines or eights or sixes but I'd forgotten they were both the same. I've been to nearly every house. And you didn't call me? I told you I would have to be dead to not turn up."

The whole room jumped again as more thunder boomed above them.

"If you'll excuse me, I'll be going back downstairs," George said.

"You should have gone home hours ago," Sugar said to him, ignoring Theo. "I worry about you standing out there for too long."

"It's me standing up here that you should worry about," George said. "My head is starting to spin so I'll bid you all good night."

"Please, Sugar," Theo said.

"Ah, let the poor fecker in," Mr. McNally said. "You've invited every other Tom, Dick and Harry."

"I saw the balloons," Theo said, pushing his wet bangs out of his eyes. He was taller than Sugar remembered and, inconceivably, even more handsome when wet. "And I remembered you talking about a balloon shop when we were in McSorley's. And then I found George, and I know I'm late but I'm not usually. I'm actually very punctual."

"You have to let him in," Ruby said just as Lola emerged from the bathroom with a towel, and passed it over her head to Theo, who took it and started to dry his face. His handsome, worried face with its square jaw and irresistible dimple.

Sugar had been as rude as she was able. The Ping-Pong ball

bounced back in to Theo's court. "All right then," she said, standing back and letting him through. "Everybody, this is Theo."

"Sit there," Mr. McNally said, pointing to a sleepy Ethan slumped in the chair next to him. "And I'll put the little fella on the couch. His eyes are hanging out of his head as it is."

He picked up the boy with a tenderness that surprised Mrs. Keschl and Lola, though Ruby and Nate were too busy concentrating on Theo to notice.

"You missed the soup," Sugar said, "but you're in time for honey-roasted chicken and sweet potato."

"I'm fine with anything," said Theo. "Honestly, I'm just happy to be here, inside, out of the rain, where I'm totally meant to be. And I'm not even going to mention that you had my number and you didn't call me while I was out there looking for you. That's how happy I am."

"She was worried about brain cancer," Ruby told him. "And she thought you were standing her up."

"I'm addled but my brain is fine. Honestly. The address melted!" Theo protested. "I've pressed nearly every buzzer in the street. I was offered dandelion wine by the man at number eighty-six and I'm not sure what I was offered by the woman at number thirty-eight."

"She is not a natural blonde, the woman at number thirty-eight," Mrs. Keschl said.

"I like your dress," Theo told her. "My grandmother had a dress like that and my grandmother was one of my favorite people."

"Can you dance?" asked Mrs. Keschl, blossoming. "I feel like dancing."

"I'm a keen but supremely untalented dancer," Theo answered

cheerfully as lightning struck again. "Great apartment, Sugar. Cozy."

"Aren't you the silver-tongued devil?" Mr. McNally sniped, his tenderness evaporated. "You know cozy is just another word for too small."

"He might be nervous," Ruby said. "He told Sugar he wanted to spend the rest of his life with her, even though they only just met. He told her she was the one. And so she asked him to dinner but then he never turned up."

"Ruby!" Sugar was mortified.

"I didn't not turn up," Theo said. "I was late and it was an act of God. And you make it sound worse than it was about the wanting-to-spend-the-rest-of-my-life thing. It was different the way I said it."

"Whichever way," said Mrs. Keschl, "you're pretty hard to understand. I've only just worked out you're speaking English."

"He's from Scotland," Ruby told her.

"So you dance with your arms straight down by your sides," Mrs. Keschl said, disappointed.

"No, that's the Irish. We have our hands above our heads," Theo said. "Plus we wear kilts."

"Now you're talking," said Mrs. Keschl.

"Highland flinging aside," Theo said, smiling at Sugar, "this chicken is delicious."

Once again, she melted. Now that he was here, he just fit right in, was the thing, without hardly any fuss or bother.

"You know, one yard that way and this would be a different sort of party," Mrs. Keschl cracked, looking at Sugar's bed.

"But on the plus side, I can reach dessert right from where I'm sitting," said Sugar, trying not to think about her bed and what she would like to happen in it sometime soon. She turned and lifted across the cake stand on which she had displayed the nutty, syrupy offerings Ruby had brought her.

"What is that?" Mrs. Keschl asked.

"It's baklava," Nate said, cheeks aflame. "It's Turkish. Made of phyllo pastry and nuts."

"And honey," Ruby said. "That's why I bought it, because of the honey."

"It's really good," Nate said, licking his lips after trying a mouthful. "Where did you get it?"

"At Poseidon Bakery up on Ninth Avenue," Ruby said. "It's my favorite."

"Oh," Nate said. "Mine too."

Mrs. Keschl looked from one to the other. "Well, one of you needs to go there more often and the other one needs to walk straight on by."

Sugar made a note to up the rose oil quotient in Mrs. Keschl's next batch of candles.

"I have never had baklava before," Sugar said, "but you're right, Nate, it's delicious. I wonder if we could make our own?"

"Of course," Nate said.

"They have really good pistachios at Kalustyan's on Lexington," Ruby said. "I think they're the best."

"Or you can order them at Nuts.com," Nate said.

"Yes, but I did that once and they mixed Californian pistachios in with the imported ones."

"The Californian ones are easier to open, but they don't taste as good," Nate added.

"Exactly," said Ruby.

They looked at each other then, finally, and something akin to a smile settled on each face.

"You have the most excellent taste in sweet, nutty, syrupy, flaky pastry things, Ruby," Theo said, striking Sugar with his kindness at speaking that way to a girl who clearly never ate such things.

Then, as suddenly as it had started, the rain stopped, and the clouds scooted across the skyline, leaving the city horizon sparkling and clear in their wake.

Sugar opened the doors, breathing in the sweet fresh perfume of recent rain on scented blooms, and turned to her guests. "If y'all want to take the table and chairs back out on the terrace, I'll clear up in here and prepare a little something special by way of a nightcap."

Her guests shuffled around, picking up the furniture and passing around the empty plates and then she and Theo were alone in the tiny kitchen. Their arms touched, and once again the electricity shot right through her.

"Did you feel that?" Theo asked, his dimple deepening as he smiled.

His hair had dried a little crinkly and, for a moment, Sugar wondered if the electricity between them had done that as well. He was so close she could feel his breath on her lips, almost taste the honey syrup from the baklava.

"You look beautiful," he said. "May I?" And he took her in his arms and kissed her again, their hearts thumping in perfect time, like two lost musical notes finally finding their place in an unexpected harmony.

It was the belonging that so surprised her; the belonging that had been missing from her life, and she hadn't even known it. His hands on her body, his lips on her lips, it was so simple. So right. He did not feel like a complication that would ruin her life or threaten the world she had built for herself.

What had she been thinking?

In his arms she felt his strength, she craved his strength, but she felt her own too. In that moment Sugar let the sun shine in on the last of the wounded parts of herself that she'd kept hidden for so many years. Under the warmth of those rays, she did not try to protect her poor broken heart; she just let herself believe that what Theo had told her was true, that it was sudden and foreign and catapulted her out of where she felt safest but it was also what being truly alive was all about.

"There's time, Sugar," Theo said. "There's forever. Don't worry."

Again, she wanted her guests to disappear. She wanted him to herself, in her bed, for a long time with nowhere else to go and nothing to do but discover each other. But her guests showed no sign of going anywhere and, much as she wanted to stay in the kitchen, lingering on each kiss, she took Theo's hand and pulled him out onto the terrace.

Ruby stood and looked as though she was going to give them a round of applause but Sugar shot her a warning look, so she sank back into her seat and just beamed.

"This is my little piece of paradise," Sugar said, her arm sweeping around her rooftop; as Theo's eyes followed he was yet again thankful for the therapist who had cured his aggression toward all things horticultural.

This was nothing like the sprawling Hamptons spreads that his wife had envied so much she ran away with someone who created them. It was contained, crowded almost, and colorful, but not in a way that had been worked out on a pie chart. Plus it smelled good, which he guessed was due to the heavy rain drying now on the flowering vines that grew up the wall and the blooming shrubs in pots by the wooden box in the corner.

With a start, he realized exactly where he was. But before he could comment on that, he noticed the hive.

"What's in there?" he asked.

"That's my beehive," Sugar said. "They're my bees."

The color drained from his face. "Your bees?"

"Yes, my bees. I'm a beekeeper."

"You're a beekeeper," he repeated. "A keeper of bees?"

"Yes, a keeper of bees. That's how I make my living. I sell my honey and whatnot at the greenmarket."

"That's how you make your living?"

"Yes, I guess we never talked about that," Sugar said.

"She's had her bees for fifteen years," Ruby piped up. "She got them from her grandfather."

"Her honey got my kid to quit whining," Lola added.

"It fixes acne," said Nate, blushing.

"It goes great with bourbon," said Mrs. Keschl. "She's nuts about those bees."

"But what about the ice cream?" Theo asked. "At Tompkins Square? I thought that was your job. I thought you were nuts about ice cream."

"No, I was just getting to know the ropes before I started selling my honey there. Why? What's the matter? Theo, are you OK?"

He let go of Sugar's hand and started plucking at the front of his banana shirt. He was sweating, his breath coming short and uneven. He backed away from her toward the open French doors, still looking around the terrace, his eyes skimming over the heads of everyone sitting there staring at him, wondering what was going on.

"Fuck," he said.

"Excuse me?" Sugar had never heard him swear. She'd really liked that about him.

"You look like you just pooped yourself," Mrs. Keschl told him.

"Fuck," Theo said again. He couldn't breathe. He couldn't think. Panic had robbed him of all common sense as he stepped inside the apartment. "Sorry. I just, I think . . . I can explain. I need a moment. But not . . . I'm . . . It'll be . . . I'll call you."

Before Sugar could say anything else he was gone. They could all hear his feet thumping down the stairs, two or three at a time, as fast as they could carry him. Then, finally, the faint squeak of the first door and the distant bang of the second out onto the street.

"Well, what a jerk he turned out to be," Mrs. Keschl said. "I thought we were going to dance."

"'I'll call you'?" Lola repeated, rolling her eyes. "I hope you hadn't picked out a china pattern."

Sugar took a deep breath and forced the agony back down deep into the shadows of her heart. She'd opened it so briefly yet still the pain seemed insufferable. "All right now," she said. "Who wants what? I can make coffee, or I have a dessert wine chilling inside. Any takers?"

Elizabeth the Sixth was bamboozled by the goings-on outside her hive. Bees hated the rain, for a start. A raindrop might be a nuisance on a human head or an irritant on a windshield but for a bee it meant plummeting to a watery grave. Luckily foraging had finished for the day by the time the skies opened so the workers were back in the hive.

And when the rain cleared there had been a brief window—as long as it took to lay sixty-three eggs, to be precise—where it felt to Elizabeth the Sixth as though everything was falling into place.

She could tell the moment Sugar stepped out onto the terrace that Theo was there with her, that happiness was tantalizingly close. But no sooner had the promise of it danced in the rain-scented air than it was snatched away again. As the stars twinkled above her, however, waxing and waning into yesterday, the queen found that far from being discouraged by the night's ups and downs, she was nothing but exhilarated. She had been right, after all, about the object of Sugar's desire. And he'd been there, barely ten feet away from her, right in her range long enough for her to sense all she needed to sense, to smell all she needed to smell, to tell her everything she needed to know.

Happily-ever-after was still in the cards for Sugar, she knew it. She issued her instructions to her workers, then set about her business, as usual.

28TH

Sugar's stand had already become one of Tompkins Square greenmarket's most popular, with its jars of gold, amber and dark honeys sitting delectably in their fall-hued rows. On one side of the honey jars she kept her salves and lotions, her lip glosses and face creams, and on the other her tinctures, her throat sprays, her tiny tins of precious bee pollen, her ambrosia and her candles.

At either end of the stand she kept delicate flowered bowls filled with honey-roasted pecans for her customers to nibble on as they browsed.

The stallholders on either side, known to her as Mr. Apple and Mrs. Lavender, might have been miffed had they not both fallen a little in love with Sugar as soon as she started at the market. The first day she worked her stand, Mr. Apple had crunched his hand in the door of his truck, and Sugar had closed up and taken over his sales while he had it seen to. Then she'd bought dried flowers from Mrs. Lavender and made lavender honey, half of which she put in tiny clear plastic vials and gave to her to hand out as free gifts with purchase. It was Mrs. Lavender's best day ever.

The Sunday morning after the dinner party, neither of her market friends would have noticed she was not her usual self because it was such a busy day for all of them. Sugar was glad to be run off her feet. She even welcomed the crackpot who kept up a fast-paced nonsensical rap for the entire morning.

By four she was heading home to lose herself in the soothing aromas of the essential oils and gums and creams that needed mixing up to replace her depleted stock. But when she got to 33 Flores Street, George was standing at the top of the stoop, as usual, with Theo crouched at the bottom. He sprang to his feet as she approached.

"He's been waiting for hours," George said, "although I gather from Miss Lola that you might not entirely appreciate another one of his visits. Not that she put it quite so politely."

"I didn't go to the market because I knew you wouldn't want—" Theo began, but Sugar held up a hand to stop him.

"I hate to be rude—I really do, I'm not just saying that—so that should give you an idea of how much I mean it when I tell you that whatever you have to say to me, I am sorry, but I do not wish to hear it. Not one tiny little itty-bitty whisper. Not a word. Nothing. So I'm going up to my apartment and I would very much like you not to be here when I come back out, or indeed ever again."

"Please, Sugar, you have to let me explain," Theo pleaded.

"No, Theo, I don't believe I do. I don't believe that at all. I believe I have already listened to all the explaining I need to from you and whatever kind of game it is that you are playing, I am not playing it with you."

"Oh God, I'm so sorry. I—"

"I'm sure you are sorry, but you can go and be sorry someplace else because I need you to leave me alone."

"You don't understand—"

"I'm asking you politely, Theo. George, could you please get the door for me?"

"Of course, Miss Sugar. Speak quicker, Theo," George said.

"I'm allergic!" Theo cried. "I'm allergic to bees! Not just a little bit allergic but as allergic as you can get. I nearly died when I was a kid. Twice! I have a bracelet! I'm terrified of them. I panicked when I saw your hive. I didn't have my antidote with me. I know that's pathetic. I am pathetic, but only when it comes to bees. You never mentioned the bees. It threw me. It doesn't mean I'm not certain about you, or us, or any of that. It just means I'm really scared of bees. That's all."

Sugar's heart, already as low as she thought it could get, sank to the bottom of her shoes. "That's all?"

She moved swiftly in through the door George was holding open for her and climbed the stairs, thinking about Elizabeth the Sixth, about her Puget Sound wildflower blend, about her rosemary oil, about the chai tea she'd just had with the smiley man at the Punjabi deli around the corner, about the sweet peas she was trying to train up between the clematis and the moonflower . . . about anything but Theo Fitzgerald.

She was done thinking about him.

But the next morning the tiny hall outside her apartment was covered in a sea of red roses. There must have been two dozen bunches of them stretching from her doorway to Nate's. She kneeled down and opened the card on the nearest bouquet. *I'm sorry*, it read, as did the next and the next, and every one of them.

She took a pair of scissors and snipped off all the cards before sweeping up as many bunches as she could hold into her arms and dropping one outside Mr. McNally's door, then doing the same outside Mrs. Keschl's, Lola's and Ruby's. She gave two to the smiley Punjabi man, and the rest to the girls in the Tibetan handicraft store. Not one single petal made it inside her apartment.

"I tried to get the delivery company to take them back," George told her. "But Theo must have paid them off."

His flowers did nothing to soften Sugar's heart, which was set firmly back in protective mode.

But his money wasn't entirely wasted.

Ruby thought that Nate had sent her the roses and, although she didn't even know him, or particularly like him, or want to, not really, she put the roses in a crystal vase her mother had given her for a birthday (the lamest twenty-first birthday present anyone could imagine) and sat them in her front window. She also made plans to walk up to Kalustyan's to buy some pistachio nuts to give to Nate for homemade baklava if she bumped into him.

Lola couldn't work out who the flowers had come from. She just didn't know the sort of people who sent flowers. Unless it was the guy she'd met on the Internet and had one far from enthralling date with before she gave up on any hopes of having a halfway decent social life. She couldn't even remember his name but he had admired the garden of wildflowers that she had tattooed up her arm and had not seemed too disgusted when she told him about Ethan. Most men ran a mile when they found out she had a kid but he said he was one of seven himself so children never bothered him. And now she came to think of it, he hadn't

201

disappeared to the restroom to do lines, or stiffed her on the check, or got drunk or creepy or anything. He'd seemed . . . polite. She'd thought it was boring at the time but now she wondered if she might find his number and send him a text in case he wanted to go for a drink.

Mr. McNally checked his roses carefully to see if they had been sprayed with poison or peed on by a dog, only to find they hadn't so he came to his own conclusion about who they had come from.

Actually, it made his day, and it had been a long time since a day of his had been made. He put his roses in a water jug and sat them next to the flat screen. Well, I'll be jiggered, he thought, every time he looked at them. I'll be jiggered.

Similarly, when Mrs. Keschl found her red roses, her heart skipped a beat, and not in her usual arrhythmia. She picked up the flowers, and in so doing dislodged a card that Sugar had missed. She opened it with gnarled fingers. "I'm sorry," she read out loud.

She lifted the plump blooms to her nose. Actually, she didn't smell too well these days but she could still imagine. She started looking for a vase and was surprised to find that she did not own one. She'd lost half her furniture in the divorce and had never replaced anything so she only had two armchairs (he took the couch), two chairs for the Formica table (he took the other two and the coffee table) and just one nightstand in her room although she had kept the bed.

She still slept on the same side too. And although she had bought a new television a few years before, it sat on top of the old Zenith Console in the living room. She had fought hard for that TV and she liked looking at it and remembering her victory.

Searching for something else she could use for a vase, Mrs. Keschl caught sight of her reflection in the hallstand mirror (hers; the dresser in the bedroom, his).

She had been a beauty in her day, everyone had said so, with high cheekbones, big dark blue eyes and thick beautiful chestnut hair that had been the envy of all her friends. Her cheekbones were certainly not high now, and her hair was thin and gray. Between the loss of her looks and that failed marriage still sticking in her throat like a chicken bone it was no wonder she had been in a bad mood since the eighties.

But there was something about the red of the roses that picked at a corner of her memory. She'd been seventeen, it came to her, he not much older, and he'd brought her a single red rose and taken her dancing. She'd completely forgotten! She hadn't thought about that rose for years, or that night. Coney Island, the music, the dancing, the kiss. The kiss? She had believed in it then: the joy of living, love, family, companionship. And seeing those fat flowers sitting there now, the red like a slash of lipstick on a pretty girl's lips, just for a moment she felt like the slender head-turner of her youth.

They were married just a month after the Coney Island kiss and had moved in to this very apartment where for at least five minutes she thought that life would be a bowl of cherries and she the ripest of them sitting smack-dab in the middle to be admired for eternity.

Well, that hadn't happened. She'd been there on her own for almost three decades and didn't even own a vase. Flowers were for sentimental sissies, she'd always thought, but now she had some, she realized that this wasn't true—*she* didn't have a sentimental sissy bone in what was left of her crumpled old body, yet the roses had given her back a taste of something wonderful from her youth.

She looked in the mirror again and tried to raise her cheekbones and widen her eyes. God knew her eyesight was kaput, but even squinting or closing one eye at a time she still looked like a silly old woman. Nonetheless, she thought she might put rollers in her hair and maybe even change into a different dress before going over to the pierogi shop on First Avenue.

Out in the hallway, she bumped right into Mr. McNally but before she could gather her wits to think of an insult, he said, "I like your hair all poufed up like that."

"What?"

"I said I like your hair. Jaysus, can you not even take a compliment?"

"I can't remember what they sound like, especially coming from you. Are you drunk?"

"I haven't touched the stuff since June '87, you know that."

"So now he has a sense of humor."

"Would it kill you to believe a single word I ever said?"

"Would it kill you to tell the truth?"

Lola emerged from her apartment and hissed at the two of them to shut up or they'd wake Ethan and if they weren't careful she'd make them babysit him.

"I'll babysit the brat anyway," Mrs. Keschl hissed back.

"No, I'll babysit the brat anyway," Mr. McNally argued.

"Well, I'd like to go out for a couple of hours while he's asleep so what about you both come down and babysit him?"

Mrs. Keschl and Mr. McNally stared at each other, neither of them wanting to be the first to commit, or refuse.

"So?" Lola asked.

"So, it's all right with me if it's all right with her," Mr. McNally said.

"Of course it's all right with me, I suggested it!"

"Then get down here," snapped Lola. "Come on, I can't wait all week."

The next morning, George sent the deliveryman up to Sugar's apartment to tell her himself that he had been paid to bring roses to her door every morning for a week.

"I'm terribly sorry," Sugar said politely, "but if I ever see you again I'm going to have to take out a restraining order."

"Whatever you say," the deliveryman said. "These stairs are a killer anyhow."

"She's a tough nut to crack in 5B," he said to George on his way past. "Most chicks would kill for all these flowers."

But Sugar was not most chicks, and George did not think she was a tough nut to crack, either. He thought she was a very soft nut.

"The cheek of him, sending unwanted extravagant floral arrangements," she said later in the morning on her way out to the Union Square greenmarket, ostensibly to check out the honey sellers up there but also because she couldn't stand her own thoughts alone in her apartment.

"I don't think Theo means to be cheeky, Miss Sugar. I think he means to apologize—and before you get snappy with me, just remember I'm only an honorary doorman so you can't fire me because I'm not hired in the first place."

"I would never get snappy with you, George, and I would never fire you either, even if I could. But please don't entertain Theo on my account. The kind thing would be to let him know he is wasting his time and money on me because I am not interested. I do not want to see him again. No matter what you think about him, or me, or matters of the heart, you can't let him up. I can't take it. I need your help and I need to trust that you will give it to me."

"Of course I will, Miss Sugar. A doorman you can't trust is worse than no doorman at all."

But Theo was crushed when George passed on her decree. "If I can't go to the greenmarket or see her here, how can I fix this?"

"Where there's a will, there's a way," counseled George. "Although you could try toning down those shirts for a start. Are you color blind? Anyway, you can't go asking me to help. I promised Sugar I would keep you out of the building and I intend to keep that promise. But goes without saying you can do whatever you see fit outside the building. That's none of my business. None at all. Not a bit."

"Perhaps I should scale it," Theo suggested, looking up at the fire escape.

"I think as far as Miss Sugar is concerned, being on the building is the same as being in it," said George. "If not worse."

The next day, Sugar was in the kitchen making beeswax candles for Mr. McNally, whom she felt could do with a little ylang-ylang scent in his life, when there was a loud knocking on her door. It was Lola, Nate and Ruby and they were all holding helium-filled balloons that bobbed above them in a variety of colors and shapes.

"What in heaven's name?"

"We need to come in and get in the right order," said Lola, pushing past her. "Out on the rooftop, you guys."

Nate slunk past, embarrassed, but Ruby—holding just one giant inflated red heart—looked delighted.

"Am I the only person in New York not allowed in your store?" Sugar asked Lola.

"Be quiet," she snapped. "And turn your back. Ruby, you stand there in the middle and Nate, you need to separate yours—they're tangled, dude—and if I can just get these to stay in line . . . OK, we're ready. You can look now."

Sugar turned around to see Lola holding the number one in her right hand, and a "c", an "a" and an "n."

Ruby had her enormous heart and Nate had a collection of about a dozen "b"s and "B"s, all in different colors.

"One can heart 'b's?" Sugar asked.

"Yeah, I fucked up with the one," Lola said.

"She doesn't like that," Ruby said.

"Sorry, sorry, sorry," Lola grumbled. "It's supposed to be an 'I.'"

"What is?"

"The 'one.' It's supposed to be an 'I' as in 'he.'"

"An eye as in he? Have you been drinking?"

"A 'he' as in Theo," Ruby said. "Theo can."

"Theo can what?"

"Theo can heart bees, Sugar! The balloons are from Theo. He's saying he can heart your bees!"

Lola pulled a piece of paper from her pocket. "Actually, he wanted to say 'I AM SO SORRY' but I had no 'S's so we tried it with '5's but that was too weird so we decided on this."

"'I CAN HEART BEES,'" Sugar said, shaking her head.

"It's pretty cute, don't you think?" asked Lola.

"I'm not sure what to think, to be perfectly honest. Now, does anyone want a slice of honey pie? I just made one. With extra nutmeg. It smells divine."

They looked at her.

"The guy gives me two hundred bucks to inflate you this little love letter and all you want to do is eat pie?" Lola asked. "That's harsh."

"It's not a love letter," said Sugar. "Although I do commend you on the inflation, Lola. It's very . . . pert. And good for you for the money too. But I'm not sure I really get it. Maybe it's missing an exclamation point?"

"I don't even know how you would do an exclamation point with a balloon," said Lola.

"You could attach a little round balloon by an invisible string to a big long one," suggested Ruby.

"Yeah, whatever, there isn't any such thing and he didn't ask for one in the first place and I'm off." Lola tied her "1 CAN" to the back of a chair. "The Crankles are looking after Ethan while I go to a movie with this dude I met online. And yes, I know it's 'rude' to call them the Crankles but that is what they are and yes, I know his name. It's Johnny. Or Jimmy. See ya!"

"So about this pie," Sugar said.

"I should get going too," said Ruby, although she didn't want to, she just didn't want the pie.

"Yes, please, I'll have some," Nate said quickly, feeling bad for Sugar. He didn't want her to think everyone was abandoning her.

"You can let your balloons go if you want to," Sugar said, going in to get the pie. "She opened her store for Theo? I'm surprised, I must say."

"I think it's nice that he would do that for her," Ruby said, wistfully, to Nate as they tied their balloons to their chairs.

"Me too," he answered, going crimson. He was starting to get more of a feel for his type and thought Ruby might be kind of close. "Are you sure you don't want to stay a bit longer?"

Ruby went a lighter shade of beetroot herself. "OK," she said.

Sugar heard this small but significant exchange from where she was standing in the kitchen gripping the counter with whitened knuckles and wishing she had never laid eyes on Theo Fitzgerald.

Theo would never heart bees. She was never going to let him.

The moment her neighbors left, she got out her sharpest knife and popped every last balloon, very gently, so as not to alarm the bees. But the ruined colored carcasses hanging from their strings ripped a hole in her she couldn't quite explain.

She had thought it would feel good, but it didn't. It felt terrible.

29TH

The following Monday Ruby was back leaning against the jamb when Sugar opened the door, her scrapbook pages bejeweled with Post-it notes.

The layers of sweaters sagged between the younger woman's shoulders and Sugar thought she could see every tiny bone and vein in her neck, the pulse beating too quickly at the base of it beneath the ghostly white skin. She had black rings under her eyes and her lips were the same color as her face.

"Welcome, honey, come sit on the terrace with me. It's such a beautiful morning."

Outside Ruby sank into a chair and her eyelids drifted closed. For a moment Sugar thought she'd gone to sleep and she was more frightened for her friend than ever before, but then her eyes opened and she managed a little smile.

"I thought I heard bagpipes," she said. "Can you hear bagpipes?"

"No, honey," Sugar said as a forager bee flew past her and over to the hive entrance, where the usual collection of bees was hovering, before going inside. They looked as though they were talking to each other, like washerwomen at a well, putting off the moment when they had to leave the socializing behind and get to work.

Sugar also had something she could no longer put off.

"Ruby, you have become a very dear friend to me, you know that?"

Ruby nodded. "And the bees," she said, looking over at the hive, with the shadow of that same sad smile. "I'm a friend to the bees too. I already heart them."

"I need to talk to you," Sugar said, "about the thing we never talk about."

Ruby kept watching the bees. One was doing the waggle dance by the entrance to the hive. She wished with all her heart she was a bee, that she could just fly off to where the nectar was and bring home food for the queen, simple as that. Eating was so uncomplicated for a bee. She did it without even thinking. Ruby could barely remember what it was like to eat like that, to just put something in your mouth because it was there. That seemed like a pleasure from a distant past that did not belong to her, although she knew that once upon a time she'd been just like everyone else in that regard.

Now, every mouthful she chewed had probably been pondered over for at least an hour and there were many more hours spent pondering mouthfuls she didn't end up eating. No wonder she was tired. And she was tired. "I know what you're going to say," she said. "And it probably seems to you like it's an easy thing to fix but it's not. I try. In my mind I try but then I just can't. When it comes down to it, I can't."

"So what do you think is going to happen?"

"Someone will put me in the hospital," she said. "Then my mom will have every shrink in New York talk to me and she will get mad and it will be the same mess it was last time and the time before that until she ends up hating me more than she already does."

"Your mom doesn't hate you, Ruby."

"You don't know her."

"I know mothers don't hate their daughters," Sugar said. "They just don't understand them is all."

"It feels like hate," said Ruby. "Trust me, if she gets involved, everything will just get worse."

"Ruby, it can't get much worse. I'm not sure what the right thing is to say here so I'm just going to plow right on in because I can't sit still any longer. You have so much love in that body of yours. Why I bet it's having trouble keeping hold of all that love. And you have a wonderful, amazing future waiting for you but we need to figure out a way for you to get to it. You are just at the beginning of your life. Don't you see that, Ruby? Don't you want to live it?"

Ruby's eyes rolled slowly to hers. "Not always," she said.

"Oh, honey." Sugar fought back tears. She reached for Ruby's small, cold hand. "The world needs gentle souls like yours. Don't you know that? You can't leave us here on our own. You just can't. There's enough of us. We need more of you."

"I wish I was a bee," Ruby said. "I wish I could just come and go and not think about anything."

"Bees think," Sugar said. "Bees think a lot. A bee can count to five—did you know that? And a bee has to think about her queen, all the time. She has to think about living. Every creature in the universe has to concentrate on staying alive, honey. It doesn't come natural to anyone."

"Don't cry, Sugar," Ruby said. "Please don't cry."

"Well, of course I'm going to cry. You're breaking my heart."

"But your heart's already broken," she whispered.

Sugar let go of Ruby's hand to dab at her eyes. She was the only person Ruby had ever met who always had a clean handkerchief.

"Well, even if that was true, which it isn't, you shouldn't go worrying about me," Sugar said. "Because my body is strong and I'm going to be OK. But your body is not strong. It's not going to pull you through unless you help it. This is serious, Ruby. And you can't expect the people who love you to just sit and watch you fade away, so we're going to have to work out what to do."

"I'm watching you too," Ruby said, with more than a glimmer of steel. "And Theo."

"Oh hush, sweetie. It's not the same thing."

"I'm not doing something you want me to do and you're not doing something I want you to do. It is the same thing."

"But you could die, Ruby. That's the difference."

"Being dead isn't the worst thing."

"Please don't speak like that, Ruby. You can't imagine how it upsets me."

Sugar stood up but Ruby reached for her arm, her grip strong despite her frailty. "We had to talk about my thing," she said. "So it's only fair we talk about your thing."

Sugar sat down again.

"It's like Gwen Currie and John Doogan before they got married last year in Vegas," Ruby said, holding up the scrapbook. "She thought he loved baseball more than her and he thought her friends were snooty so they broke up but then they met again at the opera and realized nothing else mattered."

"I see."

"Or Jason Lee and Wendy Yang," Ruby said. "They split up because his job took him to Seattle and hers took her to Orlando and neither of them wanted to give up work but after a year they missed each other so bad they met up in Denver and both decided to stay there."

"You don't say."

"It's normal. Stuff happens and things get all messed up but it's like what happened with Mary-Jane Stewart and Reuben Johns before their wedding last fall. Mary-Jane said that everyone could tell from the moment she and Reuben first met each other that they should be together forever and ever but they were the last ones to see it."

"That's real cute, but I really don't see—"

"That's the point! You don't see! Because the other night when Theo found you in the rain and he kissed you in the kitchen and we were all here, we saw it. Everyone saw it. Everyone saw that you two should be together. Everyone except you."

"You saw the kiss?"

"Mrs. Keschl saw it and she told us but we could tell anyway. We could all tell."

"Am I the only one who remembers that he ran off like a scalded cat?"

"He was scared, Sugar. Don't you know what it's like to be scared?"

"I think that's enough, Ruby. Theo's nothing in the great scheme of things."

"He is totally not nothing," Ruby said, looking at her scrapbook. "Nobody is nothing. Love is totally not nothing."

Sugar wanted to tell her that if she would just get help in battling whatever demons were making her starve herself half to death if not completely, she would find love herself and could stop finding it for other people. "I'm going to fix us a drink," she said instead. "You sit right there."

"Dinah Phillips and Greg Steiner met through the personal ads and eloped to Hawaii," Ruby told her, not to be put off.

"Well, I hope she's going to keep her own name," Sugar called from the kitchen. "Otherwise she'll be Dinah Steiner."

"They were married by a Hawaiian woman who danced the hula and blew into a conch shell," Ruby continued. "And her mom was pissed that she wasn't invited." She put the scrapbook down. "Would you invite your mom to your wedding, Sugar?"

"I'm not going to have a wedding," she answered. "But if I did, I think it's fair to say that my mother would be unlikely to attend."

"But would you invite her?"

"Of course. She's my mother."

"I'm not going to have a wedding either," said Ruby. "But I would not invite my mom anyway."

"Ruby, honey, you are twenty-one years old," Sugar said when she came back with the drinks. "The Mr. Steiner of your dreams is out there looking for you somewhere and if you would just get strong enough to find him, you could have all the weddings you want. You could get married by a hula dancer in Hawaii or a Masai elder in Tanzania or a rabbi at the New York Public Library."

Ruby shot her a mischievous look and bit her pale bottom lip.

"What are you looking at me like that for?"

215

"I read that," Ruby said slyly, "about the Masai elders in Tanzania."

"Well, that must be how I know about it."

But Ruby had read it at home, on her own, which meant Sugar was reading the *Times*'s wedding pages without her.

Elizabeth the Sixth, as always, was cheered by the presence of Ruby, the love sponge, up on Sugar's rooftop but she was feeling pretty positive anyway. A swell had been building in the hive all day and was about to reach critical mass.

That sometimes happened with the approach of big news. It might start, for instance, with one trio of bees flying back with a piece of crucial information, which they imparted at the entrance to the hive with a waggle this way and a waggle that way. Another trio or two or ten foragers might then fly off to the spot that first trio was talking about, and on their return tell another dozen or so. In this way, the queen herself would eventually get to hear about what her bees had discovered.

And as Ruby sat on Sugar's rooftop talking about the Steiners and their Hawaiian elopement, so Elizabeth the Sixth became aware of the crucial key to solving her big problem. Sugar was closer to happiness than the queen could possibly ever have imagined.

30TH

Early the next morning, Sugar stepped out onto the roof terrace with her cup of mint tea. The sun was rising over the neighboring rooftops, the vanilla scent of her heliotropes hung heavy in the air, and the hard, sharp edges of the rooftop jungle around her softened in the morning light.

Mrs. Keschl ribbed her for always "mooning" over the city's modern towers and turrets but Sugar never tired of her view. Everywhere she looked she was reminded that there she was, on top of it all, in New York City.

She would take her blessings where she could find them and her home was a blessing.

George's leg was almost completely healed, that was another, and Nate was doing less midnight gardening, plus Lola was happier now Ethan was quieter; she'd seen the baby out walking with Mr. McNally and Mrs. Keschl—together and laughing—and if that wasn't a blessing, she didn't know what was.

Ruby, on the other hand. She was so worried about Ruby. And Theo?

"I do not even want to think about Theo," she said, clasping her favorite cup in both hands. She'd brought it from her grandfather's cabin, one of the few mementos that she had from her old life, and it was as smooth and comforting against her fingers as it had been the morning before and the morning before that and all the mornings since she left South Carolina.

But despite her blessings, and the beautiful morning, the day did not hint at better things to come. Something in the air was a little off-kilter.

She absently swatted away a bee that was hovering just out of eye line, then another. When the third and fourth bees started buzzing around her, she looked over at the hive where—to her amazement—the busy contingent of bees that usually lingered in front of it had thickened and was thickening more and more as she watched.

The bees streamed out of the tiny entrance and gathered in a growing fat black ball, then in front of her very eyes, they started to stretch out and move upward in a steady column.

"What in heaven's name?" Sugar asked, as the column grew denser and denser with more bees pouring out and joining it, rising in the air, upward and upward, and then they stretched out, like a fat garden hose, toward her.

"What's going on?" she asked, as the bees re-formed into a perfectly round dark cloud above her, then stretched horizontally like a bubble blown into a wobbly oblong, before lazily circling her head half a dozen times . . . at which point Sugar realized that Queen Elizabeth the Sixth was in the lead.

The queen?

A queen typically left her hive just once, not long after her birth, for the sole purpose of mating. It was no fun for her and even less for the drones who sperminated her and died immediately afterward as a result.

But this was definitely Elizabeth the Sixth, her unmistakably elegant body flying slower than the workers normally would, them keeping a respectable distance behind as she led them in a graceful swirl around the terrace, over to Nate's window boxes, back to the hive, once more around Sugar's head then over the railing, across the gap where some building had long ago disappeared, across the street and then directly onto the vast empty rooftop with the fat naked sculpture.

There the bees landed, covering the nude's elbow—at least she hoped it was the elbow—like a suede patch on an old tweed blazer.

Sugar's precious cup dropped from her hands and shattered on the tiled terrace, bringing Nate to his window, bleary eyed, to see what was happening.

She could only point, and, when his eyes followed her finger, he still didn't understand.

"What's going on?"

"Elizabeth," Sugar said. "She's gone!"

Nate squinted as the elbow pad on the sculpture changed shape and then changed shape again. His jaw dropped. "That's your bees? They ran away from home?"

Sugar looked at him, bewildered, then went to the hive and lifted off the lid. She'd only checked the queen the day before so knew that there was plenty of honey, plenty of space, and plenty of brood. The hive was in perfect condition.

But it was empty.

Not one single bee had stayed behind.

There was no reason for Elizabeth the Sixth to swarm. None at all. And in the morning, right in front of her eyes. Bees just didn't do that.

"I can't believe it," she said. "I just can't believe it."

"I'm coming over," said Nate and moments later he was there, peering in at the brood box.

"Have they done this before?"

"I've seen other bees swarm," Sugar said. "But usually it's because they're too cramped or the weather's too hot or too cold or because the queen is weak. But then there's usually a new one left behind and there isn't. You can see a new queen clear as anything. The workers build special breeding cells for them. That's how you know what they're up to. The queen just doesn't leave the hive."

Well, not usually.

"Do you think it's been too hot?" Nate asked.

"No. And the bees are very good at keeping everything the right temperature. They've been so happy here. She was off-color a couple of weeks ago but everything has been going just fine since. She's been laying her rear off. Look at all that honey! She's taken every last bee, Nate."

She looked across at the scene of Elizabeth the Sixth's betrayal. "That's not even swarming, that's absconding."

"It's different?"

"With a swarm, they leave enough bees behind so you can keep going. She hasn't even done that. She's taken all of them."

"What are you going to do?"

"I'm going to go over there and get them back," Sugar said. "That's what I'd do if it happened anywhere else."

Agitated, she kneeled down and started to pick up the broken pieces of her cup. "I've had this cup as long as I've had them," she said. "This is terrible."

"I can pick that up," Nate said. "You should go and get the bees."

She stood up, putting the shattered remains of the cup on the table, her hands shaking as she fingered the pale blue daisies, another link with her past now lost. "Any chance you could come with me?" she asked. "It's pretty easy to catch a swarm but a second pair of hands never goes astray and I need to work out where that building is and get into it somehow."

"I won't get stung, will I?" Nate asked.

"I wouldn't think so but you could wear my bee suit."

Nate blushed. "It won't fit."

"Then you could just wear the helmet and veil and your own shirt with long sleeves and long pants. It'll be just like playing the front end of the horse in the school play."

This didn't do much for Nate, as he had not even been picked to play the back end of the horse in the school play. But once he had the helmet on, and the veil down in front of his face, he found that he liked it in there. It smelled good and the world looked better through such a filter.

Sugar did not even brush her hair or put on her lipstick, just dashed out the door in jeans, T-shirt and sneakers, her thoughts scattered to the wind as she hurried down the stairs.

It wasn't that swarming bees were usually in that much of a hurry to go anywhere; as a rule they camped overnight on their way to wherever they were headed. But the whole abscondment was such a departure from Elizabeth the Sixth's usual behavior that Sugar didn't think it was safe to take any risks. She wanted her bees back, pronto, before they upped and did anything even more upsetting, although she was hard-pressed to figure out what that would be.

"The building must be on East Fifth Street," Nate said as they reached the bottom of the stairs. "About five from the corner, I'd say."

George did a double take as he reached to open the door for them. "I'm not even going to ask," he said. "Although others might."

Sugar waved a cardboard carton at him as they turned up Flores Street and headed for Avenue B.

"What's the box for?" Nate wanted to know.

"That's what I'll bring the bees home in. They're not hard to capture. Not that it's the catching them that worries me, it's why they would abscond in the first place."

They took a right at Avenue B, another into East Fifth Street and soon found the building. Luckily for them, someone was coming out of it just as they approached.

"Excuse me, ma'am, would you be so kind as to tell me how I might get up on to the rooftop?" Sugar asked.

"Are you the exterminators?" the woman asked. "Because you were supposed to come a month ago."

"No, ma'am," answered Sugar. "We're the opposite of exterminators."

"You're bringing rats into the building? Oh great. Maybe you could add some bedbugs while you're at it."

"No, I'm sorry, we're nothing to do with your building, as such. We live in one of the places out back and something precious—which is not in need of extermination—has sort of gotten stuck up there and we're just trying to figure out what to do."

The woman looked at her uncomprehendingly.

"Her bees ran away," said Nate. "She inherited them from her grandfather."

"Oh, I got a painting when my grandfather died," the woman said. "I sold it and went to Paris for a whole summer."

"I can bring you some honey," said Sugar, "if you tell us how to get up on the rooftop."

"Well, it's private," the woman said. "Belongs to the guy in 4P. I don't know him that well but if I let you in the building, you can take the elevator up and just knock on his door. It's probably harder for him to turn you away then. Tell him Carol sent you. And I'm in 3A if you're serious about the honey."

"Yes, ma'am. I'm serious. And thank you."

Nate straightened his helmet, Sugar hitched up her cardboard carton, and up they went.

"Now, some people get a little antsy if they think a big old bunch of bees has just landed in their backyard for no apparent reason," Sugar explained outside the door of the penthouse apartment. "So if it's possible, we keep 4P in his apartment while we or at least I go and get them. You got that?"

"I got it," Nate said, bold inside his hat and veil, and Sugar knocked robustly on the door.

As soon as the door opened, however, she knew getting a little antsy was more than just a possibility because the guy in 4P was Theo.

224

31ST

O
h, shoot," said Sugar.

"Oh, Sugar!" said Theo.

"You live here?" Nate asked from inside his veil.

"Who's that?"

"This is Nate. I think you met him at my apartment before you, you know, ran off and all. Listen, Theo, I don't want you to go thinking that—"

"Why is he wearing that hat?"

Sugar and Nate looked at each other. The beekeeper's visor was possibly not the best idea in the world given that the bee rescue was secret.

"He can't be in the sunlight," Sugar lied, trying to cross her fingers without dropping the carton. "Like that boy on *60 Minutes*."

"And I feel faint from being out in the street," Nate said, rather woodenly, although Sugar had to hand it to him for quick thinking. "Can we come in?"

"Of course." Theo stood back and let them in. "With pleasure. Be my guests. I'm so surprised. But pleased! Surprised and pleased but obviously more pleased. What can I get you? A soda, a coffee, anything else that isn't alcoholic?"

An awkward silence mushroomed as Sugar found herself lost for words.

"What a cool apartment," Nate said. "It's, like, fifty times bigger than mine."

"Perhaps you would like to show us around," Sugar said. "Then we can decide what we'd like to drink."

Theo's apartment was indeed fifty times bigger than Nate's, and twenty-five times bigger than Sugar's, and had two bedrooms, two bathrooms, a gourmet kitchen, a vast living area and a separate office.

The space was modern and cool, but it was furnished in a way that befitted a man who had abandoned corporate law to wear Hawaiian shirts. There was actually a palm tree in one corner, although it doubled as a basketball hoop, and a small pinball machine in another. But there was a comfortable old worn leather sofa too, and bookshelves heaving with books, mostly well-read paperbacks, plus drawings on the wall that Sugar thought might have been done by his niece. At least she hoped so.

"Don't you ever feel like going outside?" she asked.

"Not really," Theo replied. "We Scots are not known for our sun-worshipping skills. Actually, we don't really have sun in Scotland, but I do have a roof terrace that you get to by the stairs next to the spare bathroom."

"Do you have hot chocolate?" Sugar asked immediately. "The real sort that you boil the milk for and then mix in the chocolate and then wait a few minutes until it's perfect drinking temperature?"

"Um, maybe, somewhere," said Theo. "Would you like one?"

"I certainly would," Sugar said, "and if you've a mind to boil the milk real slow, that's how I prefer it. Don't you, Nate?"

"Yes, I do," he said. "Although I see you have an espresso machine so a cappuccino would be good too. As well as a hot chocolate. Just in case."

Sugar smiled at him as Theo started opening cupboards to look for the hot chocolate.

"If you boys will excuse me," she said. "I'll just use the powder room."

"Do you want to leave that carton here?" Theo asked.

"No, I need to take it with me," said Sugar, groping for an excuse. "My new kitten's in here." She then scurried around a corner, straight past the powder room and up a narrow staircase before opening the security door and emerging onto Theo's rooftop.

"Elizabeth the Sixth!" she said when she reached the sculpture around whose elbow indeed her bees were still, thankfully, huddled in their heaving elbow patch. "What in the heck are you doing here?"

She looked back across the gap at her own rooftop, at the thriving oasis of greenery she and Nate had created in the higgledy-piggledy morass of the city. Why would her queen want to come here to Theo's bland empty space and sit on a fat bronze arm when she had always been so happy wherever Sugar was, surrounded by nectar and pollen and good old-fashioned beekeeper hospitality?

Often when bees swarmed it was to a tree branch, which could be shaken or chopped off, but in the case of Theo's sculpture, Sugar had to use her hands to gently brush the bees off and into the carton. Luckily they fell in easy clumps, the last of which she could clearly see contained Elizabeth the Sixth.

"I don't understand," Sugar said. "You're not even putting up a fight. What's this all about?"

It wasn't the first time she'd wished a bee could talk back.

"I look after you, don't I? You know how much I care. I'd be lost without you, Elizabeth, especially at the moment. Truly, I would."

She taped up the box and headed back down to Theo's apartment, opening and slamming the spare bathroom door on her way past.

"I'm sorry," she said, clutching the carton. "I'm not feeling so good all of a sudden. Do you mind if I skip the hot chocolate and just get Nate to take me home?"

Theo's face fell and she resolutely ignored the full force of the tug at her heartstrings. She simply did not have time to consider the complications as far as he was concerned.

"But you came looking for me," Theo said following her to the door. "Didn't you? I was hoping that maybe you had found it in your heart to forgive me."

"No, that's not why I'm here. I just wanted to check something and now I've checked it, so we can go."

"Plus you're not feeling well," Nate reminded her. "Remember?"

"You checked something in the spare bathroom? Wait, Sugar, please, just tell me what's going on so I can fix it. I can change the spare bathroom. I can move the spare bathroom. I can seal the spare bathroom up forever. Please! Just tell me what I can do. And Nate, shouldn't you be carrying the kitten since Sugar's not feeling good?"

Nate obediently reached for it but Sugar hugged it to her chest and waited for Theo to open the door.

"I went and talked to an allergist," he said, touching her lightly on the shoulder. "That's what I meant with the balloons. I told him about you, about the, you know, bees, about the nearly dying thing and he says it's different now. He says I probably wouldn't die now, not if I carried this new doohickey from Sweden. Hang on, don't go—I'll get it! I want to show you."

Sugar could feel the spot where he touched her burning beneath her T-shirt and found her staunch outlook on the subject of Theo suddenly seeming perilously unstable. She tried to remember that feeling in the pit of her stomach from when he ran out on her at the dinner party because a feeling like that went a long way toward not repeating a terrible mistake. But instead all she could grasp was the unfamiliar sensation that had so deliciously claimed her when he kissed her in her kitchen. She needed to forget that kiss.

"Come on, let's scram," she said to Nate, but he shook his head just as she caught sight of herself in Theo's hall mirror and saw what a state she was in. Her mother would garrote her for being in someone else's house looking like that. It was a fine thing that Sugar particularly didn't want Theo to care for her because if she did, she would be mortified.

Before she could juggle the box of bees to open the door, however, Theo came back holding a crayon-sized white stick.

"This is the new antiallergy EpiPen. If I carry one of these around with me all the time, then I probably wouldn't even need to go to the hospital. You know, if I was stung. It means I could visit with you."

His handsome face suited being hopeful far more than crestfallen. His eyes had brightened, his smile was closer. Forget the kiss, Sugar told herself. Forget the kiss.

"Thank you for your hospitality, Theo, and that is a particularly lovely soap you have in the powder room but you will not be visiting with me. You tried to get me drunk, remember? You stalked me, then you ran out on me. So I'm sorry to say that I meant it when I said I never want to see you again."

Nate's eyes were bulging under his visor and Theo's smile had retreated once more.

"But you came here," he said.

"Well, that's completely different and not related to the not wanting to see you again at all. Because that starts now." She was getting flustered and it felt like the bees were getting that way too. They couldn't stay in the carton too long—it would overheat. She had to get them home.

"If you could just tell me—"

"I'm sorry. Theo, but we need to go. Nate, would you be a honey and get the door?"

"I like your kitchen," Nate said, before following Sugar to the elevator.

Theo watched as it swallowed the two of them up and took her away from him again.

"Who the heck does he think he is?" Sugar seethed as they made their way back to Flores Street. "You can't just pester a person into liking you. It doesn't work that way and even if it did, why hasn't he got so much as a sad old rubber plant up there on that enormous rooftop of his? Does the man have something against gardens?"

"Can't stand to think what your mission was but I hope it's accomplished," George said as he opened the door for them.

"Certainly is," Sugar said. "Thank you for asking."

Back on her rooftop, Nate helped shift Elizabeth the Sixth and her subjects back into the brood box, then place the honey-filled supers on top. They were getting heavy with drying nectar but Sugar filled up the hive-top feeder to sweeten the bees more anyway. She wanted to make sure they didn't stray again.

"You going to take that visor off and tell me what this silent treatment is about?" she asked Nate when they had the bees settled.

Nate really liked the visor. He wished he could wear it to work. It made him bolder.

"Theo is not pestering you," he said. "His wife ran off with a gardener so he does have something against gardens. He really likes you, that's all. And he's doing everything to show you that but you're being mean."

Sugar's mouth fell open. "You think I'm being mean?"

"I know you are. It's not easy to tell a girl how you feel about her. It's hard. Some people can't even do it at all."

He really was just about the sweetest neighbor she had ever had. And she'd had some honeys.

"You're right," she said. "I'm sorry. I don't mean to be mean; that's the last thing I want to be. I apologize, and it won't happen again, but it can be just as hard to hand your heart over to someone as it is to ask for that heart in the first place, Nate. Especially if you've done it before and it hasn't worked out so well."

"That's the same for everyone," Nate said. "Theo too."

"He told you about his wife and the gardener?"

"He told Lola," Nate answered. "When he bought the balloons. He said he didn't think he would ever fall in love again but he did with you, only then he lost his shit—I'm sorry, he lost his shizz—because he's allergic and he made a big jessie out of himself. That's what he said. A jessie."

"Is that a Scottish thing?"

"A scared Scottish thing, I guess."

"Well, whatever it is, I won't be mean again, I promise. But enough about him. Did you think any more about the job at Citroen?"

Nate looked at her through his veil. "It'll be gone by now," he said. "And I wouldn't have gotten it anyway."

"But if you're not even going to try how will you ever know? That's defeatist talk where I come from and you are such a star, Nate."

"It makes me feel bad when you keep asking about it."

"Oh, I'm sorry, honey. I'm just trying to help."

"It doesn't feel like help," said Nate. "There's too much of it."

"Oh," said Sugar.

Nate took off the hat and was just himself again.

"Um, I gotta go," he said. "Bye."

32ND

Sugar's plan to never see Theo again came unstuck almost immediately when she woke up the next day and, before she could even get out of bed, saw her bees rise up out of their hive as one and abscond right back to his rooftop.

It was as if they had been waiting for her to wake up and do it in front of her.

"You have to be kidding me," she moaned, after leaping out of bed and reaching her rooftop railing just as they took up residence this time on the rear end of the sculpture.

Again she checked the hive and saw Elizabeth the Sixth had taken nearly every last living creature with her save, this time, a few lazy drones who were chewing at the honeycomb.

"Nate? Honey? Are you there?" she called out, but she had woken in the night and heard him gardening, so wasn't surprised that he was still sleeping. She didn't have the heart to wake him now, especially after what he'd said the day before.

"Why, George, you look extra-specially distinguished today, you know that?" she said, down on the stoop, batting her eyelashes in a way she thought would make any southern mama glow with pride.

"You got something in your eye, Miss Sugar? Better do something about that real quick before the wind changes and leaves you blinking like an owl in the sunlight forever."

"All right then, no, I don't have something in my eye," she said. "The truth is I need your help."

"And I like helping so just tell me what I need to do."

"You know that mission I told you I accomplished yesterday?"

"Yes, ma'am."

"I need to accomplish it all over again."

"Certainly explains why you have that cardboard carton."

"Do you think you could come with me?"

"Do I have to wear a helmet?"

"No, I think it would be better if you don't."

"Then I can come with you, but only if you let me carry the carton. And only if I may say that you look particularly pleasing to the eye today. Particularly."

It was true. She had brushed her hair, put on her lipstick, and was wearing her favorite dress and her nicest summer sandals. It wasn't because she wanted Theo to see her in a better light than the day before either. She had no interest in what Theo wanted. None whatsoever. It was because everyone on the block would smell a rat if she turned up looking like an exterminator without actually being one two days in a row.

That's what she told herself as she and George headed around the corner to Theo's building.

"Would you be a sweetheart and buzz Apartment 4P for me?" she asked him.

"Who lives there?"

"Theo does."

George looked at her, eyebrows raised.

"It's not what you think," Sugar said quickly. "Not at all. I have a situation, a difficult situation, which I can't explain and which I can't fix on my own, so I would appreciate it if, when we get up there, you do all the talking so I can go use the powder room."

She pushed the buzzer herself and nudged George toward the speaker, knowing that women and powder rooms were a combination he would likely avoid.

"George Wainwright and Sugar Wallace," he announced when Theo answered. "Do you mind if we come up?"

Theo, of course, did not mind, which moved George to raise his eyebrows even farther.

"I told you," Sugar said as they stepped into the elevator. "It's not what you think."

When Theo opened the door, however, he was grinning from ear to ear, but it was the panting black retriever dog at his feet that caught Sugar's immediate attention.

"You brought your kitten back," Theo said, his smile disappearing. "I'm not sure how that's going to work out."

"You have a dog?" The dog was looking up at Sugar with large, black, baleful eyes. If Sugar had one really truly soft spot for anything other than lame ducks and bees, it involved canines.

"Dogs, heights; this is not a good day for George Wainwright," George said, stepping backward.

"This is Princess," Theo said. "I got him through the dog rescue program. Remember, I told you I was thinking of getting a man's best friend?"

"You called a 'him' Princess?" George asked.

"The people who abandoned him called him Princess," Theo explained. "They walked out and just left him to starve, didn't they, Princess?" The dog looked up adoringly as Theo scratched his ears. "I'm just not sure how he is with kittens."

"Kittens?" George repeated.

"Don't worry about the kitten," Sugar said, wishing she had never mentioned the nonexistent creature, her eyes still on Princess. He could have been her faithful old hound Miss Pickles's twin sister.

"Can we come in?" George said to Theo. "I need to talk to you about something."

"Of course," Theo said, ushering them inside. "And can I just say that you look much better today, Sugar."

She bridled but remembered her promise not to be mean. "Well, of course you can say it but you know those jeans were clean and that T-shirt has great sentimental value," she said.

"No, no," Theo said. "I mean you were unwell yesterday, when you brought the kitten."

"Is it the kitten we need to be talking about?" George asked, confused.

"No, but now you come to mention it, Theo, I'm perhaps not as well as I may appear so can I please use the powder room again?"

Not waiting for a reply, she resisted the urge to stop and pat the dog, headed past the bathroom and up the back stairs. But Princess had already sniffed her out as a potential source of affection and followed. As Sugar pushed open the door to the roof terrace she felt the warm pressure of long soft fur against her legs.

236

"No! Princess! Go back," she hissed, but it was too late, the dog was already outside, bounding around the empty space like a colt in spring grass.

Sugar couldn't help but smile. Miss Pickles had been similarly willful; indeed, she left most human southern belles for dead with her demands regarding the kindness of strangers and the quality of sirloin.

Sugar called Princess over and he came straightaway, bent tail wagging maniacally, and sat down, just the way Miss Pickles used to, ready for some quality petting.

"You got to help me out here, boy," she said, crouching so she could lean into his neck, smelling the expensive dog shampoo that Theo had used. "I need to get my bees and take them home so if you could just sit here quietly while I collect them, I'll soon be on my way."

Princess seemed to understand and sat obediently, tongue hanging out, his eyes following Sugar, who was horrified to spot Elizabeth the Sixth crawling over her subjects as they writhed between the substantial butt cheeks on the bronze nude.

"You can't keep doing this," she told her queen. "And especially not in there! You are going to get me in a whole lot of trouble, Elizabeth. You just don't know who you are messing with here. It's going to end in tears, I can assure you, and you know how I feel about tears."

But it wasn't Elizabeth the Sixth, in the end, who caused the trouble, it was Princess. He didn't want to sit quietly while Sugar collected her bees, as it turned out. He didn't want her to be on her way.

The moment he realized it was real live insects she was scraping into that cardboard box, he started barking fit to wake the dead.

And although the bees seemed unperturbed at such a vocal interruption, Theo was not. Theo was most perturbed.

"How did Princess get out on the roof?" he asked George, who had been halfway through a very involved story about a particular inhabitant of East Sixty-Seventh Street who had gone sixteen months, by George's calculations, without once leaving the building and had also, he thought, been called Theo.

"And where's Sugar? Do you think she's all right?"

"Can't speak for the dog but Sugar seems to know what she's doing," George said.

"I'd better go and see what's happening," Theo said, getting up from his chair, and George, who had just realized the shut-in on East Sixty-Seventh Street had actually been called Leo, decided the game, whatever it was, was up, and stood to follow.

Up on the rooftop, Princess was dancing around Sugar and her carton half full of bees with all the pride of having rounded them up himself.

"What are you doing?" Theo asked her, approaching the sculpture and seeing the large black mark at the top of its butt cheeks. "Are you defacing my Fernando Botero?"

"Stop, Theo!" Sugar cried. "Stop right there!"

"I don't have to stop anywhere: this is my rooftop. What's going on?"

"Stop, Theo. Please!"

But Theo was already just a couple of yards away from what he thought was the site of Sugar's bizarre vandalism.

"If you don't like it, you just have to say; I should sell it anyway, it's worth a fortune but it was never really . . ."

He realized, at that point, that the dark tattoo on his priceless sculpture's bottom was not paint at all. It was moving. It was alive. It was bees.

"Bees," he said, the air squeezing out of his lungs. "Bees."

"It's not my fault," Sugar insisted, trying to scrape the remaining insects off the sculpture. "It's nothing to do with me. They were right as rain over at my apartment but then they just started coming over here of their own accord and I have to keep coming and rescuing them and taking them home again and I would have said, I mean I hate to be anything less than truthful, despite the little white lie about Nate and the boy from *60 Minutes*, but I thought it would upset you to know so—"

"Your bees are running away from home?" George asked.

"I wish people would stop saying that," Sugar answered. "They're not running away, they're just—"

"Vacationing?"

"Bees," Theo repeated, followed by six short, shallow breaths. He scrunched up his eyes and dug his fingernails into his palms.

"I'm real sorry," Sugar said. He looked so distressed and it alarmed her that she hated so much to see it. Why should she care? But she did. She cared a lot. "This must be awful for you."

"No!" Theo wheezed. "Good!"

"This is what good looks like?" George had found the middle of the rooftop, the spot farthest from any possibility of falling over any of the edges. He held on to the knee of the sculpture and tried not to sway.

239

"In therapy," Theo said through gritted teeth. "Bee therapy."

"Now I swear I have heard it all," George said. "A male dog called Princess and a man in bee therapy. Are you finished with me now, Miss Sugar? I'm as giddy as a schoolgirl up here."

"I'm OK," said Theo. "I'm OK. I'm OK."

"If he's OK then we are all in trouble," George told Sugar. "You'd better get those bees out of here before the poor guy bursts a blood vessel."

"I'm trying, I'm trying," Sugar said, sweeping the last of them into the box and taping it shut. "All right then. We're good to go."

Princess, finally, stopped his barking and calmly started licking his nether regions; Theo remained where he was, sweating like a galloping horse and carving holes into his palms with his nails.

"I'm OK," he repeated, and his breathing seemed to even out a little. "I'm OK. Kitten?"

"Shoot, no need to worry about the kitten," Sugar said, unable to meet his eyes. "I can't apologize enough for this, Theo. We'll leave you alone now and I will make certain this never happens again."

"Welcome. Congratulations," Theo said, frozen to the spot.

Sugar's deep desire to not cause him any pain was alarming, to say the least. What she really wanted to do was take him in her arms, kiss away his fear, soothe and assure him. Instead, she took control of herself and bustled over to the door back into the apartment, indicating that George should come with her. "Thank you for your hospitality," she called brightly. "And have a nice day!"

240

"He was just standing there," she said as they stepped into the elevator. "He's allergic and he was just standing there, and Elizabeth the Sixth and her girls didn't even bat a wingtip. I don't get it. I don't understand, George. What the heck is going on? What does it all mean?"

"It means it's time you told me the rest of your story," said George, as they stepped out in to the street where he could breathe freely again. "You take that poor little kitty cat and those bees back home and do with them whatever you need to. I'll get some shrimp pancakes and we'll meet in Grace's Garden in an hour. And don't even think of leaving me waiting there either, Miss Sugar. I'm old. I could go at any time. And you don't want that on your conscience."

Sugar had enough on her conscience to last her a lifetime. "I'll be there," she said.

Elizabeth the Sixth's great-great-great-grandmother, Queen Elizabeth the First, knew when there was a threat in the neighborhood, whether it was a bear or a wasp or a person wearing too much aftershave.

Each potential predator carried its own set of smells and vibrations and as soon as Elizabeth the First picked up on them, she communicated to the rest of the hive to be on high alert. It didn't take much: just a flick of her pheromones and the guard bees ramped up their electric charge while the foragers stayed closer to the hive in case they were needed.

All the bees knew Sugar: they carried their feelings for her with them in their genes, they could sense her from more than half a mile away and would no sooner find her a threat than fly to the moon. But Elizabeth the First sensed Grady Parkes from half a mile away too, and her resulting hum was not one of blissful content. It was his smell, partly: an aftershave with base notes of tobacco and cedar and a hint of bitter herbs, and his natural scent, which was too sour for Elizabeth the First's liking. She registered him as something to watch out for and passed this on through the realm.

But it was the chill in the air she picked up when Sugar and her grandfather were standing by the hive, talking about him, that alerted the queen to the fact that he could pose a far more lethal danger.

The queen and Grampa Boone were close. He knew how she felt, it was as simple as that, and what's more, it was mutual. She knew he was fearful for his baby girl. And she knew the reason for his fear was sitting in the car just a stone's throw away radiating overpowering smells and an oppressive disposition.

Not long after, Grampa Boone was gone, and Elizabeth the First knew then that it was up to her to keep the hive intact until Sugar came and got them, which she finally did. What's more, Elizabeth the First liked her new home in the garden in Church Street. In the pretty corner south of Broad behind the big magnolia there were so many more scents to interpret, blooms to visit; she was happy about the water feature and looking forward to getting to know her new neighborhood.

Then Grady arrived and started cursing and kicking at her home, and one of the worker bees who knew he was not to be trusted acted on her own behalf and launched a minor attack. When Grady caused Sugar to fall, his pheromones fizzing, the other workers went on high alert.

This was not what Sugar's grandfather had raised his bees to witness.

It would not be tolerated.

33RD

George was waiting on their bench beneath the oak, with that same bluebird perched on a bough behind him, and Sugar's pancake and a soda waiting on a napkin beside him. He smiled when he saw her and although Sugar was so churned up inside she could barely even contemplate food, a sliver of that same comforting calm she'd felt last time in the garden slid around her shoulders like a stole.

"I haven't told anyone this before," she said, sitting down. "So if it doesn't make sense, or I start to cry, or run for the hills, you'll have to forgive me, I'm doing the best I can."

"Your best is all you can do, Miss Sugar," said George. "And yours is better than most."

"It was the last Saturday in August," she said. "Usually too hot to get married in Charleston, according to Grady's mama, anyway, but mine just wanted us down that aisle as soon as she could possibly arrange it."

Actually, the morning had been blessedly cooler than those of the previous days and weeks, cool enough for Etta to stop fussing about the flowers at the Yacht Club where the reception was to be, and the green of the lawn in the Legare

Street garden where she was hosting a postwedding luncheon the following day.

The hairdresser had come early and piled Sugar's long hair in a graceful updo; the dressmaker herself had made one last-minute alteration and fitted the gown like a whale-boned glove.

Her makeup was immaculate, her eyes soft and clear, her lips pink and perfect.

She'd even been practicing walking in heels to make sure that she didn't tumble and fall off her father's arm, revealing the satin La Perla underwear Etta had given her to wear beneath the dazzling dress.

Afterward, everybody would agree that, despite what happened, Sugar was the most beautiful bride they had ever seen.

The sunlight was filtering through the elegant arched windows of St. Michael's Episcopal Church on the corner of Meeting and Broad Streets, the intersection at the very heart of Charleston where City Hall met the Courthouse and the Post Office.

The pristine white St. Michael's was where Sugar's parents had been married thirty years before, and her father's parents before them. In fact, the bells of St. Michael's had been chiming at Wallace family weddings since 1764.

Sugar and her father arrived from Legare Street in a white carriage pulled by four glossy gray horses, their manes long and silky, their black oiled livery glistening.

The organist lit up as she stepped out of the coach, the choir bursting into the psalm Etta had chosen as Sugar entered the church and started slowly down the aisle on the arm of her proud father.

Her mother stood in the front row wearing a stunning suit of the palest draped cream silk, knowing she was stopping just short of outshining her daughter, and pleased with that.

Ben and Troy were groomsmen, their girlfriends bridesmaids, as Etta thought that would save anyone else from being offended and they were both exceptionally blond and pretty.

The church was full. The mother of the bride had outdone herself in the wedding preparations with everything from the first invitation to the promise of Cristal champagne at the reception to the details of the barbecue to be held the following day.

No one who knew that the Wallaces' only daughter was getting married that weekend wanted anything other than to be right there with them, sharing in the festivities, from beginning to bitter end. It was going to be some party.

"Grady looks like the cat that got the cream," his cousin Luke muttered under his breath to his brother, Ed.

"He always looks like that," Ed replied.

"He's had a lot of cream," Luke said and they both laughed, which earned them a poke in the ribs from their mother. But they envied Grady too. Sugar Wallace was just about the tastiest-looking cream they had ever seen and the two of them all but drooled as she glided past them toward the altar.

A veil of the finest French silk tulle showed a glimpse of exquisite shoulder beneath the fragile lace of her gown. Every eye was on her as she kissed her daddy's cheek and slowly turned to Grady, who was standing there with tears glistening in his own eyes, as overwhelmed by her beauty as everyone else.

They made a stunning pair, everyone remembered thinking that. This was the sort of coupling every parent dreamed of for their child: two of the city's finest joining hands in holy matrimony in front of everyone who was anyone.

They all remembered thinking that, but no one could remember when the first bee arrived.

It was definitely somewhere after "Do you Cherie-Lynn Antoinette Wallace take Grady Johnson Howell Parkes to be your lawfully wedded husband," but before "I now pronounce you husband and wife."

Sugar was standing there listening to the words and repeating her vows when she heard a familiar buzzing. A bee had flown in through the open top window above the door to the sacristy and was circling the pulpit.

She stiffened as it came closer. Where there was one bee there were usually more.

Sure enough, another bee flew in through the same window, and another, and another.

Grady was holding both her hands by then and didn't seem to notice them fly once around the altar and then head straight for him.

There were still only four, making a big lazy circle just a few feet above his head, so Sugar relaxed a little until she noticed that the bee at the front was bigger than the other three.

Grady cottoned on to them then, or cottoned on to something, and puffed out a lungful of air as if to blow them away.

They moved a little higher, but still they circled him.

Sugar couldn't keep her eyes off them. The one in the front was definitely bigger. In fact, she looked like a queen. She pulled her hands away from Grady's.

The rector shot her a warning look, but she ignored it.

"Grady, where did you take my bees?" she asked.

The people in the first few pews started to whisper, their murmurs rippling to the back of the church, where no one could see what exactly was going on, just that the bride was distracted.

"For Christ's sake, not now, honey," Grady hissed, and flapped his hand above his head to shoo the bees away.

But they weren't going anywhere and the more Sugar looked at her, the more she was sure that the big one at the front was Elizabeth the First. Of course it was impossible to be completely sure. It was impossible to be completely sure about anything. About knowing if you were marrying the right man, for example.

You are strong, her grandfather had told her, standing beside his hive. *And never let anybody make you feel like you are not.*

He'd been standing right by his favorite queen bee when he said that. Could it be that the queen had now somehow sought Sugar out to remind her of those words?

She felt panic rise deep in her chest beneath the lace of her beautiful bodice.

But the panic wasn't about what would happen if she married Grady Parkes. It was about what would happen if she didn't. She would hurt him, humiliate her family, alienate their friends and create a stir the likes of which she had spent much of her life avoiding.

The rector flapped his notes vigorously at the bees then, and him they took notice of, circling Grady in wider faster loops before heading once more around the pulpit, then flying out the sacristy window from whence they had come.

"Give me your hand, Cherie-Lynn," Grady said, as the guests

craned their necks and began to talk openly among themselves. "Stop fooling around."

Sugar was a good person; she always had been. She truly believed in doing unto others as she would have done unto her, just like Grampa Boone had always told her. If everyone did that, he said, the world would be a better place and Sugar wholeheartedly wanted the world to be a better place.

But something had gone wrong. In trying to fit in with what was expected of her, she'd lost touch with what was really important, deep down inside herself, a place that lately seemed as far away as the craters of the moon. She'd been there just a few days before, though; in the car with her bees flying along Ashley River Road with the Spanish moss waving her on. That was who she really was; a slightly out-of-kilter beekeeper who took the scenic route, not the quickest, who liked gardening in cutoffs more than cocktails in heels, who preferred the company of her bees to just about everybody in that church.

That was the real Sugar, not this flawless spectacle standing on an altar promising to love and obey a man of whom she was, if not afraid, then certainly unsure. And he might at times make her feel dizzy with love but he did not make her feel strong.

She felt the thrust of Etta's hand at her elbow. "For God's sake, pull yourself together," she said through gritted teeth.

"Does she need a glass of water?" Grady asked.

Standing there looking at him, feeling the lump in her poor bruised heart where the disappointment of love had already left its callus, Sugar could only think that becoming his wife was not going to make the world a better place, certainly not her world.

Being seconds away from marrying him, of course, was hardly the ideal time to reach such a conclusion. There was limited scope for her to work out exactly what to do. In fact, she really had only one choice.

So it was that in front of two hundred and fifty of Charleston's most privileged and popular citizens, Sugar Wallace turned and fled her own wedding.

Before Etta or Grady or the rector or anyone knew what was happening, before she could even whisper a heartfelt, "I'm sorry," she had kicked off her heels and bolted out the side door next to the altar. Once outside, she ran through the cemetery, into the courtyard of the church offices next door, and jumped over the fence at the back of the hall and into the car park beside it.

Sugar had grown up south of Broad Street. She and Miss Pickles had walked every one of the hidden side alleys of downtown Charleston a hundred times over, so she knew the back lanes and secret passageways of the scented city better than the people who put them there in the first place.

From the hall car park she dashed across St. Michael's Alley, then ran through an open gate and up the garden path beside an old grade-school teacher's ivy-covered cottage, emerging out of the rear of the property into the open green space at the end of Ropemaker's Lane.

From there, she spied another open backyard opposite. It was in the middle of a messy renovation and had no gate, just a muddy space full of rubble and building detritus behind the house the local pharmacist had just had repossessed because of his little problem with the ponies.

She stopped inside the crumbling brick fence just to catch her breath and again she heard them before she saw them: more bees! The buzzing was coming from the far corner of the yard, on the other side of a pile of rubble. She scrambled awkwardly in bare feet across the heap of broken bricks and yanked-out foliage, and there she found her grandfather's beehive, the one Grady had had taken away. The brood box and two supers were stacked neatly on top of each other, taken there, she imagined, by the workers creating the garden she would now never tend in Church Street.

A healthy collection of drones hovered at the entrance but she had no time to check and see if Elizabeth was in there. Instead, she pushed back her veil, hitched up her dress, hurried down the side of the half-renovated house and emerged out into Tradd Street. Her brother Troy's house was four doors down on the opposite side and his Explorer was parked in the driveway beside it, keys in the ignition, gate unlocked, as usual.

Climbing up into the cab, Sugar suddenly knew what she was going to do.

She reversed back up the street and into the driveway beside the pharmacist's house. She loaded her grandfather's beehive into the rear of Troy's Explorer; she jumped back in the cab, pulled out into Tradd Street, turned away from her brother's house and put her foot on the gas.

She yanked off her veil and threw it on the passenger seat in case any of the wedding guests were out on the street looking for her. She pulled the pins out of her hair as she drove up through the French Quarter, shaking out her curls and heading for the I-26, driving carefully around the tourists on bikes and the horse-drawn carriages full of wide-eyed visitors to this beautiful city that she had always loved so much.

The sunlight sparkled on the Cooper and she opened the window to breathe in that sharp, sultry salty air for one last time. It would have a hold on her forever, this southern city of her birth, squeezed between two mighty rivers, with its pretty houses, its lush gardens, its rich history and its proud past. But in the interest of her own ripe future, Sugar had to leave.

The freeway would be quicker, she reasoned, in case anyone came looking for her at her grandfather's cabin. She had to move fast.

As soon as she got there, she opened up the hive and there was the queen, looking exactly like the bee in the church—but how else would she look?

Sugar had no time to ponder this further as she took off her $5,000 wedding dress and hung it in the closet in the spare room, pulling on an old pair of jeans and some sneakers left behind from one of her visits.

She transferred the hive into the back of the old pickup, loaded up her grandfather's tools, a few spare supers, a bottle of Maker's Mark, the spare cash he always kept at the back of the bread bin, her favorite cup, her grandmother's prized collection of medicinal oils and a map from the spare room wall.

Then Sugar Honey Wallace and her bees hit the road.

They were about an hour and a half up the I-95 when she realized her hands were shaking on the wheel, her teeth were chattering.

She'd left Grady Parkes at the altar! The devastation, the scandal, the outrage—she was ruined.

And she was saved.

"Thank you, Elizabeth the First," she said, tears of relief sliding down her cheeks. "Thank you."

The queen passed this on to all her subjects and replied, in her own way, that the pleasure was all hers.

34TH

"That is some story," George admitted. "You just kept on going?"

"Yes, sir. I called, soon enough, to let Mama and Daddy know that I was OK, not that that particular piece of news seemed to please them, but it would have been rude not to. And I'd been rude enough."

"But how did you get by, Miss Sugar? To begin with, how did you ever get by?"

"I stopped in Virginia to see Jay, my best friend from high school—you met him that first day although he may have seemed a bit snippy. Anyway, he wasn't at the wedding owing to he'd been kind of run out of Charleston for refusing to stay in the closet, or that's how he saw it. I kind of figured he would understand, which he did. He even went back to pick up a few things for me. It's never as easy as just up and going. But I couldn't stay with him, he was still running away himself, and so the bees and I, well, we just followed our noses and kept following them, year after year after year."

It sounded like such a small thing when she put it like that—half a lifetime, almost, of arriving and leaving, with nothing but a few cases of honey and an address book full of grateful friends and neighbors to show for each stop. And Lord knew it hadn't always been easy, especially to begin with when she was full of shame and secrets and had yet to work out that fitting in wherever she landed felt better than not fitting in where she started out.

But despite that, she had never regretted leaving Grady at the altar. She regretted causing him pain, and humiliation, of course she did, because no one deserved that, and she did love him. She just didn't love him enough to be bullied into putting aside everything she liked about herself in order to make him happy. A life with bees and pockets of emptiness was and always would be hands down better than that.

"For what it's worth," said George, "I think you did the right thing. For you, at that time. You had to pay the price, sure, but the fact is, Sugar, it may just be about time you stopped paying it. It's pretty much the same for anyone who makes a big call like that. I know how you must have felt—I do: I ran away and never went back either. The only difference is, I had someone to remind me every day that I did the right thing. I had Eliza. And you had no one."

"I've never had no one, George," Sugar insisted. "I don't want you to think that I've been lonesome or sad or any of that jazz, because I haven't. I've had a good life. And I've made a lot of friends and seen a lot of places and done a lot of things and besides, there's always my bees."

"Strikes me those bees are no ordinary critters."

"I know; that's why I'm so worried that Elizabeth the Sixth has gone and lost her marbles. I don't want to lose her this soon. I'm only just getting to know her."

"Sugar, you're a smart woman in most respects. But you are blind in one."

"You think?"

"Those bees of yours are trying to tell you something now just like those other ones told you before."

"You mean the wedding bees? I'll never know if they were mine."

"Are you crazy? Of course they were! You think that was a coincidence? Your granddaddy told them to look out for you and that was what they were doing. They didn't want you to marry a man who was going to bully you and take away the things you loved. And you ask me, those bees are doing it all over again, but in reverse."

"Elizabeth is clever, George, but she's not that clever."

"You said it yourself, Sugar. Your bees saved you. Back then they saved you and I figure they're doing it again. Now you might want to think on that a while, that's all I'm saying."

Behind them a plume of bees rose up from behind the hydrangea bush and headed through the neighboring backyards to Sugar's own rooftop.

They had a lot to waggle about.

35TH

The following morning at precisely eleven, George knocked on the door of Sugar's apartment and informed her that he'd taken the liberty of inviting everyone in the building to one of her famous brunches and told them it was potluck.

"Goodness gracious, George," she said, letting him in. "Why?"

"Because I thought you might not have enough food."

"No, I mean why did you invite them?"

"To celebrate a special occasion," he said. "The special occasion of you not making a terrible mistake all those years ago." He was hanging on to the kitchen counter like he was in a boat on the high sea. "Such bold moves ought to be celebrated."

"It's not common knowledge," protested Sugar. "You're the only person I've told and I'm not ready for it to be out there. I will never be ready for it to be out there."

"Well, it's not exactly out there, Miss Sugar. I guess I intimated that it was more your birthday."

"My birthday is in the fall."

"You'll get to celebrate it twice then," said George. "Miss Sugar, I feel like I'm in your bedroom again and I have trouble with that."

"If you're going to ask people to my house without telling me, you'll have to live with the layout."

"I couldn't hardly ask them to Harlem. Or to Miss Ruby's. Seems to me she only eats celery. And there'll be nothing tasty at Miss Lola's. Mrs. Keschl lives on canned tuna, I know that for a fact, and so does Mr. McNally, so you don't want to celebrate your birthday in either of their apartments and poor Mr. Nate would probably have a heart attack if we all turned up at his place."

"You have a point," said Sugar. "And as it happens I like to entertain but I'm going to have to do it outside on the terrace so you'll need to sit out there if you don't want to be in my boudoir. What say I give you a job to take your mind off the whole height thing? You could set the table. I have these beeswax candles that we could sit on top of my silk magnolia blooms. What do you think?"

"I think New York looks like a different place up here," admitted George. "Sure is one fine-looking city from this angle. And you have such a beautiful garden, Miss Sugar. It's not like being up at the top of something at all."

"You're not on a pole, George. It's an apartment. Just like on the ground but higher. You were at Theo's, remember?"

"His rooftop was so big. I felt like it was harder to fall off it."

"Well, there it is right there. Look across at it."

"Across is good," said George, looking. "Down is bad, but I like across."

Indeed, he was getting a good view of Princess, who was currently romping around Theo's rooftop.

"So how are your bees today, Miss Sugar?"

"They're still here," she said, coming out with the table settings and following George's gaze. "That poor dog. Princess? He's going to have gender issues all his life."

"I'm no expert on dogs," George said, "being more of a parakeet person myself, but he seems pretty happy."

Princess proved this point by jumping in the air, barking and changing direction as though being chased by an imaginary friend.

Sugar ignored him and welcomed Nate, who was first to arrive and who came through the door bearing a mouthwateringly scrumptious-looking dessert sitting on an elaborate cake stand.

"Happy birthday, Sugar," he said, placing it carefully on the table in between the candles.

It was a giant, round, flat-topped meringue, finished with billows of thick glossy cream, topped with raspberries, fresh mint and shavings of dark chocolate.

"Oh my," Sugar and George said at the same time, as Nate beamed with pride.

"It's called a pavlova," he said.

"It looks like a beret," Ruby said, appearing behind Sugar, as pale as a ghost, bearing another cake box from Poseidon filled with baklava and finikia. "I think the Crankles are behind me."

"Would you ever get off my back about ironing my feckin' shirts?" they heard Mr. McNally roar.

"Would you get off your wrinkled old behind and iron them?" retorted Mrs. Keschl.

"Is fecking a curse word?" Sugar asked. Nate and Ruby shrugged but George said that even if it hadn't started out that way, it certainly seemed like it was now.

"Many happy returns," Mrs. Keschl said, handing Sugar an

inexpertly wrapped package. "It's a crystal honey pot. My sister-in-law gave it to me forty-nine years ago. Made in Slovenia."

"Why thank you, Mrs. Keschl, that's so sweet of you and I love that it's recycled."

"Recycled?" Mr. McNally fumed, passing over four tins of canned tuna and a jar of mayonnaise as he badgered Mrs. Keschl. "You're recycling something Maura gave you forty-nine years ago?"

"Maura never liked me, you know that," said Mrs. Keschl.

"Maura never liked anyone," answered Mr. McNally.

"Hold on there a minute," Sugar said as the pair sat at opposite ends of the table with George, Nate and Ruby in between them. She looked at Mr. McNally. "You know Mrs. Keschl's sister-in-law?"

"Maura? Of course I know her. She ruined the first eighteen years of my life."

"May I ask in what capacity?"

"In the capacity of being the screaming banshee that is my mother's firstborn while I had the misfortune to be the fourth."

George was the first to work out what this meant. "Maura's your sister, Mr. McNally?"

"Unfortunately for me, yes."

"And your sister-in-law?" George asked Mrs. Keschl.

"Also unfortunately for me, yes."

"Does that mean," continued George, "that you two used to be married?"

Mr. McNally and Mrs. Keschl raised eyebrows and shoulders in identical shrugs.

"To each other?" Sugar was incredulous.

"At the same time?" Nate was agog.

"No shit!" Ruby added. "Sorry, Sugar."

"He used to be much taller," Mrs. Keschl said, by way of an explanation.

"She used to be much nicer," said Mr. McNally.

Into the ensuing stunned silence stepped Lola and Ethan. The little boy held out his chubby arms and wiggled his fingers first in the direction of Mrs. Keschl and then at Mr. McNally, who changed seats to sit next to his ex-wife so they could both play with him.

"Did someone just fart?" Lola asked. "There's a very strange vibe out here. I made cupcakes but they didn't turn out the way I thought."

Purple cupcakes rarely did, was what everyone around the table thought, but Sugar was so touched that she had even attempted them that she knew she personally would find them delicious. "Mr. McNally was just telling us how he used to be married to Mrs. Keschl," she said.

"Yeah, right," said Lola, helping Sugar unload the uneven cupcakes from her plastic container and put them on a polka-dot platter, which improved their presentation enormously. "That certainly explains why they hate each other's guts."

"I'm not entirely sure what it explains," Sugar said. "Do you mind if I ask why you two still live so close to each other?"

The two old people looked at each other across Ethan's feathery blond head.

"I like it here. Why should I move?" Mr. McNally answered.

"Moving was never his strong point," Mrs. Keschl added. "And besides, why should I move? I own the building just as much as he does."

Little surprised George at his advanced stage in life but his jaw dropped perceptibly at this revelation.

"You two?" Lola laughed. "And I'm the Queen of Sheba."

"Why do you think the rents are so cheap?" Mrs. Keschl asked. "This is Manhattan."

"She'll only rent to people whose names she likes," Mr. McNally said. "In a song."

"Her name was Lola, she was a showgirl," Mrs. Keschl demonstrated tunelessly.

"Goodbye Ruby Tuesday," Mr. McNally added, not entirely the way the Rolling Stones might have imagined it.

"Sugar pie, honey bunch," Mrs. Keschl continued, looking at George. "What? You don't think I can pull off a little Motown?"

George said nothing, but returned his jaw to its rightful position.

"What about Nate?" Ruby asked.

"I thought it was Nat," Mrs. Keschl explained. "As in King Cole. But then when I saw he had red hair . . ."

"She's always had a thing for the red hair," said Mr. McNally.

"It's true," she said to Nate. "You have a beautiful head of hair. And looks to me like you've lost a few pounds. Now, how about we eat some of that big white hat?"

"First, please, if I could have your attention," George said, standing and addressing the astonished group. "I would like to thank our hostess, Miss Sugar Wallace, for her generosity and hospitality on this, the occasion of her special celebration."

"Hear, hear," said Mr. McNally.

"Miss Sugar," George continued, "I can only assume that it has been as much a pleasure for everyone else as it has been for me to have you enter into our lives. You have improved my health, increased my happiness and added to my good fortune, so I wish you all the very best for the next year and hope it brings all these things to you too."

Her friends stood and raised their glasses to toast her and, despite her embarrassment at having them there on what amounted to false pretenses, Sugar realized that she felt better than she had in a long time. But no sooner had she thought that than happiness moved further out of her grasp—along with her bees, who chose that very moment to again rise in a thick menacing plume from out the front of their hive. From there they formed a neat round cloud above the brunchers' heads, where they hovered, as if to make a point, before stretching out and moving slowly but surely back to Theo's rooftop sculpture.

Sugar's guests watched, speechless, as Theo himself appeared on the rooftop just as the bees settled on the plump left breast of his Fernando Botero.

Princess went berserk, running in excitable circles, barking at the bees and at Theo, who looked up and saw them all staring at him.

"Is that Theo?" Ruby asked, leaning over the railing and waving.

"The guy who flipped out at your last party?" Lola asked.

"The cute one?" asked Mrs. Keschl.

"Cute is for chimpanzees," said Mr. McNally. "Although to be fair I don't have the right glasses on."

"Are the bees running away from home?" asked Lola. "Because that would be weird."

"They're not running away from home," Nate said. "They're absconding."

Even George forgot his fear of heights long enough to move over to the railing and watch the spectacle. But it was he who first noticed that Sugar was not among them; rather she was sitting all alone at her table laden with lopsided cupcakes, cans of tuna, jars of honey and Nate's beret-like meringue.

Tears streamed silently down her face.

"Hey there, Miss Sugar," he said, coming to stand behind her, placing both large, strong hands on her shoulders.

"What are you crying for?" Lola asked. "At least your business isn't going down the drain."

"You think this birthday is bad?" said Mrs. Keschl. "Try turning sixty-eight."

"It's not that," Ruby said, slipping in next to Sugar and resting her small pale hand next to George's. "She doesn't care about that."

"Shush now, Miss Sugar," George said. "Everything's going to be all right."

"She's crying because the bees absconded?" Lola asked.

"No," said Nate, standing on the other side of George, wanting to help but not knowing how.

"It's where they absconded to," said Ruby. "It's Theo."

Sugar's face was in her hands, her shoulders shaking.

"Ah, well, now," said Mr. McNally. "That's a different state of affairs all together."

"Always with the comforting phrase," Mrs. Keschl said,

elbowing him so that he moved closer to Sugar, she moving closer with him.

"Cwying," said Ethan, putting on his own sad face and reaching his wriggling fingers out toward Sugar. "Cwying."

Sugar kept her face in her hands, the tears still falling.

"Please," she said. "I don't mean to be rude but I think I'm indisposed. You should all come back another time."

Ruby and Nate looked at each other, the arguing elderlies shrugged, Lola rolled her eyes and Ethan patted her leg.

"Miss Sugar," said George. "We don't think you're rude, but I'm not sure that we're going anywhere either."

Ruby leaned a little closer, and Nate awkwardly rubbed her back, just below her neck.

"I'm fine," she wept. "Just fine. I need to be alone for a bit is all." She took out her handkerchief and wiped at her face, although the tears would just not stop falling.

"You know helping other people is all very well," George said tenderly, "but comes a point in life when you have to accept a little help for yourself."

"I don't need help," Sugar said. "There's nothing wrong. I'm good. Truly. Please, eat some of Nate's pavlova."

Her friends looked from one to the other, at a loss, but George was unfazed.

"I would hate more than anything to risk embarrassing you when you have shown me nothing but kindness and respect," he said. "But for that same reason I am going to tell you, right here in front of all these fine people who care about you so much, that you are not fine, Sugar. You're hurting, and you're hurting because you're closing yourself off from one of life's richest and most basic human experiences and you cannot do that and expect to be fine. It just doesn't work that way."

"I have not closed myself off from anything," Sugar said. "I know what you're talking about. And I have not closed myself off from that. I absolutely have not."

"He's talking about love," whispered Ruby.

"Oh boy," said Lola.

"He's talking about Theo," Ruby said directly to Sugar. "Theo loves you. He really loves you, Sugar."

The torrent of longing that she had been trying so hard to keep dammed up inside her finally unleashed itself. "But he's allergic to bees," she cried. "And I can't live with that. My bees have stuck with me through thick and thin and I can't knowingly risk them doing something terrible to someone I may or may not care about."

"You have to admit she throws good parties," Mrs. Keschl said to Mr. McNally. "More interesting than most."

"Miss Sugar," George said, "your bees keep going to Theo's house and not stinging him. Isn't that telling you something? It's not how he feels about the bees; it's how the bees feel about him. It's time, Miss Sugar, to put the past behind you. You're not scared of knowingly risking his life, it's your own life you're afraid of."

"I can't do it," Sugar wept. "I just can't."

"Isn't that called a defeatist attitude where you come from?" Nate asked, loud and brave for him. "That's what you told me when I didn't go for the job at Citroen."

This slowed Sugar's tears as she hiccuped, gaining a few extra breaths. "I was just upset because I thought it was the right thing for you, honey. You'd make such a great pastry chef."

"It's the same thing," said Ruby. "It's the same thing as us thinking Theo would be the right thing for you."

"I'll do it then," Nate said boldly. "I'll find a job there if you go for Theo."

George smiled at him, and Nate stood a little straighter and smiled back.

"What's it to y'all if I do or if I don't?" Sugar asked, looking around them, her eyes filling with tears again. "I don't see why it has to be such a major referendum."

"Here we are with the democracy again," said Mrs. Keschl. "Just get off your tush and go get the guy."

"But you said yourself boyfriends just squash the joy of living out of you. You said you wouldn't do it again."

"What do I know?" Mrs. Keschl argued. "I live down the stairs from my nincompoop of an ex-husband! If I truly didn't want to see his ugly mug at least once a day I'd move to one of our other buildings."

"You have other buildings?" Lola's mind was set to blow.

"You want to see my ugly mug?" asked Mr. McNally.

"But you don't get along with each other," said Sugar. "You're always hollering."

"Me and Hannah, we have our differences," said Mr. McNally.

"But that doesn't mean there's no spark," agreed Mrs. Keschl.

"Hannah?" Lola repeated. "Wow. I never thought about you having a first name let alone a spark."

"Could you stop hollering at me?" Mr. McNally asked his ex-wife.

She shrugged. "Could you take me dancing?"

"Name the day and give me time to get new lifts."

"Then yes, Jimmy. I'll stop hollering at you."

"This is like the weirdest brunch," said Lola. "Especially since no one is even drinking anything."

"There's a bottle of Maker's on top of the refrigerator," Sugar said. "I think I could use some, on the rocks, half a teaspoon of my California gold, a squeeze of lime and some fresh mint, if you don't mind making it."

"I'll do it," said Nate, scuttling to the kitchen.

"Count me in," said Mrs. Keschl.

Lola, too, raised her hand for a drink. "I think romance is highly overrated," she said, "but if you do end up getting married, I think Ethan would make an awesome page boy."

"If I end up getting married?" Sugar blew her nose. "Listen, I appreciate what you're trying to do, honestly, it's real touching, but it's not as easy as—"

"I'll do something," Ruby said quietly. "If you let Theo love you, I'll talk to the shrinks. For you. I'll do it. For you and Theo. So I can be the one in the story to say I knew it, that we all knew it, that we were in the room with you and we all knew that one day you would be together forever even though Theo was allergic to bees and bees were what you cared about most in the world."

"Oh, honey," Sugar said. "The bees are what I've cared about the longest. Y'all are what I care about the most."

"So let's eat some of this big white hat," said Mr. McNally.

"And then we'll go and get the bees," said Nate.

"And put poor Mr. Theo out of his misery," added George.

Sugar rose slowly from the table. "I don't know what to say."

"Just say you'll do it," suggested Lola.

Sugar fixed her with a long, thoughtful look. "I will not promise anything about Ethan being a page boy because there is not going to be a wedding," she said, "but if I go over there would you at least consider opening your balloon shop in the morning and keeping it that way till nighttime at least for four or five days of the week?"

"Like that would ever work," said Lola. "But OK. Whatever."

36TH

"Has it ever occurred to you that your bees are trying to tell you something?" Theo asked without preamble after opening his apartment door to Sugar, with Nate and Ruby standing shyly behind her.

"It hadn't," said Sugar.

"Until now," said Ruby, placing her bony hands on the small of Sugar's back and pushing her into the room. Nate reached in behind her and pulled shut the door, leaving Sugar standing inches away from Theo inside.

"I am so sorry for such rudeness," Sugar said. "You must think I—" But before she could even work out exactly what it was that he must think, the last fifteen years of trying so hard not to have quite such a broken heart got the better of her. She felt frightened and cornered and in her confusion all she could do was stand there flapping her hands, gasping for air like a fish on a sun-scorched dockside.

"I have tea," Theo said, and led her gently to his big leather couch, Princess at his heel. "And I have honey—I got it from the Union Square greenmarket. It's rooftop honey, like yours. I would have come to Tompkins Square and got some from you but

270

I thought you might throw it at me. I've been trying all different sorts and I think I'm developing quite a taste."

She sat, still gasping and near dying of humiliation, as Princess rested his chin on her knee and gazed up at her while Theo rustled around in the kitchen.

"Did you know there's a drink in Africa called a dawa, which is just gin, fresh lime and honey? Dawa means 'magic potion' in Swahili, which I think would probably be a fairly honest interpretation of something involving just gin and honey. Not that I'm suggesting you should have one now. Now is tea time. I know that. Here, try this." He sat down beside her on the sofa and watched her as she tried to calm her breathing and sip her drink.

"I'm so sorry for all this carrying on," she finally said. "My mama taught me never to cry in front of men because it reduces their testosterone and I've just cried in front of three of them, four if you count Ethan."

"Well, my mother taught me that men have too much testosterone," Theo answered. "So we're probably even."

"I just feel so embarrassed that my bees are causing such a commotion up there on your Fernando Botero."

"Anything that brings you here is not a commotion," Theo said.

"You talk like you know me but you don't," said Sugar. "There's a lot about me you don't know and trust me, you won't like it."

"Have you killed anyone?"

"Of course not!"

"Are you on a no-carb diet?"

271

"There is no such thing as no-carb. Truly, Theo, I'm from the South. It's like oysters. Be serious. I don't mean those sort of things. I mean other things. Real bad things."

"Sugar Wallace, do you have ugly toes?"

"As a matter of fact, they are not my best feature but the thing about toes is that they are very easy to keep covered if you're having a bad foot day."

"I have nearly a full-time job containing my nasal hair," admitted Theo. "And that's bad because it's on my face, and the front of my face at that."

It's such a nice face, Sugar thought, putting her drink down and taking a long hard look at it. In fact it suddenly seemed very familiar to her, given how little she had actually been around it and how hard she had tried to avoid looking at it.

But now there it was, just waiting for her eyes to rest on it.

She felt her butterflies start break-dancing in her stomach again and fought the urge to flatten them.

What if she let herself love Theo and he didn't love her back the right way, like Grady? She'd survived that, but only by going out of her way to make sure it never happened again. She didn't know if she could expose her heart to that again. She wasn't even sure she knew how to.

What she did know was that for the first time since Grady she was sitting with a man who made her pulse race, her cheeks color, her palms sweat and her head spin.

If love was a roller coaster, she was already on it.

George was right. She had to get on with the future. The worst that could happen was that Ruby would get help, Nate would get a better job, the Crankles would stop being cranky, and more than one person a week in this particular corner of the great big beautiful city of New York might be able to buy a balloon.

"I was engaged once but I ran away from my own wedding," she said. "I humiliated my fiancé, I disgraced my family, I abandoned my friends, I left my whole life and I have not been home ever since."

Theo took this in his stride. He had anticipated worse. "So you're on the lam?"

"On a limb more than a lam."

"Well, that was bad for you and your former fiancé and your family and your friends, and no doubt the wedding planner and all right, probably the caterer too, but it's not bad for me, Sugar. It got you here, didn't it?"

"I was only twenty," Sugar said wondering what it was about sympathy that made a person feel worse rather than better for getting it. "And I have to confess I really loved him, Theo, but he turned out to have different ideas when it came to loving me back and I turned out to have a mind of my own even though I didn't particularly see it that way at the time."

"I can be a real jessie," said Theo. "But I already love your mind the way it is."

"I heard that about you being a jessie," Sugar said. "But I'm not even sure what one is."

"It's like a big girl's blouse," Theo said.

"Well, that hardly helps!" Sugar said. "I'm in real trouble here, Theo. I don't like feeling the way I feel about you. My equilibrium is all over the place and it has been ever since I met you. And you ran out on me, Theo, and I understand that now, because of being allergic and all but I don't want to feel like that ever again. And those bees mean everything to me, which is why I'm so rattled that I can't get them to stick when they've stuck with me through all sorts. I just can't believe they would up and leave me for someone who's allergic."

"I've got the super-duper pen from Sweden, remember? And maybe they're not leaving you. Maybe they're coming to me."

"They came to Grady too and that did not turn out so well for anyone."

"Grady?"

"The last man I nearly married, not that I'm saying that I'm nearly marrying you. It was Queen Elizabeth the First who told me not to go through with it. At least I think it was her. And I think that's what she was saying. You know what? It's kind of complicated."

"So, your bees stopped you from getting married?"

"I believe so."

"And you listened to them? You believed in them?"

"Of course. I'm a beekeeper. That's what we do."

"All right then." Theo stood up and held out his hand. "Let's go up right now and see what the bees have to say about me."

"I will do no such thing, Theo. Grady wasn't allergic. The bees only riled him—a lot, mind you—but they could actually kill you. And that is just not a good foundation for a relationship."

"People deal with worse problems every day," Theo said, pulling her to her feet, regardless. "It's not like you love Celine Dion or anything."

"Why, of course I love Celine Dion. Who doesn't? There's nothing not to love: she's perfectly nice. Only a monster would not love Celine Dion. It's not like not loving the guy who bites the head off defenseless little birds."

"I like that guy!"

"Well, you see, Theo, we are not compatible at all. It's just hormones or pheromones or what are those other things that you get when you're running a marathon?"

"Endorphins," said Theo, as he guided her up the stairs and out onto his rooftop. "And anyway, we're communicating, aren't we? Communication is the key to any successful relationship, everyone knows that. Compatibility with insects never even gets a mention."

Holding tight to Sugar's hand, he pulled her right over to the sculpture, whose generous bust was crawling with Elizabeth the Sixth and her subjects.

"Please, Theo," Sugar begged, trying to pull him back. "Don't."

"Sugar Wallace, you need to know that I am more sure about you than anything else I have ever been sure about in all my life and I can't think of a better way to demonstrate it."

He got down on one knee then, his head perilously close to the sculpture's moving bee brassiere and, as he did, to Sugar's horror, Elizabeth the Sixth rose from the other bee bodies and hovered above them, until one by one hundred by one thousand they all lifted off the Fernando Botero and formed a thick black ribbon in the air behind him.

"Get up, Theo, please," Sugar pleaded. "Let's go inside. We can talk about it there."

But Theo stayed where he was as Elizabeth the Sixth led the moving band of her subjects in a circular banner above his head, like a hologram halo. "No," he said, sweating slightly but firm. "I will not go inside. You think these bees are what stand between you and me and our future happiness but I am here to show you that this is not the case."

"Do you even have your pen thing?" Sugar asked. "What should I do? If you get stung—what should I do?"

"I will not get stung," said Theo; and indeed the queen and her cohorts did not appear to be getting any closer to him. "I will not get stung any more than I already have been, Sugar. But even if I do—you know what? We all get stung one way or the other. We can't hide away for fear of the same thing happening again."

"We can! That's exactly what we should do! You especially! Please, Theo—get up."

"I will not get up until you say you will marry me."

"I don't even know you!"

"I could make you happy."

Kneeling awkwardly next to a rooftop nude, surrounded by bees that could kill him, he seemed like the person least in charge of anyone's happiness. Yet she could see in those blue, blue eyes of his that unswerving certainty, the tenderness that rattled her bones, the desire that echoed in her shivers.

"Theo, I'm really scared."

"I know you are. But if you agree to marry me I will not be stung to death right here in front of all your friends watching from outside your apartment and you will not have to carry that guilty burden to your grave."

Sugar turned to see her friends waving at her from her own rooftop.

"What is this—International Blackmail Day?"

"It's not blackmail if you really want to say yes but are just too polite."

"I'm not too polite. I'm the right amount. Theo, please. The bees are not themselves; I can't speak for their actions."

"So you do want to say yes?"

"No! I most definitely don't, Theo, but maybe . . ."

"But maybe?"

"But maybe, OK, just hang on a moment here. Maybe if you agree never to ask me to marry you again, I will go out for dinner with you."

"Do you promise?"

"Do you?"

"I do."

"Then yes, I do too."

As she uttered the words, Elizabeth the Sixth swept her faithful followers up high into the air above both of them, away from Theo, away from his rooftop, up over toward the treetops of Tompkins Square Park and then back on a victory lap, swirling them eventually back down onto the sculpture and settling them in the crotch of the Fernando Botero.

On the neighboring rooftop, Mrs. Keschl, Mr. McNally, Nate, Ruby, George, Lola and even Ethan cheered.

37TH

Thanks to the new glasses Sugar had insisted Mrs. Keschl buy, she was spring-cleaning.

Without them she'd had no idea how much grime had gathered in how many places in her apartment. With them, she couldn't move without her slippers starting a dust storm or a cobweb catching her eye.

She'd found things in her refrigerator that had been there since the nineties and was just tasting a spoonful of something bright yellow and spicy from a jar she could not remember ever seeing before when she heard a knock. Thinking it might be Sugar with more cookies, or candles, or a jar of honey or a soothing cream for her roughened elbows, she shuffled over and pulled the door open.

It was Mr. McNally in his Sunday best, holding a portable cassette player.

"Oh," said Mrs. Keschl.

She was wearing her frumpiest cleaning smock, a pair of holey pantyhose, an old scarf tied roughly around her unbrushed hair and no lipstick. (She'd given up on it; it traveled too far into the canyons of her wrinkles.)

But when Mr. McNally looked at her, on this particular occasion, he saw none of that. All he saw was the seventeen-year-old girl that he had spotted right outside on Flores Street so many years before and wooed with a single red rose. She could have been wearing a sack and he wouldn't have cared. In fact, she pretty much was, and he didn't.

Hannah Keschl was slowly bringing the joy back to his life no matter how synthetic her ill-fitting frock.

And despite being on the back foot, feeling thoroughly sprung, with a spot of something yellow on her nose and a ringing in her ears she'd had for two years now, Mrs. Keschl could tell this. Something about the look in his eyes told her she need not retreat to the safety of the barbed comments that had hidden her true feelings for so many years. "Jimmy McNally," she said instead, as if she was wearing the finest furs and dripping with diamonds, "what brings you to my door at this hour of the day?"

It was, after all, only seven in the morning.

"Hannah Keschl," he said, a familiar twinkle in his eye, "I would very much like the pleasure of the next dance."

He fumbled with the cassette player, the apartment filled with music, and it occurred to her that other than the TV, there had been no sound like that in her home for a long, long time.

"'Sixteen Candles,'" she said, feeling tears well up in her eyes. It was the first song they had ever danced to.

"I got new lifts," Mr. McNally said. "Just like I said. So may I come in?"

Mrs. Keschl nodded and he swept past her, placed the cassette recorder on top of the television, then turned and held out his arms. She stepped into them, without a moment's hesitation, and they danced, slowly, around the room.

"Remember, Hannah, when you were my teenage queen?"

"That, yes," she said. "Why I bought three jars of Thai curry paste I couldn't tell you."

"You're still a good dancer, you know that?"

"I could say the same about you. You been practicing all these years?"

"Not even once. And you?"

"Never."

She rested her tired head on his shoulder. "You stopped the drinking, Jimmy? Is that true?"

"The day you threw me out. Not a drop since."

"I only threw you out—"

"I know, Hannah, I know. I can't in all conscience blame you, although I did. But not anymore. You would have been mad to keep me. I was a terrible husband and I'm sorry."

It had taken twenty-seven years, but there it was. An apology. Never mind dancing, Mrs. Keschl was floating.

"We fit together," Mr. McNally said. "So help me God, I'd forgotten."

So had she, but it was all coming back now. "Shut up and dance, Jimmy," she said.

He shut up. And they danced.

38TH

Theo and Sugar dated, just like normal people only slower.

He bought her heart-shaped boxes of candy and living plants for her rooftop and sent her cards, one every day by U.S. mail, each with a handwritten message.

Can't wait to see you tonight, the first one said.

I love your laugh, read the second.

Sorry for spilling ketchup on your dress, came the third.

She made him pork chops with honey mustard sauce and her favorite date-and-honey nut loaf and a fetching gingham jacket for Princess, who ate it the moment they turned their back on him.

Her heart had been right to take the front seat on this particular roller coaster. The more time she spent with Theo, the more perfect for her he seemed.

The only stumbling block involved the big double bed that took up half of her apartment.

She very much wanted Theo to throw her on top of it and do his worst with the hospital corners but she still was too scared to let herself go that far. It wasn't that she was worried in a getting-back-on-the-horse sort of a way. Every experience after Grady

281

had been an improvement, and she thought she could more than hold her own on that front. But sleeping with Theo was going to be the most intimate obstacle to overcome and she didn't want it to be a letdown.

The man sucked the breath out of her just with his presence, electrified her with his touch and, while she admitted now to being crazy in love with him, a tiny part of her—the scarred, vulnerable part—was still looking for loopholes. A tiny part of her wanted to hold on to the old familiar prospect of moving on and not taking anyone else with her.

Then she met his niece and came to the conclusion, once and for all, that moving on might not be an option.

Frankie and I cordially invite you for a picnic tonight at dusk in the Sixth Street Community Garden, read the handwritten card of the day.

Sugar brought her honey pie, Theo a nice bottle of rosé, plus bagels and lox from Russ & Daughters, and Frankie a dwarf lilac in a terra-cotta pot. "For your bees," she said, handing it over. She was a sophisticated girl with pink streaks in her hair. "I looked up what they like."

"You and I," said Sugar, "are going to get along just fine."

Another couple with two younger children came and sat nearby, bringing their own picnic of meatball subs and apple pie, and a pet rabbit with a Happy Birthday balloon tied to its harness.

"Now there's an idea that Lola could develop," Sugar said. The balloon shop had been open more often in recent times, but the people going in and out of it still did not strike Sugar as likely to be after balloons.

"Although I think Princess wants to eat the rabbit," Frankie pointed out.

The picnicking mother looked up and smiled conspiratorially at Sugar and she realized that she, Theo and Frankie themselves looked like a regular family. Tears tickled the backs of her eyelids. She'd kissed all thoughts of a regular family away so long ago. But now, as she sat in the last of the dappled evening sun, Princess panting on one side, Theo and Frankie playing cards and ribbing each other on the other, she opened her heart to all the possibilities.

She thought of her brothers, Ben and Troy; of their wives and the daughters she had never seen; of her once-proud father and her disappointed mother. Of the streets south of Broad where she had roamed with Miss Pickles as a girl, and where she had fled the prospect of a miserable life with Grady.

She thought of all the years she had missed out on being part of that, and then she looked at Theo, his dimple permanently in place, his broad shoulders more than willing to take on her worries as well as his own and she felt something else, something magical, like champagne bubbles dancing in her mouth, shooting hope into all her farthest points.

It was time.

"You should come back to my place after you've taken Frankie home," she whispered in his ear when the two of them dropped her off on Flores Street.

Frankie had never been taken home so quickly.

When Theo got to her apartment, Sugar had candles flickering gently all around the room: ylang-ylang, rose, vanilla and orange oil. It was a beautiful night, the twinkling lights of lower Manhattan emerging from the dusky pink sunset, the buzz of the city playing in the background like a distant orchestra.

Theo was a patient man, he would have waited for Sugar forever, but he could tell by the look on her face the moment she opened the door to him that he would not have to. She pulled him inside, over to the bed, then without saying a word unbuttoned his shirt, turned and held up her hair so he could unfasten her dress. It slid to the floor, leaving her bathed in nothing but the trembling light of the moon and her candles.

"I'm ready to show you my secret freckle," she said, and so she did, and a few more things besides.

On top of the world of Manhattan's Alphabet City, Theo and Sugar made tender, gentle, perfect love. He did not let her down. She did not tire of finding out how much.

"It does look like George W. Bush; you're right," Theo said of the freckle, on the third morning in a row of waking up next to her.

He was stroking her flat belly, looking at the blotch above her hip bone, while she was watching her bees out through the French doors, buzzing happily in front of their hive. They'd continued to abscond on a daily basis until now.

"I guess Elizabeth the Sixth really does like you," she said. "Not only has she failed to kill you, but when you stay here, so does she."

"I am adorable," Theo agreed. "All the insects say so."

He pulled her close and kissed her again.

Understandably wary of lawyers, Sugar had changed her tune when she found out Theo now worked for a nonprofit organization that helped house homeless and low-income New Yorkers.

"But when George fell on you and you thought he was homeless, you never even stopped your phone call," she said. "I saw it with my own two eyes."

"I never thought he was homeless," Theo said. "He had clean fingernails and he smelled of Old Spice."

"That's what I said!"

"And the phone call was me arranging emergency financing for a shelter that was about to be closed in the Bronx. We kept that from happening, thank you for asking."

He had spent a long time working with very rich people, he told her, and for a while he even was one. That was when he met Carolyn, the woman who became his wife, and who to begin with ticked all the boxes.

"But then I started to wonder if the boxes had been on someone else's list," he confessed.

She lived to party while he soon tired of it. She slept late but he liked to get up early. She didn't eat much and he ate like a horse. She loved the Hamptons and he always felt like an alien there. Carolyn brought out a side of Theo he didn't know he had nor ever wanted to see again.

He'd started to turn his life around, he said, about a year after his divorce, when he woke up one morning and realized he didn't have a single friend. "And I'm a nice guy. Although back then— you might find this hard to believe—I was a bit of an arsehole."

"You know, I have a problem with cursing," Sugar said. "But I don't find it that hard to believe. Although I have to say it sounds better in Scottish."

"My mother had a problem with cursing. She said it showed a lack of imagination."

"She sounds truly wonderful, Theo. No wonder you miss her so much."

"I wish you could have met her. Never a penny to her name but the original heart of gold."

"She must have been very proud of you."

"She was in the beginning, and she would be again now, but if she had seen me in the middle when I was squandering my hard-earned cash on five-hundred-dollar ties and bottles of Krug, she would have kicked me into the middle of next week."

"You're lucky to have had a mom like that," Sugar said, unable to hide the wistfulness in her voice.

"Yes," Theo said, treading delicately around the subject of Sugar's own family. "And I'm even luckier to have you."

Sugar in turn could not believe her own luck, although her ability to completely trust it was still a work in progress.

"Now don't be mad," Theo said one morning after bringing her breakfast in bed (thick slices of sourdough toast with fresh farm butter and Idaho honey—his favorite). "But I have someone I want you to meet."

Her heart sank. "Why would I be mad? You're not still married are you? Or gay? Or swapping yourself every day with your identical twin brother, also called Theo?"

"Wow," Theo said, sitting on the edge of the bed. "No. None of the above."

He took the toast away from her again and held both her hands in his.

"Nothing is going to go wrong between you and me," he said.

"Ever. Well, maybe the normal things like I'm scared of your bees and you're scared of my shirts but there are no dirty secrets I haven't already told you. There is no disaster lurking around the corner. I have nothing that can hurt you. I love you, Sugar, with all my heart and soul, and there is nothing that can change that, I promise."

She kissed him.

"Although if I was going to keep a secret," he said, "an identical twin brother with the same name would be a really good one."

They went for lunch at a new place on the Square to meet Theo's friend. She arrived not long after they were seated, a plump blond woman swathed in layers of expensive black cashmere shawls squeezing her way between the tables toward them.

Theo stood as she approached.

There was something about her that was familiar, yet Sugar couldn't quite place her. She had a Birkin bag and wore an enormous diamond ring. She did not look like an Alphabet City regular.

"Rosalie Portman," Theo said, as she checked the chair for dirt before gingerly lowering herself onto it. "This is Sugar Wallace."

Portman?

"Ruby's mother," said Rosalie.

Sugar could barely hide her surprise. Ruby painted her mother as cool and controlling and Sugar had imagined an Upper East Side version of Etta. But this woman was not cool. She was flustered. Her expertly colored blond hair was refusing to stay swept up; she had flushed cheeks and beads of sweat on her top lip. She was nervous.

"I met Rosalie here when I was looking for you," explained Theo. "All those months ago before the ice cream."

"You met here in the café?"

"Yes," said Rosalie. "I come here quite a bit."

"All the stalkers do," Theo said.

Rosalie laughed and her face lit up like a Paris streetlight, full of charm and warmth. "Yes, Theo was the first person to make me feel good about spying on my own daughter." She smiled at him. "In fact, he was the first person I told."

"You've been spying on her?"

"It doesn't sound very nice but—look, I know you've become good friends," she said, "so I'm assuming she's told you that we have a difficult relationship."

"I just tell her mothers always care for their daughters, even if it isn't always obvious."

"Thank you," said Rosalie. "That's very diplomatic. I appreciate it—and of course I care for her. I love her to distraction in fact but . . ." She lost her composure briefly, then wrangled it back. "You're obviously aware that Ruby suffers from anorexia."

Ruby never called it that, but Sugar nodded.

"I still find it hard to believe. She was such a beautiful little girl. Here, I have a photo." She opened her purse and pulled out a picture of Ruby as a chubby preschooler with long curly blond hair, holding a giant multicolored lollipop and smiling. She looked like an angel.

"And here's one of her when she was older, just before it began." In this one, Ruby was wearing jeans and a loose-fitting shirt. Her hair was thick and fell in huge glossy curls over her shoulders but the smile was gone: there was a familiar sort of distance in her eyes. Her face was round and her body was soft and feminine.

"Oh," said Sugar, swallowing the lump in her throat, because she didn't bear much resemblance to the Ruby she knew now. "She is beautiful."

"Isn't she?" Rosalie replied. "Nothing I ever said could convince her of it. She was teased at school. I made the wrong choice there, I think. And girls that age can be so cruel. I did the best I could but she blames me. I know she does. I love to eat, to entertain, to cook, to shop. It's the way my mother was too; it was a passion that we shared. But Ruby thinks I made her fat."

"She doesn't look fat to me," said Theo, scrutinizing the photo.

"Nor me. That was taken just after her thirteenth birthday. I had just remarried and actually that had gone quite smoothly but there had been this constant trouble at school. She was bullied, I suppose, and then she just stopped eating. For a while she seemed to actually like the attention. Then she got worse and worse."

"It must have been scary," Theo said, handing the picture back.

"To begin with I thought we could deal with it but then I realized it went so much deeper. Sometimes it felt like she was doing it to hurt me, to punish me for loving food so much by starving herself. But other times I could see that she really didn't want to be like that, that she was trapped, and angry."

"I'm so sorry, Rosalie," Sugar said.

"I'm her mother, I can take it," said Rosalie. "But it's a very hard disease for a family to live with. My husband has two sons and it was very frightening for them because they loved Ruby; she was such a kind, loving little girl, but the disease stole her away from us all." She turned her face to hide her tears.

Sugar reached out and squeezed her arm. "She is still kind and loving," she said. "I see that."

"Thank you," Rosalie said, attempting a weak smile. "And I'm so sorry. You probably think I'm a monster. It is not natural to send your daughter out into . . ."

"The wilds of Alphabet City and beyond?" suggested Theo, with just the right levity.

"My parents wouldn't let me come anywhere near here when I was growing up," admitted Rosalie. "They used to say Avenue A was all right, but B was for brave, C was for crazy and D was for dead."

"Flores Street is a very safe place for Ruby to be," Sugar said.

"I know," said her mother. "And I can see that she's happier now than she was at home, but she still has anorexia."

"She has promised to seek help," Sugar said. "That's what she said, and I think she really is trying."

"Ms. Wallace . . . Sugar . . . I am very grateful to you for looking out for my daughter, but I know this disease far better than you, far better than Ruby herself, and she is most unlikely to survive it by 'trying' on her own. She needs very specific treatment and, while she would never take a referral from me, she may well take it from someone like you. Which is actually why I'm here. I was wondering if I could enlist your support."

Sugar breathed deeply. "I'm not sure, Rosalie. I understand, of course, that you want to help her but I would hate to feel like I'm going behind her back."

"I don't need to have anything to do with it. I've found a woman at a clinic on the Upper West Side—she's a holistic counselor but she's also a registered psychologist—and I think she could be worth a try. I've spoken to her and she sounds totally off-the-wall to me, which means Ruby will no doubt love her. And she has been getting results. So if you would just consider it . . ." She handed Sugar a business card. "That's all I ask. You could say you found her. She knows to bill me if Ruby comes to see her. She'll say she takes pro bono clients in special cases such as hers."

"You don't want to come and see Ruby yourself while you're down here?"

"I would, of course I would, but I don't think that will help her right now," Rosalie said. "All I want is for her to get better and I'm not part of that, not now, but I hope to be one day and until then I'll just wait and, well, I will watch. It's all I can do."

Sugar looked at the card in her hands and felt the lump in her throat again. "I don't think you're a monster," she said. "I think you're a good mom. And when Ruby gets better, she'll be able to tell you that herself, I'm sure of it."

Rosalie stood up, a resigned look on her face. "I sincerely hope so," she said. "Thank you, Theo, for arranging this. And thank you, Sugar. Is that your real name? I confess I find it a little . . ."

"Yes, my mother doesn't care for it, either," Sugar said.

"What does she call you?"

"I'm sorry to say, but I'm Sugar regardless."

Rosalie reached for her hand, and held it. "Don't be sorry," she said. "I can tell you're a good daughter too."

"If only she knew," Sugar said, as they watched her leave. "Not that my mama would ever spy on me. She doesn't even answer my letters."

Theo took her hand and kissed it. "Bless you," he said, "for being the only thirty-six-year-old in the world who still writes letters."

39TH

L ola and Mrs. Keschl were having challah French toast at the Odessa diner on Avenue A while Mr. McNally was with Ethan in the park. Both women liked the vinegary white wine that was served in the old diner and had just drained their first glasses even though it was barely eleven A.M.

"Should I call you Hannah?" Lola asked.

"No, you should not," Mrs. Keschl said.

"Good. Because that would be weird, right?"

"What is weird is that you have so many patrons going into your balloon shop and none of them are coming out with balloons."

"Oh, so this is a landlady thing?" Lola plonked down her glass and got ready to be defensive. "You going to read me the riot act? Jesus, I should have known."

"First of all," said Mrs. Keschl, "I chose you to live at 33 because I like your name and you and the kid needed a break. No! Don't interrupt. This is how it works. I still choose you to live there—do you hear me? I still choose you to live there, but if you're turning the basement into a den of iniquity, that has got to stop. Those are the rules."

"A den of iniquity? You mean, like, opium?"

"You can still get opium?"

"I don't know. I don't do drugs! And I'm pretty sure I don't do iniquity either! Not anymore. I'm a single mom, Mrs. Keschl. I'm just trying to get by."

"OK, but you're not selling balloons yet you have a lot of customers so perhaps you might like to tell me what you are doing down there."

"Promise not to freak?"

"I don't think I ever have before, so yes, I promise."

"Tattoos." Lola sighed. "I'm doing tattoos. And actually I'm pretty good at it but I don't even have a diploma or a license or anything; I just learned from my ex-boyfriend back in San Francisco. I started out doing one for this guy Rollo and then his friend Rex liked it so much he wanted one and all of a sudden people started coming to see me and so I started tattooing for money. I didn't know if it was illegal, I didn't know you were the landlady, I didn't—"

"Is this you freaking?" asked Mrs. Keschl.

"I'm sorry," said Lola. "But the balloon thing isn't working out."

"You do better than the psychic."

"She was a shit psychic," Lola said. "I went to see her once and she charged ten bucks to tell me I would face many challenges."

"And did you?"

"Yes, but *I* could have told *her* that. She should have said that I would have an idea to open a store right where she was sitting and it would be the dumbest thing I ever did."

"But if you could make everyone who got a tattoo buy a dozen balloons you could take us all to Florida for the winter," Mrs. Keschl said.

"They're just not a balloon-buying crowd."

"So why not turn it into a tattoo shop?"

Lola blinked.

"You goigeous goils want another top up here?" the Odessa's pint-sized waiter asked. "I got another vat of this stuff out the back we need to get rid of and you two are the only ones who can stomach it."

"But I don't even know if it's legal to tattoo people if you're not, I don't know, licensed or whatever," Lola said, ignoring him.

"We'll have one more each and then that's it," Mrs. Keschl told the waiter. "By the way, do you happen to know if you need a license to tattoo people?"

"My cousin, Walter, was working at Fioruccio's Meats in Jersey City one day," the waiter said, "and opened Hard Knox Ink Studio two blocks down the street the next. Took one visit from the Health Department and a hundred bucks."

"That was it? Are you sure?"

"He was better at sausages than tattoos, if you ask me, but he stays on the right side of the law. These days, anyway."

"I never thought to ask anyone," Lola said as he scuttled off. "You think I could do that? In the basement?"

"You already are," said Mrs. Keschl.

"What would I call it?"

"What's wrong with Lola's Balloons? Gives it an air of mystery. 'Lola's Balloons? But why am I here for a tattoo?' Like a speakeasy, that sort of thing."

"You're a genius, Mrs. Keschl."

"That I am not," she said. "But I'm OK." They looked out the window as across the road Mr. McNally took Ethan's hand and talked him through crossing the road to the diner. "I'm better than OK."

40TH

On Sunday Sugar enlisted Theo to help her out at the greenmarket. Her stall had become so popular that at certain times of the day she needed an extra pair of hands but also she just loved having him there.

Midmorning a woman in sweats pushed her way to the front and stood, hands on hips, looking at the two of them. "Well, looky here!" she said.

"Hello, ma'am, can I help you?"

"It's me!" the woman said. "Maria. Chocolate chip, two pints, remember? Hey, Minty," she called over her shoulder and Sugar saw an old man licking at a green ice cream in the background.

It was the pair from the day she had worked Marcus Morretti's ice-cream stand.

"So you two finally got it on, huh? And guess what? Since we met that day, Minty and I are walking buddies. Hey, Minty! The cute chick finally got it on with Gerard Butler here. See?"

Minty charged his ice cream. "They always go for the loons. I seen it a hundred times before," he called.

"Turns out he's not as loony as I thought," Sugar said to Maria. "And there's no pot or poetry either," she called back to Minty.

"Excuse me, could I please have some of that Rhode Island honey?" A slim young woman was pointing to Sugar's stocks. "My boyfriend's mom is from Rhode Island. Maybe she'll like that. She certainly doesn't like anything else."

"Mothers-in-law," said Maria. "Can't eat 'em, can't shoot 'em."

"Can't shut them up for more than thirty seconds either," said the man standing next to her.

"So spit it out. You two getting married?" Maria asked Sugar. "Did he ask you properly this time?"

"I'm not allowed to ask her," Theo said, handing another customer a tester of elbow cream.

"But you love him, right?" Maria was looking at Sugar. "Of course you do. Look at the two of you. Why won't you let him ask you?"

"You know I would much rather talk about honey," Sugar said.

"Apologies in advance," Maria said to her. "But I'm a real committee person and I can't let this one go." She turned to face the other shoppers. "Hands up who wants to hear about honey?" she asked, at which no one raised a single hand. "And hands up who wants to hear about why she won't marry the cute guy in the bum shirt?" Everyone put their hands up.

"Dish the dirt, sweetheart. The people have spoken."

Sugar could not deny how happy she was with Theo, happier than she had ever been, freer than she had ever been and it wasn't that she didn't want to be Theo's wife. It was just that . . .

"I'm not ready," she said, feeling feeble, but Theo put his arm around her and kissed her delicately on the temple because he knew exactly what she was and what she wasn't.

"OK," said Maria, watching this. "Now I get it. You got your own mother-in-law thing, right?"

Sugar looked away, Theo bit his lip and Maria shook her head.

"Those bitches," she said. "Mine comes from Hoboken so I'll take the honey that comes from nowhere near there and I'll tell you this for nothing: she's not going to get a drop of it."

Sugar was unusually quiet for the rest of the day and not particularly interested in Theo's duck pancakes that night. She wanted to go to bed early, citing a headache.

"A penny for your thoughts?" Theo asked, tucking her in. He could not bear to see her sad.

But Sugar could not put her thoughts—let alone her feelings—into words. She loved Theo more than she had ever loved anyone or anything and that was just getting better and better as the days flew by. But inasmuch as he had awakened the sweetest parts of her, he had stirred up a fair share of sludge as well.

Theo, rightly, felt Maria's spiel at the greenmarket had further agitated this particular swamp. "Well, if you want to know what I've been thinking," he said, tracing the outline of her jaw with his fingers, "it's that I would like to meet your family."

Sugar sat up in the bed.

"Trust me, Theo. You most certainly would not."

"It doesn't have to mean anything, Sugar, in the strict formal sense of meeting a potential mother-in-law, because I know your feelings on that. But they're your last missing piece."

That was all he said—that they were Sugar's last missing piece—and she knew instantly that he was right.

"Oh, but it's been so long and I would be so . . ."

"Scared?"

To her dismay, Sugar started to cry.

"You can't let them haunt you, sweetheart," Theo said, pulling her into him, holding her, rocking her.

"They don't haunt me, exactly," Sugar said as she wept. But that was exactly what they did do.

"Let's go this weekend, to Charleston," Theo said. "Let's get this over and get on with our lives. Don't worry, Sugar. Everything will be all right. I promise you."

One of Ruby's bridal couples from the *Times* had married, Sugar recalled, on just such a promise. Theo had no way of knowing it was going to be all right, but he believed it anyway. "Do you really truly think so?" she asked, getting a clean handkerchief from under her pillow.

"I really truly do," he answered. "I'm not scared of them and there's nothing they can do to hurt me so I can help you. We can do this together. Trust me, Sugar."

It felt so good to be in his arms, as though anything truly were possible, and she really did like having someone to trust. "All right then," she said. "Oh, my goodness gracious me. All right."

"You have no idea how happy you make me," Theo said, leaning in to kiss her.

"Hang on to that feeling," Sugar said. "You're going to need it once you meet my mama."

41ST

The moment the taxi crossed Broad Street and slowed down enough for her to open the window, Sugar took her first deep breath of Charleston air in fifteen years.

Oh, but it tasted good.

Her native city had lost none of its sparkle while she'd been away. It dazzled, like diamonds on velvet in God's highest-end jewelry store.

The vast Cooper River shimmered to their left, the sky an impossibly Venetian blue above it, Fort Sumter's island battalions a hazy silhouette in the distance. To their right, the pastel-painted Rainbow Row colonials winked behind the palmetto trees before East Bay Street opened out to reveal Charleston's grandest mansions standing four stories tall and proud as punch, their lush gardens and musical fountains hidden behind filigreed fences and ornate gates as intricate as iron cobwebs.

"There really is no other place like it." Sugar sighed, turning to Theo. "I swear I'd forgotten."

"It's sort of like a low-slung Paris," Theo agreed. "Only with better weather and more horses."

"And the jasmine," Sugar said. "The Confederate jasmine. Can you smell it?"

Theo took a dramatic sniff. "Can I what. Leaves that Yankee jasmine for dead."

He squeezed her hand. She'd hardly spoken on the flight down and, although she didn't look quite so sick now they were in Charleston, she was still as pale as the jasmine that indeed bloomed flirtatiously over nearly every gate, railing, doorway and streetlamp in sight.

The driver slowed to turn into a cobbled street heading away from the river.

"Excuse me, sir," Sugar said, "but would you mind taking us down to Battery Park first? My friend here has never had the pleasure of seeing the tip of our peninsula where the Cooper meets the Ashley and I'd like to show him on the way."

"That's where the American Civil War started, right over there," the driver said, slowing down and pointing at Fort Sumter. "Things never been quite the same since."

"The city sure is looking fine though," Sugar told him. "Y'all have done a good job of looking after the place."

"You been gone awhile, ma'am?" he asked, checking her out in the rearview mirror.

"A long while." She smiled.

"No matter," he said. "Once a Charlestonian, always a Charlestonian."

Theo elbowed her and grinned.

"Nobody ever feels wishy-washy about Charleston," Sugar said, but they were getting close to her parents' house and she was feeling sick with nerves.

"Number fifteen Legare Street, ma'am, that's what you said?" the taxi driver asked. "This one here? The white one?"

"Yes, sir, thank you," Sugar said. "This is it."

"The Wallace place?"

"Yes, sir."

"This your folks' house?"

"Yes, sir."

"Well, you must be the Buzz-off Bride!"

"I'm sorry?"

"Shee-yoot, it's good to meet you, Ms. Wallace. They still talk about you, you know."

"I'm sorry, what did you just call me?"

"Here, let me take those bags," Theo said, paying the fare and overtipping the driver to shut him up.

"Welcome home," he said, before climbing back in his car as he counted his cash.

"Did he just call me the Buzz-off Bride?" Sugar asked as they stood on the sidewalk.

"What a lovely home. You grew up here?"

"Theo, I just can't believe that all the while I've been gone they've been calling me the Buzz-off Bride. It's beyond embarrassing."

"Ah, come on. It shows a certain sense of humor, don't you think? It's better than being called the Heartbreaking Honey or the Wife-to-Flee."

"It is?"

"Um. Look at those lovely balconies!" They were looking up at a three-story white wooden mansion that ran sideways to the street with long porches spanning the length of each floor.

"They're called piazzas round here," Sugar said, peering into the expertly manicured garden only just visible through the fancy ironwork fence.

"It looks like a very neat cake," Theo said.

"A wedding cake," Sugar added drily. She looked nervously at her watch. "You know, on second thought I think maybe we should go and check in to the hotel first, before just crashing on in here. I always liked the Vendue Inn. It's cute. Not too flashy. And it used to have a rooftop bar."

"What do you mean 'crashing on in'?" Theo asked, stepping into the shade to escape the searing heat. "They're expecting us, aren't they?"

"About that," said Sugar. "I never actually did quite get around to telling them we were coming."

Theo pulled her into the billowing jasmine. "They don't know we're here?"

"I tried, Theo! I really tried. But every time I picked up the phone to call the number just flew right out of my head or I felt like upchucking or I saw myself packing my bags and running away to Peru and in the end I just thought better to come here and let the cards fall where they may even though it is the height of bad manners to turn up unannounced and you know how I feel about bad manners."

Theo looked at her sternly. "I always wanted to go to Peru," he said, and Sugar loved him so much right then that she forgot to be scared and just kissed him. How her grandfather would have approved of this man.

This was the moment her mother chose to return from the hairdresser. She honked the horn to get the riffraff away from the front of her house as she drove through the automatic gates, glancing disdainfully as she passed, then disappearing into the property.

Theo and Sugar stayed where they were.

"Was that her?"

"Uh-huh."

"Did she see you?" Theo asked.

"I don't know."

"Would she recognize you?"

"Don't mothers normally know their daughters?"

"Can she get into the house from the garage?"

"I don't know, the garage is new," Sugar said. "But she never did like to get her hair mussed up so I'm thinking yes she can. Theo, I have a bad feeling. I think we should go back to New York. Forget about this. If she didn't recognize me she'll be none the wiser. If she did recognize me then I guess she doesn't want to see me."

"Sugar, you promised to do this and, more important, you promised me grits for breakfast! I don't even know what that is but I'm not going back home without it. Listen to me; she is not my mother and I'm not scared of her. You want scary, you should come to Barlanark and meet my aunties. They will terrify the pants off you, and not in a good way. We're just being polite, apart from the whole not mentioning that we were dropping by thing."

At that, a big shining chestnut horse pulling a blissful-looking young couple in a white carriage trotted past them, its hooves beating out sharp cracks on the cobbles of Legare Street.

"Afternoon," said the carriage driver. "Sure is a beauty. Hope y'all enjoy it." He doffed his cap and the couple waved at them.

Sugar waved back. "Thank you and the same to you," she called. Polite, she could do.

"Come on," said Theo. "We're going in," and he strode to the front door and knocked robustly. "Just remember, we're adults," he said. "We've done nothing wrong. Well, me especially. Not that your mother knows about anyway."

Sugar heard the clicking of her mother's heels across the parquet floor on the other side of the door, then she felt the breath squeeze out of her as the door opened and there she was, looking exactly as she had that dreadful day fifteen years before, only this time wearing primrose, which she always favored because it did great things for her skin and her eyes.

"Cherie-Lynn," she said without a hint of a smile, looking Theo up and down. "And friend."

Theo was wearing a plaid shirt and shorts, quite restrained for him, but Sugar knew her mama would not look kindly on such attire.

"To what could I possibly owe this pleasure?" Etta asked.

"Sorry, Mama. Sorry not to call first."

"You're sorry for that?"

Sugar got her beauty from her mama, was Theo's first impression, but this woman did not strike him as having a heart of gold. She looked rich and mean, the opposite of his own mother, and he felt proud that Sugar had turned out the way she had despite that.

"This is Theo Fitzgerald," Sugar said.

"Delighted to meet you, Mr. Fitzgerald," Etta said, sounding anything but. "But really there's no need to stand outside like encyclopedia salespeople. Although for all I know you are encyclopedia salespeople. Please, come in."

They stepped into the house and followed her to the formal living room.

Etta had aged superbly: there was no question about that. Her long blond hair was swept back into a style that had never gone out of date, her makeup was perfect, her pale yellow suit the same size she had always worn and her heels, if possible, an inch higher.

She looked stunning. And if she had wrinkles, the room was either lit to downplay them or she had dealt with them surgically. She could have passed for Sugar's older, colder sister.

"Please, Mr. Fitzgerald, Cherie-Lynn, take a seat. Iced tea for you both? I'll see to it right away. Excuse me."

"Ouch," whispered Theo, after she left the room. "She's not going to make this easy."

"I didn't think for a moment that she would," Sugar said, getting off the sofa where she had been uncomfortably perched and going over to the grand piano, a new feature in the room since she'd last been there, covered with silver-framed photos.

She wasn't in a single one. There were separate ones of her mother and father together throughout the years, and of her two brothers as they sprouted from preppy little boys to preppy young men to preppy husbands and fathers.

"Oh, this is Troy's first wife, Marianna," she said, picking up a wedding photo of her brother and a beautiful blonde in a strapless gown. "We went to high school together but she was tricky," she said. "And this must be his new wife, Lucy—she's pretty, don't you think? Oh, and these will be their daughters, Emma and Sophia. What beautiful girls. And here's my other brother, Ben." She held up a photo of a handsome man with another blond woman and two more little girls. "That's his wife, Jeanne, and their girls, Charlotte and Rebecca. Aren't they precious? Grampa's lawyer writes me once a year to keep me up to date but to see them all here . . ."

Theo took the photo from her hands and put it gently back on the piano, then wiped the tear Sugar hardly knew she'd shed from her cheek with his thumb, and kissed the spot where it had been. "If they came to your apartment, Sugar, they wouldn't find their photos either."

"That's because it hurts," she said.

"My point exactly" came his reply. They both turned as the *click-clack* of Etta's heels heralded her return to the room.

"Tea," she said, placing a tray on the table, then pouring them a glass each from a crystal pitcher. "I'm sorry I can't stay," she said. "I have a prior engagement. Had I known you were coming . . . Anyway, I've spoken to your father and he suggests we have dinner tonight—at the Yacht Club. Cherie-Lynn, I hope that isn't uncomfortable for you? He is going to see if your brothers can make it but at such short notice . . . Well, I assume that as you have arrived here without warning you have arranged accommodation elsewhere? Don't rush your drinks; Neesie, the housekeeper, will let you out; she's just finishing in the laundry. Eight tonight, Cherie-Lynn. Good to meet you, Mr. Fitzgerald.

Please accept my apologies but I have a busy schedule and anyway, yes . . . I will see you later. Goodbye now."

She swept out of the room, leaving it feeling two degrees colder than when she came in.

"Well, that didn't go so badly," Theo said as Sugar sank back into the sofa cushions, closed her eyes and wished herself back on her Manhattan rooftop.

42ND

They arrived at the Yacht Club early, Sugar unable to relax in the tasteful chintz of the Vendue Inn.

Even walking down Rainbow Row, hand in hand with Theo, the evening breeze fresh on her cheeks from the river she'd grown up beside, she barely noticed the colorful window boxes choked with spiky cordylines, trailing bacopa and the myriad brilliant hues of verbena, begonias, impatiens and petunias adding to the candy-store effect of the pretty street in the fading light.

As they sat in the bar, twiddling their drinking straws, Sugar told Theo that the last time she had been at the Yacht Club, she had been checking the table settings for her wedding reception.

"Your mother chose to bring you tonight to the place where you never had your wedding reception?"

"To be entirely fair, wedding aside, it used to be the finest dining in town," Sugar said. "And my daddy is particular about his steaks, so I don't think upsetting me would be the only reason."

Etta and Blake arrived together on the dot of eight.

"My baby girl," Blake said, walking toward her and she felt a wretched *thunk* in her stomach at the sight of him. His face had stayed frozen in time in her mind but in the flesh he'd aged much more than her mother had. He looked old, his hair almost white, his face lined and the beginnings of a paunch straining the buttons of his blazer.

She fought back tears as he embraced her, but he didn't hold her for long, standing back and shooting a quick look at her mother, who was looking stonily out through the deep Yacht Club windows at the whitecaps of the choppy Cooper.

"Daddy, this is Theo Fitzgerald."

"Pleased to meet you, sir," Theo said, shaking hands. He was wearing a dark expensive suit from his old work collection and looked devastatingly handsome.

"Likewise. Fitzgerald. So, you're Irish?"

"Scottish, actually, but I'll take what I can get," Theo answered, and her dad laughed. His laugh at least had stayed the same.

"Shall we?" Etta said, lifting a gloved hand to the restaurant captain and moving like an elegant giraffe through a herd of lesser beings toward their table.

"The boys aren't coming?" Sugar asked, when she saw the table was set for just four.

"I didn't think you'd want the fuss," Etta said, as the waiter spread the napkin in her lap. She was a beautiful woman and so clever at being rude it was hard to call her on it, but still, Theo wanted to slap her.

"Troy had a meeting," Blake said, not meeting Sugar's eye, "and Ben spends half his life running those girls of his around to ballet and violin and pony riding and whatnot. Jeanne certainly keeps him on his toes."

"They're a delightful family," Etta said, taking a sip from her glass of wine. "Jeanne is chairwoman of the garden club now. She's a golfer too. A lovely woman."

"Yeah, but she's one terrible cook," Blake said, making Theo splutter in his water glass. "Etta here had to give her our old housekeeper for fear of Ben and the girls dying of starvation. They were getting thinner and thinner every time we saw them. She was feeding them no-fat milk—even little Becca when she was just a baby. Poor thing was nothing but a shadow."

Sugar felt a pang for Ruby, her own beloved shadow. How she longed to be sitting on her big bed looking at wedding stories in the *New York Times* instead of here in this stuffy room with a family to which she no longer belonged.

"We're thinking of going to the Cordon Bleu school in Paris next spring for lessons, Jeanne and I," said Etta. "She's a doll."

"Sugar is a fantastic cook," Theo said. "She makes everything herself right from scratch: cakes, cookies, bread—even her own granola."

"You don't eat grits for breakfast up there in New York, baby?" Blake asked with genuine tenderness.

"No, Daddy, but that doesn't mean I've lost the taste for them."

"You'll get a chance to reacquaint yourself with them while you're here, I'm sure. How long you down for?"

They managed polite if stilted chitchat while they ate their meals, although nothing of any importance was said, and the white elephant of Sugar's exile remained glowering in the corner. And it was clear to Sugar, from the way Etta was showing far more enthusiasm for the chablis than the food she was pushing around the plate, that this was just the calm before the storm.

"So," Etta finally said, inspecting the pale pink nails of one smooth, moisturized hand once the plates had been cleared, "perhaps now is the time to let us know to what we owe the pleasure of your visit."

"I was just keen to see where Sugar came from, to see what turned her into the wonderful woman she is today," Theo said before Sugar herself could answer.

"Oh really," Etta said icily. "We call her Cherie-Lynn."

"Please, Mama," Sugar started.

"She might be Cherie-Lynn to you, Etta, but she's Sugar to me," Theo said pleasantly. "Your daughter has brought me great happiness and I would like to do the same for her but she misses her family. You mean a lot to her despite what went on."

"What went on is that she humiliated her husband-to-be and us and everyone she knows on a day they still talk about as one of the worst ever in the parish of St. Michael's."

"In Charleston, where the Civil War started, and the city was all but razed to the ground? Gee, I'm so sorry to hear that," Theo said, his tone still pleasant.

"Where is the wine waiter when you need him?" asked Blake.

"I didn't mean to humiliate you, Mama," Sugar said. "You must know that. I didn't set out to hurt you. I just couldn't marry Grady, was all."

"And you chose the occasion of your wedding to decide that?"

Sugar thought about that queen, circling Grady at the altar. True, the bees had opened her eyes to the mistake she was about to make, but it was Sugar herself who had done the buzzing off.

You are strong, she heard her Grampa say. *You are strong.*

"Five more minutes and it would have been too late," she said.

312

"Grady Parkes was not the right man for me and if I was about to marry him again, I would do the exact same thing."

"Blake, I told you this was a mistake." Her mother was furious. "You're unhinged, Cherie-Lynn. You always were. Ever since you were a bitty little girl. You're just like your grandma and that crazy old father of mine, your head always up in the peach blossoms, never mind the embarrassment you're causing. Well, I'm not going to sit here and listen to any more of your nonsense."

She pushed back her chair and snatched at her pale lemon clutch.

"Calm down, Etta," urged Sugar's father.

"I'm hinged, Mama," Sugar said. "I'm one hundred percent hinged. I'm just trying to do unto others like Grampa always taught me."

"He didn't teach you a thing worth knowing," Etta said. "You made that abundantly clear when you ran out on Grady."

"So how is Grady these days?" Theo surprised Sugar by asking.

"Come on, Blake, we need to get going," Etta said. "And not that it's any of your business but Grady Parkes would have done just fine if Cherie-Lynn hadn't left him at the altar and ruined him."

"So he's still in the family business then?" Theo persisted.

Blake coughed and helped Etta on with her coat.

"Dinner's on your father," she said, tying up her belt. "I hope you enjoyed it."

"It's just that I read something recently," Theo continued, "that made me think that perhaps Grady didn't turn out to be such good husband material anyway. Three wives, three divorces, four DUIs."

"The poor man could not even show his face in the street after *she* disgraced him," Etta said. "He never recovered. Never."

"I'm sorry I caused him pain, Mama. Don't think I never felt for him, I did. And for you all. But he already drank. And he was already controlling and mean. I did not turn Grady into that."

"Good evening, Cherie-Lynn, Mr. Fitzgerald. Enjoy the rest of your stay. I'll be waiting in the car, Blake."

"It's been a real treat to see you again, baby," her father said, after Etta stormed out. "And to meet you too, Fitzgerald. I'm sorry about your mother, honey, but you know how she is."

"I guess I do, Daddy. How come she holds such a place in her heart for Grady but not for me?"

"I don't know, honey. And I wish I could be more helpful but your mother's set in her ways and I'm the one has to live with her so . . ."

"I know, it's OK. Really. Just so long as you know that I always felt real bad for what I did. But I never regretted doing it."

"Of course, baby, and for that I guess I'm grateful. You OK for money and all? I know your granddaddy's lawyer still sends you a check every month but I don't know how you live on that and there's a pile of money still sitting here."

"I'm good, Daddy. I can look after myself. I'm embarrassed to cash those checks."

Her father looked sad. "Don't be," he said. "Lord knows we haven't always done the right thing by you, Sugar, so the least you can do is take what's rightfully yours without any shame."

He hugged her and held on a little longer this time. "Thank you for coming back," he said. "I know it hasn't worked out how you would have wanted but thank you anyway." He kissed her on

314

the cheek and as he pulled away, whispered: "For what it's worth, I like the new guy." Then he squeezed her arm and left.

Before Theo could even begin consoling her, a young waitress shuffled over, bright red in the face but clearly excited. "Is it true that you're the Buzz-off Bride?" she asked. "I played you in my high school musical!"

43RD

I t's sort of like soft polenta," Theo said of his breakfast grits the next morning after room service delivered. "Which is a shame because I don't really get polenta either. Why not just have porridge and be done with it?"

"Because porridge is so sophisticated and delicious, right?" Sugar asked. It was the first time he had seen her smile since they'd left the Yacht Club.

"Yes, Scotland is a country well known the world over for its sophisticated cuisine. You will have noticed all the Scottish restaurants in New York, for example."

"You mean McDonald's?" Sugar said. "I thought that was American. You know, it's a shame Mama froze us out before you got to taste her banana cream pie because for all her faults she could always make a really good pie."

"And how are you feeling about that today?"

"Five minutes with her and I feel like the same bumbling flautist I was when I was eight years old," she said.

"You bumbled the flaute?"

"The flute, Theo. And yes I bumbled it like it had never been bumbled before. My flute teacher cried tears of happiness and gave me some precious coin she'd inherited from her uncle the day I gave it up. I'm just not musical."

"You can't be good at everything, Sugar. It leads to unpopularity."

"I think I have enough of that as it is," she said. "Especially down here."

Theo smoothed her hair behind her ear. "I don't know what you're feeling exactly," he said, "because I ran out of family a long time ago. But Nina and Sam and Frankie, they've been it these past few years and they really did the trick. Plus, now I have you. Families can be small and you don't actually have to be related to them, if that makes you feel better."

"You make me feel better," Sugar said. "You always make me feel better," and she pulled him under the covers.

"Do you think you could ever live back here?" Theo asked a couple of hours later as they wandered hand in hand down the Battery seawall, the tide slapping at the stone beneath them, the wind keeping the humidity at bay, the air rich with salt and silt.

"I do love it," she said, the sounds of the string quartet playing in the White Point Garden drifting hither and yon with the wind. "And it's real good to come back and see it and smell it and feel it again because otherwise a bit of me would always be hankering after it but now . . ."

"But now . . . ?"

"But now that I'm here I think it's not about me being in Charleston, it's about Charleston being in me, and it is, and it can't ever be taken out of me, not by anybody."

"You go, girl!"

"Theo, that just sounds plain wrong the way you say it."

"Aye, it did, didn't it?"

"That's better. And you know what? *I'm* better. I stood up to her, Theo. To my mama, and I can handle being unpopular for that. So I guess I'm not running away anymore. You might not 'get' grits, but I'm going to start having them for breakfast when we get home, and I am not going to run for cover when I hear a southern accent, and we can come back on vacation and go to Sullivan's Island or—Hey! We have the rest of the day here, don't we? Let's take a drive out to my granddaddy's place at Summerville, see what's happened to it."

"For you, Sugar, I'll go anywhere."

They took the Ashley River Road scenic route to Summerville, Sugar smiling at the sight of the Spanish moss waving in the summer breeze, remembering the last time she'd driven this road, with the Volvo full of bees and the taste of freedom in her mouth.

"It's the real deal out here," Theo said, as they passed the entrance to Magnolia Plantation with its white-painted fence posts and scenic sprawl of stables and outbuildings. "There's certainly nothing like this in Barlanark."

"Or anywhere for that matter," said Sugar. "The richest people in America used to live along this stretch. Grampa used to bring me to Drayton Hall every birthday—it's like the biggest single house anyone ever built anywhere or some such. It's up that driveway there, with the big oaks so you can't see it from the road, but it's the oldest preserved plantation in the country. We'd pretend we were living in 1742 and have an old-fashioned picnic down by the river. I even wore a little crinoline—can you imagine?"

"I can imagine you wearing one now," said Theo. "A crinoline is the thing you attach the fishnet stockings to, right?"

"We're talking about me and my granddaddy, Theo. Keep it seemly! He used to say a person could learn more about American history from a single visit to Drayton Hall than a lifetime at any university. You know it survived the Revolution, the other revolution, an earthquake and Hurricane Hugo? Now that's southern spunk for you."

"The more you tell me about your grandfather, the more I like him."

"He had a heart of gold, just like you always say about your mother. And he would have loved you. I know that, and not just because the bees told me so. Now make a right here, onto Bacons Bridge Road, and then it's Tom Pike Lane, a couple of miles up on the left. Good gracious, Theo, I have a team of acrobats doing backflips in my stomach again. What on earth is that all about?"

"Do you want to turn back? We don't have to go. Or do you want to stop and take a moment? We could put on our crinolines and go back to that hall, or we could go into Summerville and grab a soda first, or we could—Why are you looking at me like that?"

"I love you, Theo Fitzgerald. That's all."

"I'm relieved to hear it," he said. "Especially since I risked death by hypothermia meeting your mother."

They both smiled, but Sugar's smile did not stay on her face as they turned into Tom Pike Lane, a country road that backed onto a large wood camouflaging the railway line that went through it. Modest houses nestled into leafy lots, most of them hidden from the road in the shade of ancient oaks, dogwoods and magnificent hydrangea hedgerows.

"His place is halfway up, opposite the big magnolia on the street," Sugar said. "Would they have had to ask me if they sold it?"

"Not if it's in a family trust, but if you are sole owner they would. Are you?"

"I think so but I'm not entirely sure," Sugar said. "Oh, shoot, here we are. It's so overgrown! Oh, he would be so disappointed. It's my fault. Oh, Theo . . ."

The house was barely visible from the road, with the hedgerow that her grandfather had been so proud of keeping clipped in a military buzz cut standing at more than six feet and sprouting shoots like electrified dreadlocks.

The gate to the overgrown driveway was not locked though, so Sugar pushed it open and motioned for Theo to come with her. And although the brambles and climbing roses on either side snatched at their clothes to begin with, when they pushed through just a yard or so it became clear that the property had not been left as much to rack and ruin as she had thought. In fact, someone was doing a very good job of keeping it spick-and-span. They were just keeping that a secret from passersby. Indeed, the house was freshly painted and what looked like her grandfather's rocking chair and two more besides were sitting on the porch.

As she got closer, Sugar heard a radio playing country music out back and to her further shock, there were bees everywhere: buzzing around the roses her grandmother had planted to grow up over the carport forty years before, flying between the oaks and dogwoods, circling the hydrangea. As she walked on she saw not one, not two but three of her grandfather's old beehives nestled behind the carport beneath the peach trees. All that was missing was the old pickup truck, which had died years earlier in California. Otherwise it was as though time had stood still.

Just then a little girl came out from the back of the house and saw her. She had dark hair tied up in a ponytail and was dressed up in a long grayish ball gown that trailed on the ground.

The little girl stopped and stared, her eyes big and brown just like Sugar's.

Sugar reached out to steady herself against the house, looking behind her for Theo, but he had disappeared around the other side.

Her head was spinning.

What had she walked into?

But then another smaller girl, this one in a fairy dress, came out from behind the house and wasted no time opening her mouth to holler: "Daddy! Come see who's here!"

Behind the little girls emerged a man in a bee suit. He was tall, just like her grandfather, with square shoulders and the same loping gait. Then he took the hat and veil off. "Sugar?"

"Ben!"

It was her brother.

His hair was a little gray at the temples and his body not quite as lean as she remembered, but his face was still as handsome as ever. The girls—of course, how could she not have seen it?—were his daughters.

They stared at each other like cowboys in a shoot-out for a moment, then Ben dropped the hat to the ground and Sugar flew into his arms.

He held her and squeezed her so tight that with each beat of his heart against her shoulder another year away from him dissolved until they were just an ordinary brother and sister separated by complications and ecstatic to be together again.

"Daddy, are you crying?" the older of the two girls asked.

Sugar pulled back, and Ben wiped his face. "Well, heck, yes, pumpkin, but they're happy tears. I'm happy to see your aunt Sugar is all."

"Hello, Aunt Sugar," the girls called in unison.

"I've told them all about you, sis. This is Charlotte and Rebecca," he said, and the girls did the cutest of curtsies.

Theo emerged from behind the house then, and Sugar introduced him too.

"Pleased to meet you," Ben said, and he looked like he meant it, which warmed Sugar's heart more than just about anything else that had happened since they hit Charleston soil.

"Y'all are keeping bees?" she asked the girls. "I used to come out here and help my granddaddy with his bees when I was your age."

"We know," Rebecca said. "Daddy told us all about you and how you live in all different places like Mary Poppins and take the bees with you wherever you go."

"Bees are responsible for pollinating one-third of the world's vital food crops," said Charlotte. "He told us that too."

"And we like honey," added Rebecca.

"Where are your bees now, Aunt Sugar?"

"They're in New York City on the rooftop of my apartment building."

"I heard something about that," Ben said, picking up the helmet.

"From Mama? I do write her on her birthday and at Christmas

time just to keep her posted but I can never be sure what gets passed on. Did she tell you I was here?"

"She's not real chatty on the subject," Ben said, looking uncomfortable. "I hear more from Phillips, the lawyer."

"Hey, girls," said Theo, "if it's OK with your dad, do you want to come to town with me to get an ice cream?"

"Ooh, yes," said Rebecca.

"Mama says we can't have ice cream," Charlotte reminded her.

"We don't have to tell your mama," said Ben. "Sure, Theo, that would be great."

"Thank you, sweetie," Sugar said, kissing him, feeling so grateful to have him.

The girls each took one of his hands and they walked down the driveway together disappearing into the camouflage overgrowth and leaving Ben and Sugar to look at each other in wonder.

"You've hardly aged a bit," Ben said. "You still look like the—"

"Buzz-off Bride?" Sugar suggested. "Yeah, I heard about that."

"Well, you created quite a stir. But it was a long time ago and I guess we have better things to discuss. Want to come sit on the porch? I have a bottle of bourbon inside and I could certainly handle a belt or two."

Inside, the house was just as Sugar remembered it, but freshly painted and with a few additions like a dishwasher and a new leather sofa instead of the old wicker furniture her grandfather had preferred.

"Who's been living here?"

"Nobody," Ben said.

"Then who's been keeping it?"

323

"I have."

"Why?"

"Why, in case you came back, Sugar."

Sugar looked at him, astonished. "You kept it for me?"

"Hell, yes," he said, checking his language. "Sorry. I mean heck yes. I guess I always thought that one day you would just turn up here and then time went on and weeks turned to months and months to years and . . . I know we should've done more to track you down and bring you home but that doesn't mean we didn't miss you. Or we didn't think about it. We missed you like crazy. Me especially. The whole family just wasn't the same without you."

"I didn't want you to find me and bring me home, Ben. And that's the truth. I knew I'd shamed y'all and I guess I got used to thinking everyone was better off without me, but I just couldn't marry Grady. I was going to have a miserable life with him and I just saw something in the church that made it clear to me it was now or never."

"The bees?"

"Yes, sir. The bees."

"Well, it certainly added a level of drama St. Michael's is not entirely used to."

"The funny thing is, the closer the wedding got, the more I felt unsure about marrying him, but I never felt unsure about running away."

"Yeah, well, Grady showed his true colors eventually," Ben said drily. "Troy still won't hear a word against him but I'm glad you didn't stay, Sugar. I'm glad you went away."

"You are?"

"I love Charleston, I really do, and I have the girls now and I want them to grow up how we did: in a beautiful city we're all proud to live in. We sail on the weekends or go crabbing with Jeanne's folks on Edisto Island or I bring them here, even though Jeanne won't come with us. We're Charlestonians, Sugar, through and through, in most respects, and I've made my peace with that, but the truth is I'm not like Troy and Daddy. There are some aspects of my life here that I hate, but it isn't being here that's the problem."

"Then what is the problem?"

"One of them is my job. I'm good at being a lawyer but the longer I do it, the less I like it, yet I'm stuck with it."

"You're not stuck, Ben. You don't have to be a lawyer—you could do anything you want."

Ben put his feet up on the porch railing and took a slug of bourbon. "I only wish that were true, Sugar, but Jeanne and I, we're used to the good life now. And I have Daddy, I have our big brother, I have a million commitments. Believe me, I'm stuck. And most of the time I'm OK with that but you don't know how I've envied you over the years, carving out a different life for yourself, going where the wind blows you. That takes guts."

For the briefest sliver in time, the world shimmered and Sugar saw her life as an enviable jewel: a shining gem radiating energy and possibility that no one but she would ever possess, no matter what its deficiencies. "The guts aren't particularly mine," she said. "I'm just doing what Grampa's bees tell me to. Every year I put my queen on his map—remember he used to have it on the wall in the spare room? It's my queen who shows me where to go and I just follow her. It seems easier than deciding for myself,

Ben, so it doesn't feel brave to me. In fact, most people would say it seems downright demented."

"So the bees brought you back here?"

"No, the bees took me to New York and when I got there . . . Well, yeah, I guess they kind of did bring me back here. It's a long story, and it's taken a long time, you know, since Grady, but thanks to my bees I have Theo."

"Hey, baby girl," her brother said. "I'm real pleased for you. You deserve it, you know?"

"He's a lawyer, I hate to tell you, and he used to be all highfalutin but he works for nonprofits now. And he's not scared of anything or anybody. You should have seen him last night at dinner with Mama!"

Ben coughed on his bourbon. "How did that go?"

"Not great. She's still so angry with me. I don't think she's ever going to forgive me and Daddy's never going to disagree with her but I'm OK with that now."

"There's something you should know about Mama's anger," Ben said. "You can't go around thinking that it's just for you. It's not. Most of it is for Daddy. He cheats on her, Sugar; he has done for a long time. She knows and he knows she knows and they stay together because he needs her and she's scared of being ruined, but she is angry. She's probably wanted to run off and live in New York herself a thousand times."

"Daddy? Cheating? Are you sure?"

"As sure as sure can be."

"But that's terrible! Does Troy know?"

"Everybody knows."

"Oh, poor Mama. Can't you get him to stop?"

"I stay out of it, Sugar. He doesn't listen much to me anyway. Troy's his wingman. I'm not nearly enough of a good ol' boy in some ways, I sometimes think, but I get by. Just look at my girls. They are the best thing I ever did. And I don't even know why I'm telling you this except I guess you always were the best person to talk to. Shoot, enough about me anyway. Tell me about Theo. Where's he from? What's he like?"

"He's from Scotland, and I thought he was plum crazy to begin with truth be told," Sugar said. "But the more I get to know him the saner he seems. Turns out the only thing he's really crazy about is me and that sure feels good."

"Are you going to give marrying him a try?"

"I don't think I'm the marrying kind."

"If he really loves you and you really love him and you're not living within spitting distance of our mother, I guess you don't need a wedding."

They sat there companionably in the shade of the dogwoods and Ben told her that he'd come out to the cabin the day after she'd fled and found Troy's truck and another swarm of confused bees. He didn't know where they came from but he reclaimed some of their grandfather's hives from the old beekeeper friend who had inherited them.

"He helped set me up to begin with and then I started coming out to check on them on my own," he said. "And I guess I got a feeling for the darn things. Then I got on with fixing up the house and taking care of the garden and before you knew it, I had a hobby that didn't involve a golf ball and every other lawyer in Charleston."

He kept it on the down-low to begin with, he said, because he didn't want Etta getting wind of it and cutting up rough but then the girls came along and he started bringing them out and they had taken to beekeeping like ducks to water.

"Guess it's in our blood," Ben said and Sugar felt a shift deep in her bones that she couldn't explain but that made her feel calmer and happier than maybe she ever had.

When the girls got back with Theo, he stayed on the porch with Ben while Charlotte and Rebecca showed Sugar the bees.

The three of them each pulled off a chunk of honeycomb and sat under the peach trees eating it, the honey dripping through their fingers and in Rebecca's case right down her front.

"I hope you don't mind," she said to Sugar. "We're usually real careful."

"Why would I mind, honey?" Sugar replied.

The girls looked at each other.

"It's your dress," Charlotte said. "You were going to be married to Mr. Parkes in it but you left it here for us instead."

It was no longer white and it didn't drape the same way on someone who was only four feet tall but it was indeed her buzz-off bridal gown.

"It's my turn to wear it today because Charlie had it last time," Rebecca said.

"It looks beautiful on you, sweetie," said Sugar. "I can't imagine a better use for it than dressing up two such gorgeous girls."

"Daddy put it in the washing machine once and it shrank," confessed Charlotte, "but we didn't mind, did we, Becca?"

When the time came for them to leave, Sugar felt a different person from the one who had thrashed her way through the overgrown hydrangea bushes hours before. She felt like part of a family again, even if it wasn't entirely hers or even a whole family. "Thank you for taking such good care of Grampa's place," she said to Ben. "I thought it would break my heart coming back here but you know what? It's done just the opposite."

"It's your place, Sugar," he said. "It's ready and waiting, whenever you want it."

"Come back for our birthdays!" Rebecca said. "Mine's on September 4 and Charlie's is on September 6 and we always go for a picnic at Drayton Hall."

"Sometimes Poppa and Ettie go too," said Charlotte. "We dress up."

"But not in this," Becky said, lifting up the trailing hem of the wedding dress. "This is a secret."

"A picnic at Drayton Hall sounds just wonderful," said Sugar. "And if I don't see you then, I still hope I'll see y'all real soon anyway."

She and Theo might not be welcome at the house on Legare Street but they could escape to this special little hidden corner of her old world if they wanted to, couldn't they? They could be part of these little girls' lives, maybe even her other brother's family too, if he was open to it.

As they sailed down the canopied tunnel of Ashley River Road, past the emerald green sprawl of South Carolina's historic finest, past the happy picnic grounds of her youth, she felt welcome anyway. Relationships could crack, never to be filled, leaving impossible chasms gaping forever after, that was the fact of it, and that was harsh.

But new pathways could also be navigated, forging their way

through uncharted territory, winding their way around those inhospitable obstacles like ribbons of tide through the low country salt marshes.

And that was just plain thrilling.

"You know, you have never actually asked me properly," she said to Theo.

"Asked you what?"

"To marry you."

Theo all but drove off the road. "Are you kidding? What about my heroic risk-taking next to your bees on my rooftop that day?"

"I don't consider blackmail that formal a proposal."

"What about the fact you told me I was never to ask you ever again?"

"Oh, well, I've changed my mind about that."

"You have?"

"I have. Not because I think we should get married, but because I no longer think we shouldn't. It suddenly seems far less complicated."

"Far less complicated? I can hardly believe my ears," Theo said, slowing down. "I'm sensing that I need to strike while the iron's hot with this one."

"Strike away," said Sugar.

He pulled off onto a verge by the glossy white railings of yet another sprawling Ashley River plantation and got out of the car, coming around to Sugar's side and opening her door.

A chestnut mare with a lightning-strike blaze trotted over to the railing to see what was going on, shaking her silky mane and snorting happily.

Theo ignored this—although he was actually scared of horses

too—and took Sugar's hand, helping her out on to the lush green grass.

Then he got down on one knee and turned to his beloved.

"Sugar Honey Wallace, beekeeper extraordinaire, love of my life, woman of my dreams, best friend forever—will you do me the great, great honor of becoming my wife?"

Sugar looked around at the vast rolling pastures in this happiest of places from her youth, then at the festoons of Spanish moss waving her gently toward her future. "Why yes, Theo Fitzgerald," she said. "After all the effort you've put in, it would be rude not to."

44TH

As love's blossoms were bearing fruit in the South, so its early buds were blooming on Sugar's rooftop in the North.

Ruby and Nate had been charged with looking after Elizabeth the Sixth while her keeper was away and had met to brave the removal of the hive lid, pulling out the honey frames and eventually finding the queen. As they put the hive back together once they saw she was in fine fettle, Ruby's shoulder touched Nate's arm and she felt a jolt so strong, she later told Sugar, it was like being launched into space.

Nate was a little further down the track with the possibilities of their friendship, however, so when he felt the electric shock of contact, he knew exactly what it was and what to do about it. Also, he was wearing the beekeeper's visor, which gave him extra powers in the field of communication.

"Can I make you lunch?" he asked Ruby. "You don't have to eat it. I would just like to make it for you."

It was hard to tell girls how you felt about them, but sometimes it was worth the risk, was the conclusion he had come to.

Ruby had no intention of eating anything but with every meal Nate prepared for her from that day on, she felt herself sliding further and further away from the lonely heart who just read about other people's happy endings, toward a happy ending of her own.

The day he got a trial at Citroen for another pastry chef position, she waited outside for the four hours it took him to find out that Roland Morant had too much in common with his boss at the diner to ever want to work for him or anyone like either of them ever again. "Out of the frying pan into the fire," he said when he emerged, his cheeks burning.

At the sight of his humiliated face, Ruby slid one small cold hand into his large warm one, and more or less never let it go.

She also had the idea that was to improve not only her fortune and his, but Lola's too.

The balloon/tattoo store was open a lot more often now and while balloon sales had barely lifted, Lola's needles were getting a thorough workout. Potential clients wafted in and out and around the basement all day long, with nothing else to do but clutter up the stoop and annoy the heck out of George.

"You should sell your pastries in there," Ruby suggested to Nate one afternoon. "That place needs good food. And coffee."

When they put it to Lola, she liked the idea but thought the combination was too weird.

"But that's Alphabet City," George protested when he heard about it. "It's where the weird people come so they don't feel so weird anymore. Sounds like a perfect fit to me."

With Nate doing the baking, Ruby making the coffee, both of them showing great enthusiasm for inflating, and Lola tattooing to her heart's content, Lola's Balloons finally took off.

"It's like a commune in there," Mrs. Keschl told Mr. McNally on their way home from a tango lesson one evening. "And they must be sharing the leftovers too, because I think the big one's getting smaller and the little one's getting, well, at least not littler."

True to her word Ruby had been seeing the holistic counselor on the Upper West Side. It was not an easy fix: for every two steps she took forward, she took one and a half back—sometimes three. Her disease was not a logical one and the cure not guaranteed, nor quick, but one thing her friends did know was that now Ruby wanted to stick around. And with Nate in her world her heart at least was no longer starving.

45TH

The morning of Sugar Wallace's second wedding dawned every bit as beautiful as the first, but this time she felt no fear, no doubt, only the blissful thrill of being certain. For reasons that had remained a closely guarded secret among her friends, she had not been able to stay in her own apartment for the preceding forty-eight hours.

Wedding preparations were taking place on Theo's rooftop and some of them were only to be revealed on the day itself, she had been told, so she had been installed in Ruby's apartment on the first floor while Ruby stayed with Nate.

This suited Sugar just fine, as she spent the two days before getting married not having facials and hair treatments and massages, but harvesting her New York rooftop honey.

She never liked to do it in sight of the bees because although they had an unspoken agreement—she looked after them and they looked after her—she was still, when it came down to it, robbing them. Of course, Elizabeth the Sixth could not have given a tinker's cuss. She and her bees had been so happy and industrious in the weeks since Sugar and Theo had been betrothed that they had enough honey to just about feed the whole of Alphabet City.

Still, Sugar wanted to do the right thing, so Nate helped her carry the supers full of heaving honey-filled frames down to Ruby's apartment, then enlisted the new couple's muscle (although Ruby didn't have much of that) to scrape off the beeswax from the capped cells and release the liquid gold.

First they decanted it into big drums, then strained and poured it into a dozen large ceramic urns from which Sugar would work her magic in the months to come.

The morning of Sugar Wallace's second wedding, she had her first mouthful ever of Alphabet City honey and it was her sweetest, most delicious harvest yet. She shared dripping spoonfuls of it with her friends as they helped her get ready, everyone in soaring good spirits.

"Nate's finikias had sold out by eleven yesterday morning," Ruby told her as she watched Sugar clip up a few tendrils of long curled hair while Lola adjusted her dress.

"And I'm tattooing my ass off," Lola said. "Sorry. My butt."

Lola might love fake fur vests and leather minis for herself, but she had made Sugar a dress the bride had been born to wear (although she refused the offer of a tattoo saying SCOTLAND 4 EVA across her back).

The gown was a pale gold silk that seemed to drip like honey itself from her shoulders to where it pooled on the ground at her feet.

"You look so beautiful," said Jay, wiping his eyes. He had not stopped crying since he'd arrived.

"You look like you need a drink," Mrs. Keschl told him. "Although I'm thinking you prefer something with a little umbrella in it."

"There's a bottle of Maker's in the cupboard next to the fridge," Sugar said, turning from the mirror to face her friends.

"You do look pretty snazzy," Mrs. Keschl admitted. "Although if I was getting married at your age I would have had a boob job."

"You can remarry Mr. McNally and get one yourself," Lola suggested.

"There's nothing wrong with my boobs," Mrs. Keschl answered huffily. "And anyway, marrying him once was a bust. And I like being a Keschl again. We're going to live in sin for a while, see how that works out."

"You saucy old dame," said Jay. "I don't suppose I can interest you in a snifter?"

"If it comes with ice and a decent buzz."

"You and I are going to be such pals."

"Here's mud in your eye," she toasted him, knocking back her drink.

"Are y'all ready?" Sugar asked, slipping on her gold sandals. "Because I know I am."

George was waiting outside on the stoop, his doorman's buttons shining so brightly the sun glinted off them and attracted attention from half a block away.

"Miss Sugar Honey Wallace," he said, offering her his arm, and together the wedding party walked up the street, around the corner, and into Theo's building where Mr. McNally, Ethan, Nate and Princess were waiting to escort the bridal party up onto the rooftop.

Once they were inside the apartment and about to step through the door at the top of the stairs leading to the terrace, George instructed her to close her eyes.

Sugar did so, feeling the nip in the air that heralded the arrival of fall. It was a day that hinted at better things to come if ever there was one, and she could not keep from smiling at the extraordinary potential of all the lives with which she was entwined.

She and Elizabeth the Sixth would now be living on Fifth Street with Theo but the hive was raising a new queen, which she was pretty sure would end up with Nate and Ruby back on the Flores Street rooftop. If that wasn't promising, she wasn't sure what was.

George stepped with her through the door.

"You can open your eyes now," said Ruby, from behind.

Sugar was standing at the beginning of a corridor of dark slender trees, each one heavily bejeweled with a million tiny white flowers and standing in its own terra-cotta pot with a white satin bow tied around it.

"How about that," said George. "Manuka trees from New Zealand."

It had taken two days and a small fortune, but Theo had created a bee's perfect haven in which to take Sugar to have and to hold, from that day forward, for better or worse, in sickness and in health. At the end of the manuka corridor he stood, wearing a kilt of the Fitzgerald family tartan, and the smile that rarely left his face. It was all Sugar could do not to run between the bees' favorite trees and throw herself at him.

Instead she walked calmly down that aisle, Jay at her side, charged with giving this beekeeper to the man of her dreams. No one else's. Just hers.

It wasn't till she reached Theo, took his hand, and looked behind him that she saw her beehive already standing in its new spot, its inhabitants making themselves entirely at home, her gardenia bushes standing at attention in front of the Fernando Botero, the magnificent Manhattan skyline rising behind them. "Oh, Theo! Are you sure? Right now? I mean, at our wedding?"

"I'm sure," he said. "I've never been surer." Then he slowly swung her around so that she was facing in the opposite direction, which was when she saw her brother Ben.

Beside him was his wife, and their girls, and next to them were Troy and his wife and their girls. And then into her line of vision stepped Sugar's father, grinning from ear to ear, behind him, her mother—stony faced and not even looking her way, but there.

On the biggest day of Sugar's life: there.

She'd been determined to remain dry-eyed but she just had so much to be happy about and, for the first time in her life, she didn't have a handkerchief. Lola's needlework didn't stretch to pockets. But Nate saw her predicament and stepped into the breach, handing her one she'd long ago given him.

And in the eyes of her true friends and family, Sugar Wallace married Theo Fitzgerald and her bees stayed politely in their hive.

Sugar Wallace and Theo Fitzgerald

Sugar "Honey" Wallace, 36, and Theo Fitzgerald, 40, were married on Saturday on the groom's rooftop terrace in Alphabet City, New York.

The two met on nearby Avenue B the day Ms. Wallace first arrived in Manhattan with nothing but a hive of bees, a birdbath and the supplies of honey that she sells from Tompkins Square greenmarket each Sunday.

Mr. Fitzgerald, a lawyer for a nonprofit company housing the homeless, said he had a feeling about Ms. Wallace from the moment he saw her but there was a major stumbling block in their relationship. "She's crazy about bees," he said. "And I'm allergic to them."

Ms. Wallace's close friend, Ruby Portman, said it was obvious to everyone who knew the couple that they were meant for each other but fate alone looked unlikely to put them together. "We had to more or less blackmail her into giving him a second chance after he sort of freaked out when he discovered her hive," Ms. Portman said. "Because a bee sting would not just hurt or be annoying. It could actually kill him."

"I knew if we could get over my allergies I could have her heart forever and beyond," said Mr. Fitzgerald. "And we did, so I have, and she has mine. She is gorgeous, kind, smart, funny and I hope I live to one hundred and forty just so I can have the pleasure of looking into her beautiful face every day for the next hundred years."

Asked if she ever worried about her husband's potentially lethal allergy, given how she makes her living and their constant proximity to bees, Ms. Wallace said:

"My bees have had plenty of opportunity to attack Theo and they have chosen not to. In fact, they seemed to know he was the right man for me long before I did. Sounds crazy, I know, but it's true."

Acknowledgments

So many people have helped me research this book that I apologize right up front for the ones that I've forgotten. I'm just of that age. Remembering where I put my glasses can take half a day and this book has been a long time coming so in the interests of getting it to you any time soon, here goes.

Jim (at least I think that was his name) in Seatoun took me to my very first beehive and introduced me to his bees looking out over Wellington Harbor. I knew then that beekeepers were going to be a great bunch of people to get to know and, indeed, almost without exception they proved to be kind, helpful and generous with their honey. Thanks also to Sylvain in Ngaio, Sarah in Wadestown and the lovely Denise and her husband at Muriwai Beach.

Julie Chadwick at Comvita in the Bay of Plenty was an amazingly hospitable honey of a woman. Thanks to her I spent the day with honey experts Dr. Ralf Schlothauer and Jonathan Stephens and have called on her often for follow-up questions. I'm crazy about Comvita 15+ manuka honey, as it happens. Not only does it taste delicious but it wards off colds and the flu and should be in every cupboard. I've even posted some to my sick cousin in Italy. Yes, she got better. Although to be honest it took two months for the honey to reach her.

The bees of the world are having a hard time at the moment, but the good news is we can do something about it—become beekeepers ourselves. For more information on the plight of the pollinators, I heartily recommend Hannah Nordhaus's wonderful nonfiction book, *The Beekeeper's Lament.*

Thank you to fellow members of the New York City Beekeepers Association, in particular to Jimmy Johnson for our afternoon at the Narrows Botanical Gardens in Brooklyn. And to my gorgeous friend Naomi Sarna; what a glorious thing it was that we met! Thanks so much for the time on your Eighteenth Street rooftop garden and, in fact, for all your time. Your company is a delight.

To Manhattan landscaper Karen Fausch, thank you for the lowdown on the Northern Hemisphere city planting cycles. Sugar's rooftop would have been nought but a collection of half-dead rubber plants without it. Jan Werner welcomed me with open arms (inside a beekeeper's suit) at the Green Oasis Garden in the East Village, as did Adam at Bridge Café. I hope these bees are now back in business after the whupping they got from Hurrican Sandy.

To my dear friends in New York, a great big kiss to Richard Ruben for the apartment in Chelsea and another for introducing me to the greenmarket all those years ago; to my favorite reindeer Rick Guidotti for taking my rooftop photo (check out his charity at www.positiveexposure.org); to Roger for improving me in too many ways to count, and to Toby because I just really like Toby. Thanks also to Nicki and Luisa at Domus for their fabulous hospitality and enduring friendship, and to Jen and Donald for sheltering me, literally, in the storm.

To Stephanie Cabot at the Gernert Company, thank you for being the person who is always waving my flag. A girl only needs one, and you never give up. I think you're amazing. Thanks to Anna and Rebecca and Will for all their hard work, too.

To Rachel Kahan and the enthusiastic team at William Morrow, thanks for having faith.

And to all the readers who answered my rather sad little cry for help at the end of *Dolci di Love* and e-mailed me—I LOVE YOU. You make my day. Keep 'em coming.

But I guess most of all I want to thank the big, beautiful city of New York. The things you can fling at that place and STILL it remains the most glittering of diamonds on the eternity ring of our planet. I've resisted buying the T-shirt but I really, really, really do heart this town. The parks, the food, the theater, the nail bars, the sales, the people and the humor just keep me coming back time and time again for more.

For *The Wedding Bees* I was lucky enough to spend almost three months in NYC researching, or "researching" as my so-called friends are inclined to put it, the part of the city where the book is set. I did this with the help of Nick Capodice whom I met at the amazing Tenement Museum (www.tenement.org) and who took us on a private food tour of the Lower East Side (seriously, the bagels from Russ & Daughters are sensational as are the pancakes from Vanessa's on Eldridge Street); and also Rob Hollander who gave me a walking tour of Alphabet City (leshp.org/walking-tours/alphabet-city).

By the way, my understanding is that everything below Tompkins Square Park used to be called the Lower East Side but gradually became known as the East Village. It's a gray area, unlike the actual area itself, which is very green. There are more community garden spaces in this part of Manhattan than anywhere else, thanks, I believe, to the fact that many buildings were burned down in the bad old days and no one wanted to build them again so the spaces became gardens. Since I was there in 2011, a public school in Sugar's real-life neighborhood on the corner of East Fifth Street and Avenue B has even opened a rooftop farm. Walking around this part of the city on a sunny day is like being Alice in Wonderland; and if you find the Creative Little Garden on East Sixth Street, please go in, unwrap your lunch, sit down and thank God that such places exist.

Readers often ask how I come up with the ideas for my books and I can't always remember (see earlier reference to reading glasses) or it's complicated, but with *The Wedding Bees* I can remember and it's simple. In 2009, my dear husband, Mark Robins, and I embarked on a wonderful trip in the United States. We started in Sandpoint, Idaho (Yoo-hoo Dan and Allison and my Scottish sister Lesley), then headed for New York, my favorite city in all the world. After that we flew to Durham, North Carolina, and drove down the East Coast to Charleston, South Carolina, a ridiculously pretty city that you should get to straightaway if you haven't already been. I could have stayed forever chatting with Martha on the porch of our bed-and-breakfast at 15 Church Street, south of Broad. We just never ran out of things to talk about. Turns out everything they say about southern hospitality is true and we got more than our fair share of it as we traveled on to Savannah, Georgia, then to Kentucky (thanks for my little bourbon habit, Kentucky), on to Nashville and Memphis in Tennessee and, finally, to New Orleans in Louisiana. These precious weeks were filled with fine food, nonstop music, laughter and newfound friends.

At the end of this incredible trip I thought about what really mattered to me in my life at that particular point and I came up with six things: love, friendship, manners, New York City, the South and honey.

The Wedding Bees is the result. For the reason that it represents a snapshot of a particularly happy period in my life (all my "research" periods are happy ones), this book holds a special place in my heart and I hope you enjoy it in that same spirit.

Appreciating what I have is another thing I seem to have trouble remembering so let this be a reminder. That's me talking to me, by the way. I do that now. Along with the forgetting.

The only downside of writing *The Wedding Bees* has been the development of an enormous honey addiction. The aforementioned Mark Robins, who continues to cook and clean and reassure his sensitive artiste wife that she does know what she is doing, has caught me many a time over the past couple of years with my paw in the honey jar. To this day he still calls me BoLBy, short for Bear of Little Brain, after my all-time favorite literary hero and fellow honey addict, Winnie-the-Pooh.

I played Winnie-the-Pooh in a high school drama production once, by the way. When I was fifteen. So not sexy. But cuddly and kindhearted still counts for something, right?

About the author

About the book

Read on

Insights,
Interviews
& More . . .

Meet Sarah-Kate Lynch

Photo by Rock

SARAH-KATE LYNCH was a journalist
for many years before realizing that
all stories could have happy endings—
if she made them up herself. Since
then she has written eight novels, a
job she combines with her regular travel
writing. She spends her time in New
Zealand, Australia, Fiji, Hawaii, China,
Singapore, India, France, Italy, Spain,
the United Kingdom, Ireland, and the
United States. But her favorite city in
all the world is New York, New York.
You can read more about her at
www.sarah-katelynch.com. ✎

Saying Yes to Love and Honey

From Sarah-Kate Lynch to Readers

CURIOUS READERS often ask if my novels are at all autobiographical and usually the answer falls somewhere between "perhaps, a little bit" and "no, not really."

But Sugar Wallace and I are joined in two vital places: at the taste buds and at the feet.

I've always loved honey and ever since I was a little girl I could be found hiding in the pantry, eating it by the spoonful. (As my husband will attest, this has not changed!) I shared this love with Sugar, which she rather cleverly turned into a career, and I also shared my itchy feet.

Just like Sugar, I love nothing more than hitting the road; the difference between us being that Sugar is running away—from her past, from her feelings, from her true potential—so in some ways she's chasing rainbows. Still, she's having a good time doing it. "A change is as good as a rest," as my mother used to say, because around every corner lie new experiences, new friends, new opportunities, new tastes and sights and sounds.

It's the newness of being in a different place that I like; the surprise, whether it be a crocodile coming around the bend in a Serengeti river scattering a herd of silly zebras or a particularly crisp sheet in a particularly bland airport hotel.

I've always been this way—hankering after the next place while barely having left the last—but this thirst to see more and go farther has only grown as the years have tumbled by. Unlike Sugar, I'm not running away. But just like her I have managed to turn my love into a career—as a travel writer. When I'm not writing novels I'm trotting the globe, happy as a clam, so excited about going somewhere new that I can even overlook the heinous hellhole that is the modern-day airport (although Aitutaki Airport in the Cook Islands is a charmer).

Some days—despite the odd whiff of loneliness or extreme hair frizz from too much airplane air-conditioning or panic at missing a deadline—I can't believe how lucky I am. Then I am reminded that like all good things, life takes time.

I was flying back from Paris recently (she says, to make her point) when the immigration officer at Los Angeles International Airport asked me what I did for a job. "Travel writer," I said, as it's a very good thing to say at border control, particularly if it happens to be true.

"Wow, how do you get to be one of those?" he asked, flicking through my passport and looking at the stamps and visas.

"I waited a long time," I said. "And I'm old."

He turned back to the first page of the passport and looked at my date of birth.

"Oh yeah," he agreed. "Good for you!"

Actually, I would have settled for "What? You can't be a day over forty!" Except that I really did wait. I ▶

Saying Yes to Love and Honey *(continued)*

waited to find out what it was I really, truly, absolutely, just-for-me wanted to do, and it took much longer than I ever would have imagined.

But it was worth it.

Don't get me wrong, I love writing— show me a novelist who doesn't: you have to like it because it takes so much time and it's harder than it looks. But when my feet aren't planted beneath my desk they itch to be traveling the globe as I soak up the myriad of spicy pockets our great big beautiful world has to offer.

In just the past year I have been lucky enough to get to the Cook Islands, Sydney and Melbourne, New York City, San Francisco, Mumbai, Delhi and the Taj Mahal, Kauai and Oahu, Paris, London, Phuket, Singapore, and Bali, plus I've traveled the length and breadth of New Zealand.

I've snorkeled and skied and wined and dined and tramped through slums and over rolling mountains and swum in oceans and rivers and fancy resort pools.

And do you know why?

Because when I turned fifty I decided I would say *yes* to every sparkling opportunity that came my way.

It's harder to say *yes* than most of us realize—we have commitments, responsibilities, we have fears and hang-ups and a thousand reasons why *no* often seems to make more sense. But deciding to say *yes* has been the single most liberating decision of my life.

I do it whether it suits others or not. As long as it suits me, I'm in. It sounds selfish but I don't think I am, particularly. There just comes a point in a girl's life when she realizes that happiness is not something that is delivered on a silver plate borne aloft by half a dozen well-oiled bronze musclemen all wearing loincloths of a certain shade of mauve.

It is something she chooses to have and goes about finding, even if other people think she's showing off, which (if she is) she's sorry about, but that's not going to stop her. Maybe she's not too big for her boots. Maybe her boots were too big to begin with and she's finally just filling them. Of course most women can't just up and go trouncing around the world at the drop of a hat. I'm lucky because (a) I'm paid to do it, (b) I have a very understanding husband who says as long as I'm happy his life is easy, and (c) we don't have children to take to ukulele lessons or put through college.

But traveling may not be what brings other women happiness. For some it's a new home, possibly without the same old dreary other half in it. Or it's a change of job, from the thankless one they've ground away at for years to one that pays less but brings them joy. Or it's getting that last lazy twenty-something offspring to move out of the house so she can have her sewing room back. It might be a new hairdo or a new sexual freedom or a new insistence on wearing unfeasibly high stilettoes, but it's still a big fat YES. ▶

Saying Yes to Love and Honey *(continued)*

In *The Wedding Bees*, Sugar Wallace has already discovered the joys of travel, and friendship, and (of course) honey, but until she says *yes* to life's sweetest elixir, love, happiness continues to elude her . . . that pot of gold always just out of reach.

Luckily for her, she doesn't even have to wait forty years to see it. ᴄᴡ

Reading Group Guide

Read on

1. When George first meets Sugar he observes: "I don't get to meet many people like you these days. You new in town?" How is Sugar different from the New Yorkers that George is used to? And even though she's a newcomer, are there ways that she fits right into her new home?

2. Sugar's father says that "Wallaces don't clean up other people's messes. That's just not what we do," and Sugar says, "I don't rescue people, that's just so sappy." But her longtime friend Jay says, "Sugar, you are a one-woman detox center stroke guidance counselor stroke bank teller stroke babysitter stroke you name it." Who is right? What motivates Sugar when she bonds with other people?

3. Why does Sugar seem so alarmed by Theo's impetuous honesty about how he fell in love with her at first sight? Do you think he crossed a line? Why does the usually free-spirited Sugar seem to think he did?

4. What do you make of Ruby's obsession with wedding announcements? What do they represent for her? Would she have approved of Sugar and Grady's fairytale wedding?

5. Early on in the novel, George tells Sugar, "Where you're from is where you're from and a person will ▶

always miss it. There's just no getting away from that." Do Theo and Sugar miss where they're from, or are they happier where they're transplanted? How do Sugar's feelings about where she's from change once she goes back to Charleston?

6. Sugar's brother Ben tells her that he feels stuck in his life as a successful lawyer, and says, "I've envied you over the years, carving out a different life for yourself, going where the wind blows you. That takes guts." Do you envy Sugar? Could you do what she did? Would you want to?

7. Food is perhaps the most important way that Sugar relates to the people in her life, from the cakes and cocktails she makes to cement her relationships with her neighbors to her observation about her mother that despite "all her faults, she could make a really good pie." What role does food play in your life? Are there certain recipes or dishes that are important to your relationships?

8. Of all the happy endings in *The Wedding Bees*, which is your favorite and why? Sugar and Theo's wedding? Mr. McNally and Mrs. Keschl's? Ruby's? Lola's?

9. The author, Sarah-Kate Lynch, opens this novel with a dedication: "In praise of random acts of kindness, good manners, and

guardian angels." Whose random acts of kindness carry the most weight? Whose good manners are most sorely tested (or most appreciated)? And which of the characters do you think are the guardian angels of this story? ∾